2/20/20

ALSO BY VICTOR GISCHLER

VAMPIRE
A
GO-GO

VICTOR GISCHLER

A TOUCHSTONE BOOK
PUBLISHED BY SIMON & SCHUSTER
NEW YORK   LONDON   TORONTO   SYDNEY

Touchstone
A Division of Simon & Schuster, Inc.
1230 Avenue of the Americas
New York, NY 10020

First Touchstone trade paperback edition September 2009

TOUCHSTONE and colophon are registered trademarks of Simon & Schuster, Inc.

For information about special discounts for bulk purchases,
please contact Simon & Schuster Special Sales
at 1-866-506-1949 or business@simonandschuster.com.

The Simon & Schuster Speakers Bureau can bring authors to your live event.
For more information or to book an event contact the Simon & Schuster Speakers
Bureau at 1-866-248-3049 or visit our website at www.simonspeakers.com.

Designed by Carla Jayne Jones

Manufactured in the United States of America

10   9   8   7   6   5   4   3   2   1

Library of Congress Cataloging-in-Publication Data

Gischler, Victor
  Vampire a go-go / Victor Gischler. — 1st Touchstone trade paperback
ed.
      p.   cm.
  "A Touchstone book."
  I. Title.
  PS3607.I48V36   2009
  813'.6—dc22   2008051381

ISBN: 978-1-4165-5227-7

For Jackie

PROLOGUE

I'm not the hero of this story.

There are a number of important things you need to know up front. Pay attention.

I'm not the hero of this story, but I am the guy telling it. It has to be me. I'm in a unique position. I know all the players, know how they mix and match and come together to make everything happen.

About me. Look, the thing is, I'll just confuse you if I get too much into me right now. You'll learn all about me later, how I fit into this. The important thing is that I know what's going on, and the plan is for me to dish it out a bit at a time so you can understand. I'll fade out from time to time, and you'll forget I'm even involved. But I'm there. Don't worry about that. I'm always there. Can't go anyplace, really. I'll explain all that at the appropriate time. I'll explain everything. You're going to have to trust me.

Let's see. I'm sure I've forgotten something. Never mind. We'll catch up as we go along.

The story begins like so many others. A fairly decent sort of guy, totally unaware of what he's getting himself into.

GOTHIC STATE

ONE

The sudden shrill chirp of a hundred birds froze Allen in place, his hand poised to knock on the department head's door. Probably it was his imagination, but then he heard it again. Maybe Dr. Carpenter had one of those soothing rain-forest-sounds CDs.

It didn't matter. He'd been summoned.

He knocked, heard somebody mumble something. He entered.

The birds went crazy, flapping between bookshelves.

"Shut the damn door," she yelled at him.

Allen hastily shut the door, stood cringing amid the bird storm, feathers brushing his face, the room alive with the swirling racket of wings and beaks.

"Sit down." Professor Cathy Carpenter gestured at the hard, wooden chair across her desk.

He sat.

She sat too, took a small wooden box from her top desk drawer, and began to unpack the contents. A plastic baggy, paper.

"You didn't have a very good semester, did you, Allen?" She unfolded a small square of thin paper, pinched the herb from a plastic baggy, and rolled it into the paper. The joint was on the small side.

Birds flapped, hopped between shelves.

"There were some distractions," Allen told her.

"Uh-huh. What's your last name? Cabbot?"

"Yes."

"Any relation to the Salem Cabbots? Good family."

"No, ma'am." He flinched as a bird swooped within an inch of his nose. The rest of the birds screeched and danced.

"The mayor's an old student of mine. Winston Cabbot of Salem. Hmmm. Winston of Salem. Winston Salem. That's odd. Isn't that a cigarette or something?"

Allen ducked another bird on a strafing run.

"So Winston is what? Your uncle or something?" Carpenter raised an eyebrow.

"We're not related, ma'am. I'm from Portland."

"Do you have any matches?" She fished around in the other drawers.

"Professor Carpenter, there are like a hundred birds in your office. Maybe more."

"One hundred and twenty-two. They're budgies. Ah!"

She found matches, struck one, lit the joint, and puffed smoke.

She stood, sucked deep on the joint, then went around the room, puffing smoke into the budgies' faces. After three minutes of this, the birds settled into sedate lines along the bookshelves.

Professor Carpenter returned to her seat. "You earned straight Cs in your classes."

"I'll do better."

"What happened?"

Allen didn't feel he could tell Professor Carpenter about Brenda Cole. The entire episode had been juvenile and ill-advised. Allen had known from the start that Brenda had been too much girl for him, a senior in Warner's poetry workshop, a rebellious girl in a black dress and combat boots and a nose ring and all those great tattoos in interesting places. They'd had three great weeks before she'd dumped him flat on his ass, and Allen had spent the rest of the semester embarrassing himself with pathetic phone calls and bleeding-heart emails, trying to win her back.

"There was a lot going on, Professor Carpenter. I fixed it."

Above him, the birds sat in a long line, looking down, hunched together like old men, some absurd jury listing to his feeble story.

"Why did you choose Gothic State University, Allen?"

The small university perched atop a rocky precipice overlooking the Pacific Ocean. The institute was undistinguished in every way. The English Department's one claim to fame had been a nationally renowned Brontë scholar named Thornton Hardwood. It was Hardwood who'd lured Allen to Gothic State. Allen loved the Brontës, wanted to write his dissertation on gender coding in *Wuthering Heights.*

Hardwood had died suddenly of a stroke six days into Allen's first semester. Allen had stayed through the second semester because he hadn't applied to any other schools and hadn't known what else to do. Brenda had happened the third semester, and Allen's scholarly ambitions had dropped straight into the crapper.

"I just like it here, ma'am."

"Uh-huh." A budgie landed on Dr. Carpenter's coffee mug. The mug had a novelty message that read, "I earned tenure, and all I got was this lousy coffee mug." Carpenter rubbed the budgie's head with her pinky finger. "Hello, Admiral Snodgrass."

"You can tell all the birds apart?"

"All the budgies are named Admiral Snodgrass."

Ah.

"I'm going to give you a chance, Allen. You'll have to bring your grades up, but I'm willing to keep your name off the academic probation list."

"I appreciate that, ma'am."

"Wait and hear the rest," she said. "It's well known around the department you have a gift for research."

Allen nodded. During his first semester, he had taken Professor Mapplethorpe's research methods class and had immediately become teacher's pet. Mapplethorpe had spread it among the faculty that "the boy can dig anything out of a library." Allen constantly endured harsh comments on his papers for sloppy writing, but his research skills were impeccable.

"I'm going to assign you as Dr. Evergreen's grad assistant."

Allen squirmed in his seat, opened his mouth to object, closed it again. What choice did he have?

Dr. Evergreen was known campuswide as a cranky hard-ass. He stank of bad cigars and gin. He was an unpleasant and demanding man, and most students only took his classes when forced to complete degree requirements.

Budgies cooed in a ganja stupor.

"I understand," Allen said.

"He's writing a chapter for a new monograph on Kafka." Carpenter stubbed out the joint in a ceramic ashtray. "You're to go with him to Prague this summer and help him with research. It's not a vacation. He'll work you hard."

"Prague? The Czech Republic? That Prague?"

"Yes."

"I was going to visit my folks this summer."

"Not anymore. Unless you'd like to drop out."

"I'll go to Prague."

"Good. Go to the party at Evergreen's house tonight. Grad students are invited, so you won't feel out of place. Tell him you're on board."

Allen stopped himself from sighing. "Okay."

"Go away now, please." Carpenter relit the joint, sat back in her chair, and closed her eyes.

I didn't like Allen at first. With instantaneous knowledge of his entire life, I figured I knew all I needed to make this judgment. He's a little weak, lets people push him around. He's apologetic when he hasn't done anything. He means well in a way somehow more annoying than if he meant harm. You know the type. Always hanging at the edge of a conversation, waiting to be invited to talk.

Allen has a bad habit of ignoring nice, bookish sorts of girls right under his nose. They like him. He's good-looking and well mannered, with brown hair, wavy and thick, a medium-square jaw and shoulders. Tallish. An open face given to a shy, reluctant grin full of straight white teeth. But Allen ignores the plain Janes in favor of exotic, fast women who ignore him, or worse, chew him up.

Perhaps I despise him for this, since I used to chase the same sort of woman. Ages and ages ago.

But having the sum total of a man's life inserted into your head like a computer memory stick isn't the same as experiencing the man or seeing him in action—or often, unfortunately, inaction. Walk a mile in his shoes—or his skin—well, sympathies develop. So I suppose I ended up rooting for Allen, hoping he'd get through all this in one piece.

It's not my job to take sides, but I am a thinking being, and I do have an opinion.

Still, it would be nice if Allen could get his head straight about women. One of these quiet, girl-next-door types could do his self-esteem a world of good.

Take Penny Coppertone, for example.

"I like that one," said Penny Coppertone as she sat on the edge of Allen's narrow bed.

Allen's dorm room was small, and there was nowhere to sit but the bed. The single chair overflowed with textbooks and dirty laundry. Allen was one of the few grad students still living in the dorms. He couldn't afford an apartment on his own and didn't want a roommate.

"This one?" He held the muted red tie up to his shirt, then held up a narrower blue tie. "Not this one." He wanted to look right for Evergreen's party.

"Actually, why don't you wear the black shirt with the tweed and no tie at all," Penny suggested. "I think that will strike the right tone."

"What's the right tone?"

"Professionally academic but off duty and ready for a glass of wine."

"I'm going to Prague, Penny. Did I mention that?"

"What? That's wonderful. When? This summer? That's when the summer writing workshops are. In July, I think. I haven't been accepted yet, but I'm hoping—"

"I'm going as Dr. Evergreen's research assistant."

Penny's face fell, all the way to the ground. She tried to pick it up again without success. "Well, but still . . . it could be fun."

Allen spared her a sideways glance as he slipped into his jacket. "With Dr. Evergreen?"

"No, I suppose it will suck."

"You'd better hurry and change if you still want a ride."

Penny's hand automatically went to her dishwater hair, pulled the ponytail loose. "Actually, I was already—" She looked down at her Gothic State sweatshirt and faded jeans, heavy wool socks and Birkenstocks. "I mean, yeah, I guess I'd better get dressed. I might be a while. How about I meet you there?"

"Okay, but hurry, or all the food will be gone."

*   *   *

Penny Coppertone was an excellent poet, but her images were quiet and subtle. If her poetry had been about sexual exploration and explosive rants against the establishment, and if Penny had died her hair jet-black and gotten her nose pierced, Allen would have been all over her.

Men can be dumbfucks. If I had it to do all over again . . .

But of course I don't.

TWO

The Pacific Ocean was just swallowing the sun as Allen left campus in his four-door, V-8 crapmobile, the red-orange rays sizzling on the water. Only a pale pink smear of daylight remained by the time he parked last in a long line of cars on Dr. Evergreen's street. He followed the cars up to the house, but it was completely dark by the time he stepped onto the front porch and knocked.

Nobody answered.

Distantly he heard muted music and the hubbub of many voices. He raised his fist to knock again.

"The party is in the garden around back."

Startled, Allen sucked breath, took a step back.

He hadn't seen her there, on the porch swing, shadows and hanging ferns making her seem as if she'd floated in darkness, only the ice blue eyes glowing out at him. She stood, approached Allen, her face coming into focus.

She was somehow light and dark at the same time, some smiling Celtic goddess, features like delicate china, skin so white it glowed, absorbing light, leaving an aura of darkness all around her. A breeze kicked up, lifted her hair, black and shining like obsidian. She seemed to float toward him, eyes flashing cold and terrible, hair streaming behind like black flame.

Like some sort of terrifying shampoo commercial.

Allen wanted to flee. He wanted to kneel and pledge his soul to her. He didn't know what the hell he wanted to do.

"You must be Allen."

He blinked. The spell was broken. Allen was aware of warm sweat in his armpits, behind his ears. *What's wrong with me?*

"Yes." He cleared his throat. "I thought there was—I was invited—"

"The party is around back." She moved as she spoke, graceful and silent, suddenly on his left, her slender arm looping into his. "I'll walk you around. It's in the garden."

Then he was on a path. He felt light, like part of him was still back on the front porch.

"You know me, but I don't . . . have we met?"

She laughed softly, the sound of delicate hamster bones crushed under the heel of a tall black boot. Like dry leaves blowing across the cold stone of an ancient tomb. Like . . . *Pay attention. She's talking.*

"I'm Cassandra."

The name was familiar. "Dr. Evergreen's wife?"

"Yes. He'll be glad you're here."

"I'm looking forward to working with him."

The slow smile on her face knew the lie.

Allen swallowed hard, felt the warm trickle of sweat down his back. The night was cool, but Allen felt flushed, a little dizzy.

They emerged from the path into a circle of light, to find a line of Chinese lanterns strung through the trees, a gazebo, people milling about a table of drinks and food, tinny music from hidden speakers. He recognized faculty, some of his fellow graduate students. He stood a moment, wondering what to do first. Maybe get a glass of wine? Or should he say hello to Dr. Evergreen?

He asked Cassandra, "Should I find Dr. Evergreen and—"

The woman at his elbow was gone.

"Okay, that's . . . weird."

He waded into the party. He did not see Dr. Evergreen or his wife. He felt awkward and wished he'd waited for Penny so he would have had someone to talk to. He zigzagged his way to the wine table, grabbed a random jug of red, and filled a plastic cup. He tasted it. Good. He read the label on the giant jug. Three Thieves' Red. Horse-riding desperados adorned the label, pistols in the air. Allen had had Dr. Evergreen pegged as too pretentious for jug wine, but maybe he had the guy all wrong. Maybe this would all be okay after all.

Allen accidentally bumped someone behind him. Purple wine spilled over his knuckles.

"Watch it, douche bag."

Allen mumbled an apology, then saw it was Kurt Ramis, one of the testosterone-driven fiction writers from the MFA program. He wore a leather bomber jacket with a patch representing a fictional squadron. Shoulder-length, auburn hair carefully arranged to seem windblown, square jaw. Kurt thought he was the next Hemmingway; most of his fiction involved shooting large animals and getting laid.

"Hey, don't sweat it," Kurt said. "How's the Jane Austen studies coming? They fit you for a dress yet?"

"You're hilarious. And it's the Brontë sisters."

The two girls on either side of Kurt giggled, but one of them said, "Be nice."

"Whatever. Come on, ladies, and sit with me in the gazebo. I'll tell you about the novel I'm working on. A rugged game hunter must guide a spoiled heiress through the Alaskan wilderness. It's got bestseller written all over it."

Asshole.

Allen decided to leave. To hell with it.

He stopped, spotted Penny emerging from the sliding glass

doors in the rear of Evergreen's house. She wore a black cocktail dress, the modest V of her neckline showing a hint of healthy pink skin. She was rosy-cheeked; hair done up and back. Allen was impressed. Penny actually looked like a girl. She was almost pretty.

She saw him, and her smile widened bright and white. She skipped over to Allen.

"You look good," he said.

"You think?" She did a little half spin. "I've had this dress for a while but not an excuse to wear it. Have you talked to Dr. Evergreen yet?"

"I haven't seen him. I was just getting ready to leave."

"Oh, don't do that. I just got here."

"I can stay another few minutes, I guess."

She smiled, and Allen did too. *When she smiles like that, she is pretty, I guess.*

He shuffled awkwardly, suddenly found it not so easy to talk to her.

"I could use some wine," she said gently.

"Oh, yeah. Okay. Let me get it."

He wriggled his way through the crowd back to the table, refilled his plastic cup with Three Thieves' Red, and filled a new one for Penny. He felt like he was at senior prom. Nervous. *Snap out of it. It's just Penny. Good old pal Penny.*

He brought the wine back, handed her a cup. They stood, drank. He put his free hand in his pocket, shuffled his feet. The party ebbed and flowed around them.

"This is good wine," she said.

"Yes." He looked at her, looked away again.

She moved in closer to him, surreptitiously pointed with her pinky at a young girl in denim across the party, and whispered in Allen's ear, "She's in my poetry workshop and wrote a poem about a professor she has a crush on. You don't think it's Dr. Evergreen, do you?"

He snorted laughter, covered his mouth. They huddled together, whispering a game guessing the life stories of the other
party guests based on how they looked. They laughed, and it was
easy. This was good old Penny. Everything was right again.

"That girl in the thrift-store dress is creepy," Penny said. "I
heard her boyfriend dumped her and she just started cutting her
leg with a kitchen knife. Just sat there, sawing bloody lines into
her thigh."

Speaking of creepy . . . "Have you ever met Dr. Evergreen's
wife?" Allen asked.

Penny shook her head. "But I've seen her with Dr. Evergreen
at parties and readings. She looked beautiful, but sort of distant.
You've met her?"

"Briefly."

"What's she like?"

"I'm not really sure," Allen said. He found he could hardly
remember her face. "She's light on her feet, I know that."

Penny grinned. "What the heck does *that* mean?"

Allen started to explain when the hysterical woman found
them.

"Oh, my God, Penny, you are *not* going to believe it." The
new girl was petite, with sharp features, short black hair, a plaid
skirt, and stylish white blouse. Pearls. Allen had seen her around
the department and thought of her as Back East pretty. Red eyes.
Tears had smeared her makeup. She swallowed great, heaving
sobs between words.

She latched onto Penny. People stared openly.

"Calm down, Blanche," Penny patted her friend on the shoulder. "Let's go this way. Come on, honey."

Penny led Blanche away from the gawkers, around the side
of the house and under a low tree. Not knowing what else to do,
Allen followed.

"Now, take a breath." Penny held her friend by the forearms,
looked her square in the eyes.

"It's K-Kurt," Blanche said. "I s-saw him kissing that skank Missy Logan in the woods next to Dr. Evergreen's house."

Penny frowned, shook her head. "I'm so sorry, Blanche. I *warned* you about him."

"Missy f-fucking Logan," spat Blanche. "She's a cow! Why would he—" Her words were lost in a new torrent of wailing and hand-wringing.

"I didn't see him with Missy earlier," Allen said. "He was with two other women."

Blanche wailed even louder, then threw herself onto Penny's shoulder, tears and snot flowing freely. Penny patted her friend's back and shot an accusing look at Allen.

Allen shrugged. "I'm just saying—"

"Well, don't," Penny said.

Allen mouthed, "*Sorry.*" Then he took a step back.

"I've a good mind to find that boy and chew his ass right off," Penny said. "Blanche, honey, stay here and pull yourself together. There's a lot of people at this party, and you don't want to give that rat-fuck Kurt the satisfaction."

Blanche sobbed and nodded.

"Allen, stay with Blanche."

"Me? But—"

"Stay!"

"Yes, ma'am."

"Hold this." Penny handed Allen her wine, stalked off, her fists clenched in righteous woman rage.

Allen looked at Blanche and cleared his throat. "That Kurt guy. He's an asshole, you know? You're better off without him."

Blanche sniffed.

"Uh . . . can I get you a drink or something?"

Blanche nodded, sniffed again.

"Okay. Stay put. I'll be right back."

Allen found the Thieves again, filled another plastic cup. Might as well top off his own drink and Penny's. He drained the jug.

Two hands. Three cups. He gathered them into an awkward triangle, tried to walk, spilling purple over his hands. He slowed his walk, hunching over, balancing the wine. He looked at the wine as he walked, so deep and dark, like fresh blood. The blood of thieves.

He wasn't watching where he was going and crashed into someone, knocking all three cups of wine down his front, staining his shirt and pants. He gasped at the splash of liquid, bit back a string of vulgarities.

He stepped back, looked at the bearlike figure before him.

"Jesus Christ, kid. You smell like a Napa Valley wino."

Allen gulped. "Sorry, Dr. Evergreen. I hope I didn't get any on you."

THREE

Allen came out of the first-floor bathroom, holding up a pair of Dr. Evergreen's Portland Trailblazers sweatpants with one hand, his wine-stained clothes bunched in the other. He swam in an extra-extra-large Gothic State T-shirt, also Dr. Evergreen's. It was like wearing a circus tent.

Dr. Forest Evergreen was lumberjack big, Paul Bunyan-ish, barrel-chested, chin the size of an engine block.

Allen went from the bathroom to the kitchen. All modern stainless steel and computerized appliances. His eyeballs ping-ponged back and forth. Tentative. Where to go next? "Dr. Evergreen?"

A voice from down the hall. "This way."

Allen went down the hall, past closed doors toward the end, where a half-open door spilled dim light into the hallway. He paused again.

"Get in here."

Allen started, went inside.

Dr. Evergreen's study was the complete opposite of his modern kitchen. It felt old, ancient in fact, like some old wizard's workroom from a bad Dungeons & Dragons movie. Very old, leather-bound books lined the shelves. Strange, arcane charts and graphs hung on the walls, and a large globe of the world during the Victorian Empire stood in one corner. Behind Evergreen's desk hung a yellowing chart, a detailed schematic of the human skeleton. The desk itself was big enough to match Evergreen—darkly polished wood with the nicks and scratches of centuries. Evergreen sat at the desk, a tumbler of amber liquid in one meaty fist. The half-glasses perched at the end of his nose looked small compared to his massive pumpkin head, like they'd been ripped off a doll.

Evergreen hunched over the desk, reading from a brochure without looking up. " 'Imbued with old-world charm, this spacious apartment overlooks the fields and trees of Letna Park. Mere steps to the closest tram line, charming pubs, and a variety of restaurants.'" Evergreen looked over the glasses at Allen. "What do you think?"

"What is it?"

"An apartment in Prague."

"Oh. Sounds good. I'm sure I won't have a problem."

"Not for you, pinhead. For me. I've arranged some dorm space for you."

"Okay."

"You're not going to spill red wine all over the Czech Republic, are you?"

"I'm really sorry, Dr. Evergreen. I'm not usually that clumsy, and—"

Evergreen motioned to the chair across from him. "Sit."

Allen sat.

"You know what I expect of you?"

"I think," Allen said. "I spoke to Professor Carpenter."

"Uh-huh. And what did ganja-head say?"

"That I'd be helping you with research. Something with Kafka."

"Yeah, that's the story, but I've got something a lot more important for you to work on. A real challenge for your research skills."

"Oh?"

"I'm getting a grant from the university for the trip, so it has to be some lit thing. I've basically written it already. But frankly, I have more important things to work on. Are we clear?"

"No."

"Don't worry, I'll fill you in later," Evergreen said. "Stop looking like that."

"Like what?"

"Like somebody pissed down your back. Don't worry. It'll be fine."

"If you can give me some kind of idea what I'll be researching, maybe I can get started right away," Allen suggested. "Get a head start."

"Save it for later. Think of it like a scavenger hunt. It'll be fun. You'll see."

FOUR

Allen went back out to the party and marched straight for the wine. He was in for a long semester. And a long summer. He gulped the wine, refilled the cup. Maybe he'd make himself drunk. Why not?

Penny planted herself in front of him. "Where the hell have you been? I told you to stay with Blanche. Why are you dressed like that?"

"I don't have time to babysit your distraught friends. Look, I don't mean to be rude, but I'm not having a very good time."

"Just tell her I'm looking for her if you see her."

"Where are you going?"

"Into those woods," Penny said. "If I know Blanche, she'll go in there and try to catch Kurt making out with whatever skank is next on his to-do list."

"The woods? Don't go into the woods," Allen said.

"Why not?"

"Because it's . . . the woods."

"If I see the big bad wolf, I'll point him toward Grandma's house."

"Just yell if you need any help."

Penny rolled her eyes and left.

Allen sipped wine. The party came and went around him. Dull.

"I hope you don't mind if I introduce myself."

Allen looked up from his wine, raised an eyebrow.

The man who had addressed him was a priest—black suit, white collar. Tall and athletic, late thirties or early forties. His hair was a deep black and just over his ears. Blue eyes. Crow's-feet. But a bright, energetic smile. He shook Allen's hand firmly.

"Father?"

"I'm Father Laramie," said the priest, "but I hope you'll call me Paul."

"Father Paul."

"Just Paul."

"Okay."

"Penny tells me you're Catholic," said Father Paul. "I didn't know if you were aware we held a Wednesday mass in the chapel on campus."

"Ah." Allen took a swig of wine to buy himself a second. He'd mentioned to Penny that he'd been brought up Catholic, but he hadn't attended mass in years. He had not even realized Gothic State had an on-campus chapel. How long since his last confession? Well, really, what did Allen have to confess?

This thought depressed him somewhat.

"I'm hoping I can convince you to come around and see us sometime," Father Paul said. "I wouldn't be doing my job if I didn't encourage you a little."

"Uh."

"I know how busy you students are, but it's often just these busy times when students need to take a break from the frenzy of the semester and refocus on something spiritual and calming. We have a surprisingly large congregation."

"Oh."

"I'd like you to have something."

Father Paul pushed something into Allen's hand. He looked down into his open palm and saw a velvet jewelry box. He opened it and saw a silver crucifix.

"That's a little welcome gift we present to all of our Catholic students," the priest told him. "We want people to know we're here and that we care."

Allen took the crucifix from the box. It wasn't small; it was heavy, maybe solid silver. Allen had a hard time believing they gave out one of these to every Catholic on campus. He started to hand it back to the priest. "I think this might be too much. I don't feel right."

"No, no, please don't worry," Father Paul said. "We pay for them out of the orphan fund."

Allen blinked.

"That's a joke, Allen."

Allen smiled weakly. "Sorry."

"There's no obligation," Father Paul said. "Why don't you wear it?"

"Well, I don't generally—"

"Wear it, Allen." The priest put a firm hand on Allen's shoulder, and an abrupt gravity descended upon the conversation. "You'd be surprised how such a simple gesture can bring . . . comfort."

Father Paul's firm gaze held him a second, and Allen's mouth fell open, speechless. *What the hell's going on here?*

Allen was about to firmly insist he didn't want the crucifix when a piercing scream split the night.

"Penny!" Allen dropped his wine and ran for the line of trees. He plunged into the woods along the narrow hiking path. "Penny!"

Thin branches slapped his face in the darkness. Allen winced but kept running. He turned a corner and smacked into somebody coming fast from the other direction. They both tumbled, went into the bushes. Allen stood, reached for the person with whom he'd collided, and pulled her to her feet.

Blanche threw herself on Allen. "Oh, my God, oh, my God." Hysterical. Gulping for breath.

Allen shook her by the shoulders. "Where's Penny?"

"My God, it's awful. He's dead. He's—he's been—it's—" She shook her head frantically, the sobbing coming back double.

He's dead, she'd said. Not Penny. Allen shook her again by the shoulders, thought about slapping her like he'd seen people do in the movies. "Who's dead, Blanche?"

Blanche made a new, even shriller, panicked sound, pushed away from Allen, and ran back in the direction of the party.

Allen followed the path in the other direction, but he didn't run now. His feet felt leaden. Fear sweat broke out on his forehead, and silver moonlight filtered through the thin canopy of leaves overhead. With Blanche's hysterical keening fading into the background, an eerie silence blanketed the woods. The bird chirps, the rustle of leaves, and the scurrying of squirrels had all been swallowed by the pall of dread that had suddenly sunk its claws into the landscape.

Allen stopped walking, his breathing coming shallow. He looked back over his shoulder.

No. Keep going. Penny is still out here someplace.

He made himself jog forward, his footfalls crunching leaves so loudly that the sound seemed obscene. A smallish clearing opened before him, and he immediately saw the body lying on the ground, looking waxlike and unreal in the moonlight. Allen took three quick steps toward the body and froze.

The head was missing.

Allen approached more slowly, fighting down a wave of nausea. A bit of spine stuck out from the ragged neck hole, as if the head had been twisted off savagely and suddenly. Blood still oozed like raspberry syrup. A thick, wet coppery smell permeated the air. Allen didn't need the man's face to identify the body. The bomber jacket told the story.

Kurt Ramis, Blanche's loudmouthed boyfriend.

Allen briefly fantasized about Blanche flying into a rage at Kurt's infidelity, wrapping her arms around his neck, and wrenching Kurt's head free of his body.

Unlikely.

Who the hell could do such a thing?

Allen heard a rustling in the bushes to his left. His head jerked around to see, and his body froze. He heard it before he saw it, a breathing and snorting, and then the low growl. Something in Allen's bowels went watery.

It poked its head through the bushes. Eyes glowed like green fire; he saw a muzzle and pointed ears, red-brown fur standing out in spikes. A dog, an enormous dog of some kind, growling, drool dripping from gigantic fangs. No. Not a dog.

A wolf.

It was gigantic, dwarfed any wolf he'd ever seen at the zoo. It snarled, lips peeled back to display two rows of yellow teeth. It crouched low, and Allen could almost feel its muscles tense, the powerful creature poised to spring.

He remembered his grandfather saying never to run from a dog. They sense fear. Make eye contact. Back it down.

Allen very much doubted his grandfather's advice applied in this situation.

It's going to jump on me now. It's going to eat me. Holy shit, I've got two seconds to live what the hell am I going to—

Voices from back down the path, several coming toward him. A group, many talking in frantic voices.

The wolf cocked its head toward the sound, listened a split second, then turned tail and vanished into the woods, departing with impressive speed.

A mob formed behind Allen. A girl screamed. Allen recognized Father Paul's voice saying, "Dear God!"

A heavy hand on his shoulder. Dr. Evergreen. "Jesus, what the hell happened here?"

Allen's head was spinning, his gaze still fixed on the patch of bushes where he'd seen the beast. "I have absolutely no idea."

FIVE

Let us leave Gothic State University and its people and environs a moment, and let us travel across the country, across time zones, the Atlantic Ocean, to Europe, and a small cobblestone street in the Jewish Quarter of Prague in the Czech Republic.

A side note: An alarming number of people still refer to it as Czechoslovakia. It's a republic now. I digress.

The Jewish Quarter, or *Josefov*. Full of old-world charm and souvenir stands. Tourists simply went apeshit for old-world charm and souvenir stands, and nothing said "old-world charm" like a plastic replica of the Old-New Synagogue perched atop a plastic base with little Czech flags around the edges and a hole on one side for sharpening pencils. The Old-New Synagogue on Maiselova Street was the oldest in Europe still actively used as a house of prayer. The spiritual zeal of the Quarter was probably best expressed by a T-shirt that read, "Prague Oy!" and was available in all sizes at a nearby kiosk. In a narrow house next to a jewelry store, mere steps from this temple of worship, lived the disgraced rabbi, Abraham Zabel.

Zabel was something of a wizard, and he sold his occult powers to the highest bidder.

There was good money in this.

Zabel is about to entertain an unhappy client.

Let's watch.

Abraham Zabel sat at the old scratched desk in the small office of his *Josefov* house. It was going on evening, and the steady din from the street of hucksters roping in tourists had relented somewhat. He thought often of giving up the house for someplace quieter in the suburbs, but the Jewish Quarter was too perfect, too close to places he needed to visit, people he needed to stay in contact with for his business. The tourists would remain a minor annoyance.

He poured himself a glass of port and returned his attention to his journal, a combination diary and appointment book. On Thursday he had a demon banishing, but then he was free for the weekend. He relished the time off but was concerned that business had been slow. Well, no worry. It would eventually pick up again. It always did.

The dark arts were ever in demand.

He opened an intricately carved wooden desktop humidor and removed a thin cigar, lit it with a thin silver lighter. The humidor was carved with symbols from ancient Hebrew—various warding spells and protections. Zabel doubted the spells retained any potency, but the box looked nice, and it was convenient for the cigars.

A knock at his office door startled him. It meant someone had let themselves into his locked home. Zabel thought briefly of the small revolver in his bottom desk drawer but decided to leave it. He was well protected in the little office. Zabel was a cautious man.

He was about to tell his visitor to enter when the door swung open and a man entered. Zabel knew him: Pascal Worshamn, a client. He had bright blue eyes, alert and energetic, and a smooth pink face that made him look youngish, although the dusting of gray over his ears told his real age.

"Hello, Pascal." Zabel motioned to the small chair on the other side of his desk. "A seat?"

Pascal didn't sit. "We haven't concluded our business, Zabel."

Zabel spoke good Czech and passable German, but he'd been born in Brooklyn to Czech immigrants. Pascal was from some upper-crust place in London, so the conversation went on in English.

"I told you on the phone," Zabel said. "You get what you pay for."

"It didn't work."

Zabel sighed. "It worked as well as it could. It killed the wrong man, I admit, but that must be because Evergreen caused some distraction. He's not without his own skills."

"Can't you control the thing? Tell it to try again."

"It can't," Zabel insisted. "It was commanded to destroy itself after the kill. It wouldn't do to have a golem lumbering around attracting unwanted attention. It probably threw itself off a cliff into the ocean."

"Make another one," Pascal said.

"Pay me, and I will. You cheaped out the first time. You should have sent me along, to make the thing on the spot, so I could control the situation, allow for changes and surprises. My resources are not unlimited."

"Neither are the Society's." Pascal pulled a small automatic from his jacket pocket, aimed it at Zabel's chest. "I must insist the Society get its money's worth. You'll make another golem."

"Only if you pay me."

"I don't think you appreciate the implications of this 9 mm pistol." Pascal stepped forward, trying to appear menacing.

"Threats, is it? Fine, let's trade threats. You're not going to leave here alive, Pascal. That's my promise to you."

"Are you deluded? Drunk? Too much port for you, my dear Zabel. I'll draw your attention to the obvious one last time. I'm the one with the pistol."

"Shoot then."

"What?"

"Go on," Zabel said. "Shoot."

Pascal lifted the pistol, stood pointing it for five seconds. Ten seconds. A light sweat broke out on his forehead. The hand holding the pistol developed a subtle tremor. Pascal laughed, embarrassed and nervous. "I can't seem to pull the trigger."

"See the tapestry behind me? The paintings on either side of you?"

Pascal turned his head, looked at them. Abstract images with intricate patterns.

"The patterns are subtle, but woven into the mix are hypnotic suggestions reinforced by powerful spells," Zabel explained. "Right now, your subconscious is being told that I am your best friend in the world and that you would never harm me. Every second you look at the pattern, the subliminal command grows stronger."

Pascal jerked his gaze away from the painting, redoubled his efforts to shoot Zabel.

"It's no use, Pascal. Even a glance is enough."

"This isn't over, Zabel. The Society won't stand for it. They'll dog your every step."

"Lars!" Zabel raised his voice. "Lars, come here."

The floor shook with heavy footsteps. The thing that appeared in the office doorway made Pascal wince and step back, a surprised gasp leaking out of him.

The wooden man was six and a half feet tall, put together with mismatched pieces of wood. He smelled like pine. The face was an agonized grimace, wide, hollow eyes carved in dark wood, the mouth slightly open, the corner of a folded piece of parchment stuck out from between the thickly carved lips.

"Lars, please dispose of our friend Pascal."

The golem advanced on Pascal, who screamed and backed against the wall. This time the pistol fired. Pascal squeezed the trigger until he emptied the magazine, the shots scarring the golem's chest, woodchips and splinters flying.

The golem didn't flinch; it grabbed the wrist of Pascal's gun hand and twisted. *Snap.* Pascal screamed again, and the gun fell to the floor. One of the golem's powerful arms went around Pascal's neck. The man squirmed and tried to pull free, panic aflame in his eyes. "Zabel, please. Zabel!"

The golem squeezed with one arm, put a gigantic hand on top of Pascal's head, and twisted. Pascal screamed in raw agony, and the golem twisted again and pulled. A wet snap and a crunch. Pascal's body went limp. The golem continued to wrench at the head, Pascal's limbs flopping around like a rag doll's.

With a final, mighty tug, the golem pulled off Pascal's head with a wet pop. Blood sprayed.

Zabel looked at his servant, who was cradling the head in the crook of his arm like a football. Perhaps he'd been hasty. Information was never a bad idea. Zabel took a large serving tray from his small closet and set it on his desk. He instructed Lars to set the head there. "Clean up the body in the usual manner, please, Lars."

The golem threw the corpse over his shoulder and carried it away.

Zabel sat at his desk, facing Pascal's head. He pulled a small velvet bag from his desk drawer, spilled the materials in front of him. He took a polished, dark red stone and placed it into Pascal's mouth. He lit a candle, mixed some powders and herbs in a small bowl, then mumbled a few syllables and blew the mixture into Pascal's face.

The head's eyes fluttered and opened. "Wha hammpned?"

"Move the stone to the side of your mouth with your tongue," Zabel instructed. "You'll be able to talk."

"What happened?" Pascal asked. His eyes darted to either side. "Good God! What's happened to me?"

"Did you tell anyone else in the Society you'd hired me to construct the golem?"

"No," Pascal said. "I was ordered to eliminate Evergreen. That's all. How I went about it was my own business. Damn, why did I tell you that?"

"You're a Truth Head now," Zabel said. "You can't lie. Who ordered you to eliminate Evergreen?"

"Jackson Fay," said the head.

Zabel sucked in breath. Jackson Fay. The name was not unknown to him. A very dangerous spellcaster. "Why eliminate Evergreen?"

"I was told he'd persisted with unholy associations and would cause trouble if not handled. Fay did not elaborate. He simply trusted me to get the job done without going through the bureaucracy of a full Council vote."

Zabel's lip curled into a mocking grin. "It seems Fay's trust was misplaced."

"The Society will still be suspicious when I don't report in," Pascal said. "They have ways. They will find you and avenge me."

"Perhaps, but not anytime soon."

"What the hell is this in my mouth?"

"A bloodstone," Zabel said. "If you spit it out, you'll break the spell."

"Then I will spit it out and damn your spell, you son of a bitch."

"Go ahead. Spit."

Pascal shifted the stone from one side of his mouth to the other but didn't spit.

Zabel laughed. "You see? It's not so easy to give up life, is it? To resign yourself to oblivion. How we do cling to hope, we pitiful human creatures. Even now you're thinking there must be some way out of this, some way to reverse what has happened. Some do, in fact, spit out the bloodstone, but not you, Pascal. Oh no, not you."

"Damn you to hell, Zabel."

"Lars!"

The golem returned carrying a mop and a bucket.

Zabel said, "Before you clean up the blood, take Pascal's head to the cupboard with the others."

The golem scooped up the head, then carried it out of the room under its arm.

"This isn't over!" Pascal screamed back at Zabel. "Do you hear me, you bastard? I might just be a head, but I'll get you. I'll get you, Zabel. I'll see you rot in hell!"

SIX

Dr. Evergreen's party was almost no fun at all after the discovery of the headless corpse.

The police showed up. Guests were questioned and questioned again. Efficient men in white coats zipped the body into a black bag and wheeled it away in an ambulance. A few special people like Allen were asked to come down to the station for further questioning. Allen dutifully went along and answered what he guessed were routine questions.

As if there's ever anything routine about a decapitation.

Allen sat in the bland interrogation room sipping tepid coffee under fluorescent lights. His stomach was upset. He was tired. He vaguely felt like the cops suspected him of something even though he'd been assured numerous times they only wanted to be as complete as possible and if Allen could just be patient, they'd wrap all this up as soon as possible.

The police evidently had a very different definition of "as soon as possible."

Another cop asked him the same list of questions for the third time. There were forms to sign. They confirmed Allen's contact information. Just as it looked like they were about to let

Allen go, a particularly dour-looking cop had one more question for him.

"You have any knowledge of what this might be about?" The cop held up a tiny glass vial, sealed at the top. It was three-quarters full of thick, red liquid. Crescent-shaped particles floated in the liquid, in addition to strands of what appeared to be thread.

"I've never seen that," Allen said.

"It's blood and fingernail clippings and hair," the cop said. "It was found in the victim's jacket pocket."

"Okay, gross," Allen said. "Hey, I have *nothing* to do with that, okay? All I did was find the body."

"You ran into the woods after you heard the scream. That's right?"

"Yes. I told you that." He'd said nothing about Penny. They hadn't asked.

"And there was a wolf at the scene, which ran away when the other party guests approached the scene?"

"It was dark. Like I said before, it was probably just a big dog." Allen was eager not to seem crazy-cuckoo.

"We appreciate your time, Mr. Cabbot. We'll call you if we think of anything else to ask."

Allen left the police station. Fast. All he wanted to do was get back to his dorm and sleep. It was after midnight by the time he got there. He slouched up the stairs, unlocked his door, and went into the dorm room, already unbuttoning his shirt, anticipating nothing but deep, dark sleep.

"Allen!"

"Jesus!" Allen clutched his chest. "You scared the hell out of me."

"Where have you been?" Penny curled on Allen's bed in sweatpants and a T-shirt. "I've been waiting for hours and worried about you."

"Where have *I* been? Where'd you go at the party? Jesus,

I heard this scream and thought you were being murdered or something. Did you hear about Kurt Ramis?"

"Of course! It's been all over the news. I went to my car to get something, and when I came back I couldn't get near Dr. Evergreen's house. The street was choked with police cars."

"It was horrible. Penny, something ripped Kurt's head right off his body. I've never seen anything like it, and I never want to again. The police kept me for hours."

Penny sucked in breath, slid to the edge of the bed. "Holy shit, Allen, they don't think you did it?"

"Of course not. But I found the body. They had a lot of questions. Something else." Allen hesitated. "Penny, I swear I saw a huge wolf near the murder scene. I thought it was going to eat me, swear to God."

Penny stood slowly. "Oh?"

"I mean, this fucking thing was snarling and going crazy. I really thought it was about to pounce."

"Wolves are not indigenous to this area," Penny said flatly.

"Well, I know what I saw, and it was—hey, are you mad at me or something?"

"It's just that with everything going on, I don't think you need to exaggerate, telling people your wolf story."

"It's not a *story*."

"It was probably just a big dog."

Allen blew out a sigh, flopped onto his bed. "Fine. A big dog."

"Listen, Allen." Penny eased down onto the bed next to him. "If you don't want to be alone . . . I mean, if you want to talk or have some company, I know what you saw was probably upsetting and everything."

"No, thanks. I'm exhausted. All I want to do is go to sleep."

Penny stood again quickly. "Of course, I mean . . . sure. I know you're probably exhausted. Right. I'll just go."

"I talked to your friend Father Paul at the party."

Penny brightened slightly. "Isn't he nice? I don't get to mass as often as I should, but I go when he's on duty."

"I don't know. The whole conversation seemed a bit odd." Allen pulled the crucifix from the pocket of his sweatpants. "He insisted I take this."

"Good. You should wear it."

"I don't think so."

"Look." She dipped two fingers under the collar of her T-shirt and came out with a silver crucifix. It was smaller but otherwise identical. "You wear yours, and I'll wear mine. We can be Savior buddies."

Allen laughed. "Maybe."

"We're friends, aren't we?"

"Mmmmmm. What have you done for me lately?"

"I'm serious," Penny said.

"You know we are."

"Then do this for me," she said. "Simply because I'm asking you to."

"But why?"

"Do it for me, and I'll tell you later."

Allen looked at her, then at the crucifix, and back to her. He hadn't figured her for the religious type.

"Didn't I get you through Professor Mayflower's Restoration lit class?"

"Yeah."

"Then humor me."

He smiled and shrugged, slipped the thin chain over his head. The crucifix hung heavy to the middle of his chest. "There. Happy? You saved my soul."

"Maybe."

Penny left him to sleep and to dream.

You've probably heard all the Freud stuff about dreams, the

subconscious stretching and giving itself a workout, all those dreams that originate from within. Going to class in your underwear. The dream where you're falling and falling and falling.

But there's another sort of dream too. The kind that comes from elsewhere, that wriggles into your mind. An invasion. Allen dreamed of eyes. Cool, calm eyes of the night, eyes he felt had been watching him for centuries. Eyes that ate the light and lived in darkness. And he was cold; he shivered.

Allen awoke at dawn, covered in sweat and burdened with some nameless dread that he couldn't explain.

PRAGUE

The rest of the semester passed uneasily. The headless murder lingered in the newspapers and on the TV news, the story catching fire again whenever the police insisted they had a lead or were questioning a new suspect. Every trail, however, led to a dead end. The mystery eventually passed into local legend, the tale becoming strange and exaggerated. For Halloween, the bloody, headless corpse wearing a bomber jacket became a favorite costume of Gothic State students.

In the meantime, Allen passed his exams (with Penny as a dutiful study partner) and readied himself for his journey overseas. The week before their flight, Evergreen peppered him with emails, reminding him of books and materials to pack. Allen was being asked to go ahead of Dr. Evergreen to supervise the arrival of some equipment about which Evergreen was very vague. He grew exceedingly cranky if pressed for an explanation. Allen did not relish the idea of being in a foreign city alone.

Here he comes now. You can see his American Airlines flight descending toward Prague airport after a three-hour layover at Heathrow. Allen is coming to me, to my hometown. I wasn't born here, no, but after so many centuries one can't help but think of it as home.

There he is coming through customs. He looks terrible, hasn't slept a wink. Poor bastard. I'd show him around town if I could, but life's a bitch when you're not corporeal.

SEVEN

The surly Czech cab driver dropped him in front of the apartment building in the little neighborhood across from Letna Park. Rain flayed the world, and Allen, struggling with his two enormous suitcases, was soaked in just the quick dash across the sidewalk and into the building. He hauled his luggage up two flights of stairs, then collapsed in front of number three, the apartment Dr. Evergreen had arranged for himself for the summer.

Allen unzipped the front pouch of the first suitcase, fished out the key he'd been given, and entered the apartment. It was spacious, with two bedrooms, a sitting area that bled into the kitchen, and a balcony that overlooked the street in front. From this vantage point he saw warm light in the windows of a neighborhood pub not even half a block away. He had a sudden, overwhelming urge to sample the Czech beer he'd heard so much about, but if he missed the delivery, there would be hell to pay with Dr. Evergreen.

And anyway, he was getting wet again standing on the balcony.

Back inside, he changed into dry clothes. He turned on the

TV, found he had three channels. One showed something in-comprehensible in Czech, and another showed something in-comprehensible in German. The third showed soccer.

Allen switched off the television and turned his attention to the present Penny had given him when she'd dropped him off at the airport.

The Rogue's Guide to Prague was intended to be an irrever-ent travel guide to the city, pointing out all the usual tourist at-tractions, offering helpful hints for travelers, but also providing tongue-in-cheek commentary about various parts of the city and its environs. He read the entry for the Letna neighborhood:

> More difficult, but not impossible, to locate a hooker in one of the local taverns of this quiet neighborhood. Better chances at the nearby Holešovice train station. The area is bordered by Letna Park on the south and Wenceslas Park to the north, known for its extensive rose gardens. There are numerous quiet grottos and shrubby enclaves where prostitutes can pleasure you if you're too cheap to spring for a room.

Allen glanced through some of the area's highlights.

> •*The Charles Bookstore and Café*: Unlike the more touristy places in the city center, you can still get breakfast or lunch here for a song. The strong coffee will crush your balls. Cold beer. Local prices. The girls with tattoos and nose rings who work at the place know enough English to refuse your advances.
> •*Metronome Sculpture in Letna Park*: This useless piece of crap gives the graffiti artists something new to deface instead of the old giant statue of Stalin. But the view here is magnificent. You can look down into the heart of Prague where things are actually happening.

The constant racket of skateboarders will make you long for the old days of the iron-fisted Communists who would have sent these punks to the gulag without blinking.

• *Kjyeilkle's Pub*: No English. Very few hookers.

Allen closed the book, wondered if Penny had meant it as a gag or if she'd really thought Allen would be able to get useful information out of it. He waited another hour, dozed off to the sound of the rain against the windows and balcony. A harsh knock on the door woke him with a start. He rubbed his eyes, stumbled to answer it.

He opened the door to four grumpy, rain-soaked men, who babbled at him in Czech until he got the message they wanted him to move the hell out of the way. He stepped aside, and the men grunted and heaved a long wooden crate into the middle of the apartment. They shoved a clipboard into Allen's hands and mimed for him to sign it, which he did right before they left, muttering and frowning.

The wooden crate was nearly seven feet long and came almost up to his belt. He'd been told to wait for some things Dr. Evergreen was having shipped, but Allen had figured it was just miscellaneous luggage and books. An overwhelming curiosity seized him, a strong desire to crowbar the thing open and take a look.

He ran his hands across the rough wood, knocked. Thick planks, something heavy inside. He tried to push the crate off to the side but couldn't budge it alone. He sat on the crate, let his legs dangle. The rain continued its hypnotic splat against the windows. After signing for Evergreen's package, Allen was supposed to see to his own accommodations, but he was loath to trek through the downpour.

A whiff of something wet and pungent caught his attention. Allen leaned over, put his nose close to the surface of the crate, and sniffed an earthy smell, like freshly tilled soil, moist and rich.

Allen stretched out on top of the crate, yawned. He was jet-lagged. His eyelids grew heavy, and in seconds he was drawn into deep, dark slumber.

Night had fallen. Allen rose from the crate, the full moon casting a pale blue light through the open balcony door. He shivered, a cold wind flowing around him. He saw his own breath fogging between his lips.

It's summer. I didn't pack anything warm. He hugged himself.

A creak of floorboards. Allen jerked his head around, looked at the front door, saw nothing. The room seemed to groan under its own weight, and Allen suddenly felt the immensity of the apartment building, an eerie self-awareness of himself as an insignificant part of a greater whole, sleeping minds in other apartments, people eating, screwing, watching television.

A gust of cold wind on his neck and he turned back to the balcony. Allen gasped at the figure standing there.

Her skin glowed white, the frigid wind lifting the midnight hair off her shoulders, her eyes blazing with cold fire. Cassandra. It was Evergreen's wife, wearing some shimmering, silky gown, her figure clear beneath the sheer material, soft white breasts threatening to overflow the gown's plunging V-neck. She stretched her hands out to him, the red of her glossy fingernails like radioactive raspberry fire. The color matched her lips, the contrast of the bright red against her white skin doing strange, animal things to him.

Allen. Her lips didn't move; the voice echoed in his head.

She drifted closer to him, her feet seeming not to touch the ground, the gown billowing around her. The wind howled now, washing the apartment intensely cold. The drapes flapping violently, bits of paper and debris flying around the room.

Allen was unable to move his body or rip his eyes away from Cassandra's gaze.

She moved close to him, rested her hands on his thighs. An electric shock went to his groin, his sudden anticipation growing. He trembled as her face inched toward his, felt her breath on his mouth. She sank into him, breasts pushing against his chest.

Allen trembled, his erection straining painfully against his jeans. Her lips pressed frozen against him, a violent mix of cold fire, pain, and ecstasy. He tried to push away, but Cassandra's tongue pushed its way into his mouth, invading him.

He wrenched himself away and scooted back on the crate. He opened his mouth to scream but couldn't draw breath. He worked his mouth, tried to get air. *Allen.* Her voice filled his mind.

Allen's eyes popped open. He sucked breath and screamed, rolled off the crate, and landed with a thud on the hard wooden floor.

He raised his head slowly, looked around. It was still day. The rain had eased but still fell in a drizzle. He was alone. His fingers went briefly to his lips, the dream images lingering and disturbing. Arousal and dread hung on him in equal portions.

He backed away from the crate, gathering his luggage as he went. He left the apartment, flew down the stairs two at a time, and sprinted from the building, out into the drizzle.

Prague lay before him like a mysterious stranger in an old hat.

An exotic woman waiting for him in poor light.

Like an inviting gypsy with a brand-new iPod.

Anyway, it was Prague.

EIGHT

Allen overpaid a cab driver to take him to Charles University.

The housing administrator spoke good English and sent Allen to a crusty brick building, down a narrow dim hall, to a ten-by-ten-foot room with a barren desk and a set of cold war bunk beds. It resembled a prison cell more than a dorm room, the walls an industrial sort of faded green, the tile floor gray and cold. The view from the window was the brick wall of another building five feet away.

The university had been founded in the 1300s. The dorms didn't seem much more modern. Naked pipes ran up the walls and across the ceiling. They clanked periodically.

Allen unpacked a length of thin line and stretched it across the room, draped his wet clothes over it. He changed again, this time into khaki shorts, white ankle socks and Sketchers, and a dark green Gothic State T-shirt. He'd been told there were laundry machines in the basement of the dorm. If he kept getting soaked, he would probably have to visit it sooner than planned. He put the rest of his things into the tiny closet.

Jet lag pulled at him, but the haunting nightmare of Evergreen's wife still fogged his brain. He would not be able to sleep. Not yet. Maybe a jolt of caffeine would help. Allen consulted *The Rogue's Guide* for a nearby coffee shop.

> •*The Globe Café & Bookstore:* Convenient to the National Theater and a number of tram and metro stops, the Globe is a favorite of expatriates tired of struggling with their Czech language books. Patrons enjoy a cold pilsner or a strong cup of coffee all while luxuriating in the English language. Tired of chicks rebuffing you in some foreign tongue? Come get shot down in English. It's all so comfortably familiar. Hey, you might even get lucky with some coed from Long Island, away on her first trip, putting the whole thing on Daddy's American Express card, and man, there you are buying her all the absinthe she can handle until BAM she wakes up in Wenceslas Park without her panties. What's really cool is that most of the American chicks won't know where you're from, so quick thinking and a passable fake British accent will smooth the way. I mean, what's with these chicks and British accents? Maybe they like to pretend you're James Bond. Who knows? What happens in Prague stays in Prague. A selection of English language books and email terminals available.

A chalkboard sign outside the Globe advertised a poetry reading that night, reminding Allen that soon the summer-program fiction and poetry students would descend upon the city. Penny would arrive in a few days, and Allen brightened at the thought. It would be nice to have somebody with whom he could pal around the city. He absentmindedly touched the crucifix under his T-shirt. Somewhere back in America, Penny wore hers. He'd kept his promise; he put the thing on every day when getting dressed. He was even starting to like it.

Inside, Allen purchased a strong cup of black coffee and rented one of the computers for twenty minutes to check email. The first message from Dr. Evergreen reminded Allen (for the fiftieth time) how important it was for him to make sure his crate was delivered safely. Allen replied, assuring the professor all was well.

The next message, from Penny, asked if he'd arrived safely. He wrote back that he had but was exhausted. He sipped the coffee, which burned down his throat like acid. It would either wake him up or kill him.

Another email from Evergreen—a perplexing list of research tasks that seemed to have nothing whatsoever to do with Kafka. Allen put them off for later.

He deleted a dozen spam emails before arriving at the final message:

> *You don't know what you're getting into. Be alert. Be cautious. We shall be in contact soon. Trust no one!*
> *The Three*

The email address was concerned4u@hotmail.com.

Allen raised an eyebrow, hesitated, then replied,

> *Who are you and what the hell are you talking about?*

Allen glanced over his shoulder. Nobody was taking any particular notice of him. Indeed, the idea that there was anyone within a thousand miles who even knew his name was utterly ridiculous.

Allen finished his coffee, walked out the front door, and ran smack into a priest.

"Allen!" Father Paul greeted him enthusiastically. "Imagine running into you here."

NINE

"Come back inside," Father Paul insisted. "I'll buy you a drink."

Allen checked his wristwatch. "Already?"

"It's nearly dinnertime," Father Paul said.

Allen's body was all screwed up. He couldn't tell if it was morning or evening. While he was contemplating his jet lag, he found that Father Paul had him by the elbow and was gently guiding him back into the café.

Beyond the computer terminals, the café opened up to tables and a long bar. Artwork of various types hung on the stucco-brick walls, little price tags in the corner of each frame. Father Paul selected a table under a large painting of a block-headed three-breasted woman, the artwork a seeming cross between Picasso and Jack Kirby.

"Those pilsners look good. Hang on." Father Paul went to the bar and came back with two beers. He set one in front of Allen. "These are brewed in the town of Plzen. Czech brewers have been perfecting their art for centuries, and Czech beer is counted as some of the best in the world."

Allen sipped. "It is good."

"Damn right. Oh, hey. Smokes. Be right back."

Father Paul went to the bar again and returned with a pack of Pall Malls. He lit one, puffed. "There we go. That's the stuff."

"What are you doing in Prague?" Allen asked.

"I'm surprised Penny didn't mention it."

They drank two beers each, and Father Paul smoked five cigarettes while they exchanged stories. Allen explained he was here to do research for Dr. Evergreen, and Father Paul told Allen he was attending a conference on St. Augustine.

"All pretty boring religious stuff," said the priest. "I'm hoping to sneak away and see the sights."

Father Paul looked at his empty pint glass, pushed away from the table, and started to rise.

Allen motioned him to sit. "My turn."

He took the empty glasses to the bar. Somehow the place had become crowded with a mix of bohemian expatriates, locals, older, younger, frat guys in Ping golf caps, art-fags and greasers, tweed academics, hipster throwbacks, a smelly Bulgarian, and an old, old man in a black beret, smoking a dark pipe. An eclectic crowd. Not quite as diverse as the cantina scene in *Star Wars*, but close. The place smelled of cloves and pipe tobacco and beer and sweat.

"What can I make for you?" asked the twenty-something girl behind the bar. She had a thick French accent. She had streaks of hot pink in her brown hair, numerous earrings, a flimsy black tank top. Too much eye makeup.

"Two more pilsners." Allen set the glasses on the bar.

She took the glasses, filled them one at a time. "You're new."

"Just got in today."

"You're not a poet, are you? I do not think I could stand it if you were another poet."

Allen laughed. "No."

"I am Katrina."

"Allen."

"I'll be seeing more of you in here, no? All Americans come to the Globe."

"Sure."

"Someone has taken an interest in you perhaps." Katrina motioned with her chin as she topped off the beer.

Allen followed the gesture to the girls in a corner booth: three of them, looking straight at him, no attempt to conceal that they were openly observing his every move. The pale one with black, spiked hair, looked scary. She lounged with one combat boot up on the table, a cigarette dangling from her mouth, dark eye makeup making her look like a raccoon. Brutally pretty, the expression on her face said she resented the world.

The blonde would have looked at home at any sorority fund-raiser, but even among the Globe's eclectic patrons, she seemed out of place. Pink, close-fitting T-shirt, white jeans, corn-silk hair in long braids. Very Reese Witherspoon-ish.

The third wore only black. She had an olive complexion, hair cut short like a boy's. Hawkish nose. She smoked a thin cigar like she dared anyone to ask her to put it out.

All six eyes drilled into Allen.

He turned back to Katrina, still feeling the watchers at his back. "Maybe they've just never seen such a staggeringly handsome specimen before."

Katrina snorted.

Allen carried the beer back to the priest.

"You talk to the barmaid?"

Allen nodded. "She's French."

"You gonna hit that?"

Allen sputtered beer, coughed. "What?"

"Hey, I may be a priest, but I know how it works, you know? Besides, I can't indulge myself, so I like to hear about what everyone else is doing. Hearing confession is a big part of my week."

"I only talked to her for a minute."

Father Paul sucked hard on his cigarette, blew a big gray cloud over Allen's head. "We should do some shots."

Allen grinned. His face felt warm and numb. "No, we shouldn't."

Father Paul laughed.

They did shots.

Something amber that burned Allen's throat and set fire to his belly. Allen grabbed Father Paul's disposable lighter and lit one of the cigarettes.

The night, very slowly, began to blur.

The Globe became impossibly crowded. Allen was forced to squeeze in between people as he maneuvered to the bar and back or made trips to the restroom. Men and women pressed up against him, greeted him in a variety of languages. The place had become a United Nations of booze and musk and animated chatter.

It was during one of Allen's claustrophobic treks to the men's room that he felt the hand on his ass. He turned, saw the impish face of the blonde in the pink T-shirt as she melted in the other direction back into the crowd. Allen thought for a moment he'd been the victim of some petty crime, like maybe he'd been pickpocketed. He checked. His wallet was still there.

In his other back pocket, he found a folded piece of paper.

In the men's restroom, he folded himself into a narrow stall, sat, and read the note. It was written on hotel stationery in sloppy red ink.

In the next stall, another of the Globe's patrons vomited violently, spewing chunks all over the next toilet and the floor of the stall. Allen flinched and lifted his feet. The acrid smell slapped him in the face like a fetid mackerel.

The note read:

> Don't trust the priest. You have to meet me in the alley
> right now. Your life depends on this.
> The Three

Allen tried to read the note again, but the words went blurry. The guy in the next stall spewed more vomit. Allen closed one eye, and in this fashion was able to confirm the note's message. It seemed like some outrageous prank, but he was feeling drunk and dizzy, and the puke stench in the small restroom was over-whelming. A short trip to the alley out back seemed like an op-portunity to suck some clean air into his lungs.

He stepped carefully as he left the stall, slipped in some of the puke anyway.

"Hell."

The café beyond the men's room was still crowded and smoky. His face slick with sweat, Allen felt he might be sick now too. He pushed through the crowd and found a narrow hall, which lead to an old wooden door. He opened it, stepped out into the alley. The night air was cool relative to the interior of the Globe. Allen closed his eyes, breathed in through the nose, out through the mouth. He felt better. Slightly.

When he opened his eyes again, he saw the blonde with the braids at the end of the alley. There was just enough street light to see it was her. She held her hand up tentatively, a shy wave. Allen waved back.

She lowered her hand slowly, regarded him a moment, then gestured for him to follow as she disappeared around the corner. Allen stood a moment, baffled, then looked over his shoulder. It was still and silent in the cobblestone alley, the dim light casting lumpy shadows. The blonde in braids might almost have been some kind of ghost, except Allen doubted the tourists would tolerate a ghost that looked like a California sorority girl in a centuries-old city like Prague.

He headed toward the mouth of the alley, turned the corner.

She stood there waiting in front of a parked car, some foreign model Allen didn't recognize. The trunk was open. She gestured toward the trunk.

What the hell is this?

"Tell me your name."

She shook her head, put her finger to her lips in a *shhhh* motion. She nodded at the trunk.

Allen inched forward. "You want me to look in there?"

She nodded. Her smile was warm and inviting.

"Sure." Allen stepped to the edge of the trunk, looked inside. It was empty.

"Okay," he said. "I guess I'm not getting it. Did you want—"

Something heavy slapped him at the base of the skull. He tumbled forward into the trunk, felt somebody lifting his feet. His eyes went crossways, and he saw the fuzzy image of the blonde leaning into the trunk, touching his forehead, her lips moving with unspoken syllables.

Then the trunk *thunk*ed him shut into darkness.

He thought he might pass out. The base of his skull throbbed with a deep, nauseating pain, but he didn't lose consciousness. He heard a group of muffled voices, some heated conversation, but only one word came through clearly. *Zizkov.*

Where had Allen heard that word before? He faded a little as the throb in his head worsened. The next thing he knew the car was moving. He shifted and slid in the trunk as the car accelerated and made turns.

Allen had the fleeting thought that he'd left Father Paul stuck with the check back at the Globe.

TEN

The car continued to bump along, and Allen remembered where he'd seen the word Zizkov. He pulled *The Rogue's Guide* out of his back pocket, along with the disposable lighter. He sparked the lighter, which dimly illuminated the interior of the trunk, and flipped through the guide until he found the page he wanted.

> •*Zizkov*: This working-class neighborhood is rich with authentic pubs, serving a variety of Czech beers at working-class prices. Although they are unlike the more touristy pubs of Stare Mesto, it turns out they are still more than happy to accept tourist money. Smelly backpackers can stretch their drinking budget here. The area is named for one-eyed general Jan Zizka. Stumble around long enough and you can probably find a few statues of him, both on horse and not. One of the area's primary sights is a giant, blocky Commie monument at the top of Zizkov Hill (known as the National Monument). The monument's architecture is of the typical "look at us, we're big" Soviet variety,

but the view from the top of the hill is actually pretty decent. The monument's tomb, formerly occupied by party dignitaries, now lies empty—presumably waiting for somebody important enough to kick off.

There was more, but Allen broke off from his reading when he felt the car stop. He extinguished the disposable lighter, held his breath, and listened.

Footsteps on gravel. More muffled voices. The footsteps retreated, and Allen found himself alone in the silent darkness.

He pushed up against the trunk, tried to give it a kick but couldn't maneuver for leverage. He was going nowhere. He waited, drifted off.

Allen's dreams swam with cold blue eyes. He ran through mist, the smell of moist earth all around him. He ran through the deserted streets of Prague, the night pressing in on him, and wherever he went he felt colder and colder. He ran faster, a freezing wind at his neck.

His eyes popped open. Allen shivered. He was stiff and cold and his head ached, probably a combination of getting hit and too much Czech beer. Shots. Good God, he'd done shots of some unknown booze with the priest.

How long had he been out? He couldn't tell if it had been two minutes or ten hours. Maybe Father Paul would call the police. Maybe after he noticed Allen was missing, he'd tell somebody, get some help. But how would help find him? For all Allen knew, he was five hundred miles from the Globe.

No. Surely he hadn't been out that long, and they hadn't driven that far. Someone had mentioned Zizkov, a neighborhood that wasn't so very far. And anyway, The Three had warned him against trusting the priest.

Who warned you, dumbass? The nice people who smacked you on the head and shoved you in a car trunk? What the hell am I in the middle of?

If only he could get out of the damn trunk.

The trunk opened.

A flashlight seared his eyes, and Allen winced. The outlines of two figures beyond the flashlight.

"He'll be fine," said a female voice. "I put a spell of well-being on him when we put him in."

"Well, he looks like hammered shit," said a male voice. "Let's get him out of there."

Allen felt hands under his arms lifting him out of the trunk. He felt weak, and his legs were wobbly as he felt his feet touch the ground. "Who are you?"

"Friends, Mr. Cabbot," said the man. "Although that might be hard to believe at the moment."

Allen felt a cool hand on his forehead. It was the braided blonde. "You'll be okay," she assured him.

"So you can talk."

"I couldn't speak during the luring spell, or I would have muddled the magic."

Allen pulled away from her hand. "Luring spell?"

"To lure you to the back of the car. So we could put you in."

"I'm full of beer, and a pretty girl wants to meet me outside. More like hormones than a spell." Allen looked down, saw a small automatic pistol in the man's hand. "You don't seem like friends to me."

"Yes, I see what you mean," he said. "It's important that you don't give us a lot of trouble until we've had an opportunity to explain ourselves. Amy, show Mr. Cabbot into the house, and we can all get comfortable. I'll be right behind you."

Allen followed the girl, the man with the pistol bringing up the rear. Allen expected to feel the gun stuck into his back like in the movies, but that didn't happen. He was acutely aware of the pistol anyway.

They were in the cramped, gravel parking area behind a small house. There were tall hedges on one side and a stone wall on the other, so Allen wasn't able to get a good look at the surrounding neighborhood—not that he'd be able to recognize anything in any case. He'd been in Prague less than a full day, and so far he'd had bizarre nightmares, gotten drunk with a priest, slipped in puke, been hexed by a sorority girl, and stuffed in a trunk.

And there was still the jet lag.

And the man with the gun right behind him.

He followed Amy into the small house. It was unimpressive, utilitarian, and drab, probably built during the iron curtain days. They ushered him into a small sitting room, and the man pointed him toward a threadbare easy chair with the pistol. Allen backed toward the chair and sank into it. The man sat across from him in a stiff-looking wingback.

"Amy, I could really murder a pot of tea right about now," the man said. "Can you come up with something while I have a word with Mr. Cabbot?"

"I'll see what's in the kitchen." She left the room.

Allen got a better look at his abductor. Middle-aged, wire thin, a gaunt red face, lined along the jaw, closely shaven. He had a head of thick hair that was pure white; his watery eyes were faded and blue. He wore nice clothes but nothing ostentatious—a light blue jacket, gray trousers, pressed white shirt. He could have been one of Allen's literature professors back at Gothic State.

"My name is Basil Worshamn," said the man with the pistol. "And I'd like to tell you a story." His accent was vaguely upper class and British.

"This doesn't end with you trying to sell me Amway, does it?" Allen said.

A tolerant smile. "I don't know what that means, but I take it as some kind of quip. I'm no traveling salesman, Mr. Cabbot. I'm in Prague on very important business."

"I can't imagine it involves me."

"Indulge me," Basil said, "and I'll stretch the limits of your imagination."

"As it happens, I'm in the mood for a good story," Allen said. "And also, you're the one with the gun."

"You're here to assist Professor Evergreen in some sort of research, correct?"

"He's writing a book chapter on Kafka," Allen said.

"Have you had the opportunity to meet his wife?" Basil asked.

Allen cleared his throat, swallowed.

"I see by the expression on your face that you have met her."

"At a party hosted by Dr. Evergreen," Allen admitted. "Briefly."

"Yes, well, we'll return to that in a moment. Are you familiar with the legend of the philosopher's stone?"

Allen paused. He looked toward the kitchen at the sound of clanking dishes. At that moment, the small house seemed absurdly normal, not the kind of place he would have predicted he'd be when interrogated about the philosopher's stone at gunpoint.

Basil cleared his throat. "The philosopher's stone, Mr. Cabbot?"

Allen jerked back from the kitchen noise, met Basil's gaze. "It's some kind of magic stone that alchemists thought might turn lead into gold. Isn't that right?"

"That is the popular understanding," Basil said. "Scholars more learned in the subject understand that the philosopher's stone is not actually a particular mystical rock but rather a symbol of enlightenment, standing for knowledge beyond the ordinary. The ancient alchemists were unafraid to seek knowledge in places where others feared to tread. These alchemists were often condemned. Sometimes as charlatans, other times as practitioners of the dark arts."

At the words "dark arts," Allen flinched. He wasn't exactly sure why.

"In 1583, Holy Roman Emperor Rudolph II moved the seat

of the empire to Prague," continued Basil. "Rudolph was a bit eccentric, and his interest in astrology and the occult became legendary. His court swarmed with thinkers and men of science."

While Basil's story unfolded, Allen's eyes darted around the room. Perhaps he could make a dash for a door or window.

"In 1599, Rudolph invited alchemist Dr. John Dee to join his court," Basil said. "Dee led a team of dedicated alchemists to solve the challenge of the philosopher's stone."

"This doesn't have anything to do with me," Allen said.

"I'm afraid it very soon might," Basil said. "For you see, your very own Professor Evergreen has come to Prague, not to write a chapter on Kafka as he'd have you believe, but rather to plunder the secret dungeons of Prague Castle in search of the philosopher's stone."

Allen went slightly pale, the surprise plain on his face.

"I can understand that this might be a lot for you to digest," Basil said.

"It's not that." Allen swallowed hard. "It's just that there's a priest at the window with a machine gun."

Before we witness the inevitable gunfire and breaking of things that's about to happen, let me just return briefly to something Basil told Allen. Basil mentioned Dr. John Dee and a team of alchemists.

Horseshit.

Team, my sweaty ass. There was no team. And John Dee. Let me tell you something about John Dee. Asshole. What an *insufferable* asshole. If I never lay eyes on that son of a bitch again, it will be too soon.

So yeah, I'm a little bit more interested in this part of the story.

Because this is the part about me.

THE BAD ALCHEMIST

(PRAGUE 1599)

ELEVEN

I am the ghost of Edward Kelley.

I am—was—an alchemist at the court of Holy Roman Emperor Rudolph II.

Impressed yet? Wait until you hear the rest of the story.

Okay, let me slow down lest I get ahead of myself. One thing at a time.

First let us address this idea of a "team" of alchemists mentioned by Basil Worshamn. There was no team. There was only me. I suppose if you count the maid who emptied our chamber pots every day and the young girl who brought us refreshment in the afternoons, you might consider we were all part of a team. But mixing just the exact right amount of milk and sugar into a cup of tea hardly counts as alchemy.

No, the entire team was yours truly, good old long-suffering Edward Kelley.

Man, did I hate being the team.

Dee was the worst sort of boss. Any dim-witted peasant girl could have cleaned the glassware and equipment every night, but Dee insisted that I do it. He trusted almost no one to handle his precious equipment. Make sure those herbs are put up just right,

Edward. Don't heat the mixture in that beaker too long, Edward. Hurry with the monkwort, Edward, we're losing the moonlight. Measure that sulfur into exact portions, Edward.

Fuck you, Dr. John Dee.

So I was Rudolph's other alchemist. I mean, I never get any credit. You always hear about Dee. At best, old Edward Kelley is an afterthought. A minor blip in minor historical texts.

And I *hate* the picture they have of me in the Wikipedia entry. It's one of those generic old man pictures with some fucked-up hat like I'm half wizard and half Oxford professor. One of those long Gandalf beards. As if.

Look, there I am now. Young and strong and up to no good. Zoom in there at that window in the White Tower where my room is. Come have a look.

Come hear my story.

TWELVE

K elley had the dress bunched up around her hips.

"Hurry," said the serving girl.

He was naked, climbed between her legs and put himself inside. She gasped, wrapped her legs around him, the heels of her shoes digging into his bare ass cheeks.

"Oh, Edward." She threw her head back, arched against him. "Oh, my Edward."

Kelley thrust, felt the heat building in his groin. He'd come to rely on these daily visits with the serving wench to break the relentless tedium of castle life. What was her name again? Brianna or something, wasn't it? Something with a B.

The serving wench's climax started as a low moan and built into a banshee scream as Kelley grunted with his own orgasm. He thrust three more times as his climax subsided. He sighed and rolled off her. She leaped off the bed, smoothing her dress down.

"I've got to hurry, my lord," she said. Now that the passion had passed, she no longer called him Edward. "Those great sweaty men in the courtyard will be wanting biscuits and grog, and it's all me and Miss Sarah can do to keep up with them. I don't know what sort of infernal machine they're building out there, but they work up a terrible thirst doing it."

"It's a moon machine," Kelley said. "When they're done, they'll shoot a man all the way to the moon. Straight through the air and past the stars."

The wench stood up straight, eyes wide. "Really?"

"No," Kelley chuckled. "I'm having fun with you." In fact, Kelley had heard vague rumors about the construction in the courtyard but nothing that made any real sense.

She rushed to the edge of the bed, grabbed Kelley's face in her hands, and planted a wet kiss on his lips. "I can't bear to be away from you, my lord. Until tomorrow."

"See you then, sweet." Kelley slapped her butt as she departed.

Red hair and skin so white it might have been milk. Already Kelley looked forward to tomorrow's visit.

He climbed out of bed and went to the window. The White Tower afforded a good view of the lane below, where a number of Rudolph's goldsmiths labored day in and day out. Kelley couldn't quite see the courtyard where the men labored, but the clank and hammer noise of work in progress drifted clearly up to the tower. Kelley was sure Dr. Dee knew what was going on, but so far the old alchemist had been as tight-lipped as a monk.

Kelley put on a shirt, slipped into a plain doublet and breeches. He hated the billowing slops Dee and the other fancy men wore around court. It made them seem preening and slightly feminine. He stepped into his shoes, sighed, and sipped the now tepid tea left behind by the serving wench. He winced. The primary failure of this tea was primarily that it refused to be wine.

Kelley chuckled. Some alchemist's trick, turning tea into wine. Then he remembered his New Testament and frowned. A similar trick, but it was water turned to wine, not tea. No, that was something beyond mere alchemy.

Not for the first time or the last, Kelley wondered if his work here at Rudolph's court wasn't in fact a terrible, terrible idea.

Did Kelley even believe in all that trumped-up mumbo jumbo? Basic mind tricks and sleight of hand to dupe the simple-minded rabble. Wasn't it? And anyway, it was better than pushing his mystic heal-all and bowel remedy back in Ireland, wandering from village to village, putting on his wizard act. Not that he'd actually been swindling anyone. Not really. Fish oil and beet juice and a few other special ingredients. It really had been quite a good remedy for constipation. It just hadn't been what anyone would normally have thought of as *alchemy*.

So when Dr. Dee had said he'd needed a pair of good hands for something special in Prague, well, the offer had been timely, seeing as there had been this pregnant farm girl in Cork, and, well, it had been a fine time to take a long, long trip.

Kelley choked down two more sips of tea, then gave up. After sundown he'd trot to the bottom of the castle steps and settle into his favorite pub. Sometimes he'd get too potted to make it back up again. There were quite a few steps, and it was steep going.

He opened his chest, wondering if he still had a flask hidden somewhere. He'd all but given up when a knock at the door startled him.

"Yes?"

The door creaked open, and Dr. Dee entered. He wore a ridiculously ornate doublet, and the sleeves of his shirt sported intricate braiding. His shoes were so shiny that they hurt Kelley's eyes. The expression on Dee's face was the worst—sort of a tight, haughty, contemptuous snarl. Dee could definitely benefit from some fish oil and beet juice.

"Good God, Edward, it smells like ass in here."

Kelley admitted to himself he was overdue for a bath, and the room was lousy with his dirty laundry. Still, Dee needn't have been so rude. More than anything, Kelley wanted to ball up his fist and punch all of Dee's teeth down his throat. He settled for saying the following:

"Fornicate with yourself."

"Yes, very amusing," Dee said, unperturbed. "If you can make yourself halfway presentable, we have an audience with His Highness in twenty minutes."

Kelley's eyes went wide. "Rudolph?"

"No," Dee said. "Another Highness. The king of the pixies has summoned us to a banquet. Of course Rudolph, you fool."

"But why?" Kelley had only met Rudolph once, when he'd come with Dee to Prague. Kelley had stood behind Dee, saying nothing and trying to appear intelligent. There had been no need to meet with the Holy Roman Emperor since then, and that had suited Kelley just fine.

"He's calling a number of his scientists and scholars together for a counsel," Dee said. "This might be the big one."

"You go," Kelley said. "Tell me what happens."

"You are summoned as well."

"I don't want to go. Tell him I'm ill."

"I'll do no such thing," Dee said. "There will be a number of engineers and astrologers. We're the only two alchemists in the castle, and I intend for us to make a good showing. Comb your hair, for the love of God."

"The love of God has nothing to do with any of this," Kelley said.

Dee rolled his eyes. "Spare me your squeamishness. I am not afraid to reach into the abyss where other men fear to look."

"I hate it when you talk like that."

"Nevertheless." Dee sniffed. "I am an expert in my field. And I won't let peasant religion or any other superstition stem my quest for knowledge. And I will stay on the path for answers . . . *wherever* that path might lead."

"And what if it leads us to hell, Dr. Dee?"

"Then we shall see what we shall see. But I'd be less worried about hell if I were you and far more concerned with a proper doublet. You look like a common tinker. My tailor dresses better than you. Where's the doublet I had made for you? The one for formal occasions."

"I'm not wearing that ridiculous costume."

"Wear it, damn you."

Kelley sighed, went into the wardrobe across the room, and came out with a doublet of fine material. It was deep blue, embroidered with yellow moons and stars. Kelley shook his head as he put it on. He stood in front of Dee, spread his arms. "Happy?"

"Placated," Dee said. "Follow me."

They spiraled down the stairs and out of the White Tower, Kelley following behind Dee reluctantly as they went down the Golden Lane and through the archway into the main courtyard, where dozens of men labored.

A monstrous construction of gears and flywheels caught Kelley's attention. "What is that supposed to be?"

"All will be revealed in time," Dee said.

"You don't know, do you?"

"Uh . . . no, actually. Not a clue."

They strode across the courtyard and into the castle proper. Various dignitaries and lords scurried to and fro. The castle hummed with activity, dozens and dozens of independent projects going like mad, all presumed to come together sooner or later in some kind of grand scheme.

Only a select few knew the ultimate goal of this scheme.

Kelley was in no way one of the select few.

Frankly, he was starting to wish he'd been back in Ireland selling constipation remedy. Spain. He'd always thought about Spain. Maybe Kelley could ply his trade in some of the warmer towns and villages along the Mediterranean. Ah, sun and sea. Kelley shuddered at the thought of winter just a few weeks away. Prague would become white and dead, bitter heavy snow sealing him into the castle for a month at a time.

Tonight. Kelley had a little money stashed away. He'd pack a small bag and slip out of the castle tonight, maybe sweet-talk a fisherman into taking him down the Vltava. He tried to calculate how long it would take him to make his way to Spain. His Spanish was weak, but it would get better living in the place. Kelley had a knack for languages. Already his Czech was passable, and if he did stay, it would be as fluent as a native's in another three months.

On the other hand, Spain might not be the best place for an alchemist. He'd heard the Inquisition had eased a bit in the last few years, but the thought of getting burned to a crisp as a heretic was enough to put him off Spain.

Sicily. He'd always wanted to see Sicily.

Kelley followed Dee into Vladislav Hall and abandoned all thoughts of sneaking away into the night.

The grand hall was alive with activity, the vaulted ceiling echoing with animated conversation and debate. A line of iron chandeliers hung low, with hundreds of candles spreading warm light. Men stood in groups of twos and threes. Some stood at tables, zealously pouring over elaborate drawings and design plans. A small group of men crowded an alcove, holding a thick, curved disc of glass as big as a dinner plate. Sunlight streamed in through an open window. The beams hit the glass disc, distorted, and splashed the men with rays of color, blue, red, green, yellow.

No, Kelley wasn't going anywhere. Something amazing was going to happen at Rudolph's court, and Kelley admitted he was eager to understand. Edward Kelley had been called a swindler, a cheat, a womanizer, and a drunkard. But the small part of him that was the alchemist could not bear the thought that something historical would happen here in Prague and he wouldn't be a part of it.

So Kelley kept his mouth shut and followed Dee the length of the hall.

The small audience chamber off the far end of the great hall was crowded with dour-faced men. But this was no audience, no diplomatic meeting of politicians and emissaries. This was a working meeting, men with sleeves rolled up, parchments, maps, and drawings spread across the table.

At the far end of the table sat Rudolph II, emperor of the Holy Roman Empire.

There was nothing remarkable about the emperor. Short, slightly pudgy, bland eyes. He sat with his shirt open, doublet unbuttoned, listening intently to an old, old man in monk's robes and a skullcap discuss the problems involved in removing tons of rock and dirt. Two men at the other end of the table, close to where Dee and Kelley stood in the open doorway, debated the best way to feed and house the hundreds of laborers who had descended upon the castle. There were other conversations that Kelley couldn't follow.

Rudolph spotted Dee and raised a hand. The din ceased abruptly.

"Gentlemen, I'm afraid I need the room," the emperor said. "If you could excuse us."

They stood, gathering parchments as they went.

"Stay just a moment, Hans," the emperor said.

A gaunt, pale man in his fifties nodded and resumed his seat.

Kelley followed Dee into the room after the others departed.

"Your Highness." Dee bowed slightly.

Kelley hastened to mimic the gesture.

"Gentlemen, be seated," Rudolph said. "Dr. Dee, I want you and your associate to make the acquaintance of Hans Vredeman de Vries."

The men nodded to one another.

"Hans has been designing fountains for the palace grounds," Rudolph explained. "He can work miracles with water flow and drainage. We've recently put him on to something a little more ambitious. Some of my scientists have suggested a new way of generating power, something that might aid your own research. I simply wanted you to meet. I think in the future you might be working closely together. Hans, excuse us, won't you?"

Hans stood, nodded again, and left.

The emperor turned to Dee. "Progress remains slow?"

Dee's smile was painful, embarrassed. "Highness, considering the difficulty of the task, a slow approach is certainly to be expected."

The emperor pursed his lips, nodded. Kelley detected no signs of emotion either way. Had Dee and Kelley been summoned to a dressing down? Were they to be chastised for slow progress, or was Rudolph simply after a routine progress report? Kelley had been relegated to cleaning beakers and checking measurements, but it was his firm opinion they would never turn lead into gold. Not if they kept at it for a thousand years.

Sicily. Definitely Sicily.

"What do you see as the key to success?" Rudolph asked. "On a fundamental level."

"It concerns the manipulation of matter on a level of pure essence, Highness," Dee said. "I've tried a number of chemical compounds in an attempt to sunder the cosmic energies that hold an essence in place."

A brief pause.

Then Rudolph said, "I have no idea what you're talking about."

Neither did Kelley.

Dee cleared his throat, squirmed in his seat. "It is a difficult concept to communicate clearly, Highness."

"Try."

That nervous laugh again. Dee wiped his brow with a handkerchief. Kelley had to admit he enjoyed Dee's discomfort. On the other hand, anything that happened to Dee would surely also affect Kelley. Like it or not, he and Dee were a team. *Come on, Dr. Dee. Let's see some smooth talk, and make it fast.*

Dee grabbed a silver cup from across the table, set it in front of him. "Consider this silver goblet, Highness."

Rudolph leaned forward, looked at the cup.

"If you broke it in half, each piece would be smaller," Dee said. "But both pieces would still be silver."

"Obviously," Rudolph said.

"Uh . . . yes. And if you kept breaking the goblet into smaller and smaller pieces, each piece would still be silver. Now imagine you break it into a thousand pieces. Ten thousand pieces. Ten thousand times ten thousand individual pieces."

"That would be impossible."

"In theory, Highness."

Rudolph shrugged. "In theory then."

"Your Highness is most patient," Dee said. "Imagine you've somehow broken the goblet into as many pieces as you can possibly break it. Pieces so small they cannot even be seen. Now take one of these pieces—a piece that cannot be broken any further—and break it again. You are now breaking it past the point where it continues to be silver. Break it any more, and it will *no longer be silver.*"

Rudolph considered a moment, then asked, "Then, if not silver, what is it?"

"Ah." Dee thrust a finger in the air. "Therein lies the mystery, Highness. What, indeed? But a more pertinent question, I would contend, is, once having deprived this infinitely small piece of matter of its innate . . . *silverness*, what then can be done to change it, manipulate it into something else? Could we not build it back as something different? What I am attempting to do with our experiments is to attack the very force that holds the silver together."

The pause this time was much longer. Kelley would not ask Dee to come to Sicily with him. The deranged alchemist was on his own.

"I do not fully understand what you say," Rudolph admitted. "But I sense you have an understanding of this matter that is simply beyond me, and I am intrigued. The lodestones you asked for. I take it they are another attempt to manipulate these energies you speak of?"

"Your Highness is most insightful," Dee said.

Rudolph said, "What if I were to tell you that my astrologers might have discovered another possible way for you to address these energies?"

Dee spread his hands. "I would naturally be most grateful for any additional tools that would aid in the pursuit of Your Highness's ultimate goal."

Rudolph nodded. "Stand ready, then. It could happen at any time. Thank you, gentlemen, that will be all."

They stood, bowed, and left. On the way out, Kelley became determined to make Dee talk. What in blazes was this ultimate goal? No, Kelley was tired of being in the dark. He'd need to figure some way to loosen Dee's tongue.

He put his hand on Dee's back, an uncharacteristically friendly gesture. "Well done, Dr. Dee. I think the emperor was impressed with your explanation. How about a quick drink to celebrate?"

THIRTEEN

Dr. Dee might have been a gigantic prick, but I had to give him credit. I'd had no idea at the time that he'd been speculating about the nature of matter on an atomic level. Nobody had had the vocabulary. Protons and electrons and so forth had been centuries away.

And then there had been the darker forces, which science has yet to explain.

I should have gone to Sicily.

It's true that I have a facility for languages. In the hundreds of years I've haunted Prague Castle and its environs, I've become more fluent in Czech than any Czech. I've learned German and Russian. Even a smattering of Japanese. The castle draws tourists from all four corners of the globe. My French is good, but even now, my Spanish is still weak.

There is a room behind one of the gift shops where the cleaning staff can lounge and have a smoke. They have a TV in the lounge. I've seen every episode of *Hogan's Heroes* dubbed into German. Prague gets German TV. It's easier to spy on TV than it is to read a book over somebody's shoulder, but I've done that too.

The problem is that I can't touch anything, so it's hard to turn pages. I can float through walls and doors, drift the night gardens, haunt the tombs beneath St. Vitus Cathedral. There is no nook or cranny of this place I haven't seen a hundred times. But I can't turn pages. I still haven't made it through all the Harry Potter books. For the first three volumes, I stood over the shoulder of this nice woman who worked in the kitchens. She'd take her break on a bench outside and read while taking a quick lunch. She was a slow reader. But she got married and moved away, so I don't know when I'll get a chance to read the rest. I think Harry and Hermione will get together. I just have a feeling.

I am confined—mostly—to the castle and its grounds. I experimented with this quite a bit the first few decades. With great effort, I can make it to the little pub I loved so much at the bottom of the castle steps. On certain nights, when the moon and stars align just perfectly, I'll feel the cosmic energies stir. On these occasions I can make it into the tourist areas below the castle.

I've never made it as far as the Charles Bridge.

When I attempt to leave the area the cosmos has approved for me, things go gray. The real world bleeds away, and I feel myself in a fog. I try to trudge forward, but it's like walking through mud. I feel a tug at my back, like there's an invisible line hooked to my belt.

I always turn back. I am here. I will be here forever.

The Hapsburgs fell, and I remained. I watched the Nazis come and go. The Communists. The latest invasion has been the tourists, men and women from the UK and the USA. So many students. They all flock to cheap beer and old-world charm. The prices are starting to go up now, and Prague isn't the bargain it used to be. Travelers are discovering Budapest and Warsaw.

But Prague is mine, or the castle—the symbol of the city—is anyway.

There are other ghosts in Prague Castle. I've talked to them. Well, I've *tried* to talk to them. They seem to lack the gift of conversation. These spirits are stuck in some kind of loop, acting in the same play over and over again, saying the same lines. They spend eternity reenacting their unjust murders or roam the halls looking for the road to the afterlife. They're only half there. Insubstantial even for ghosts.

Only I see all. Only Edward Kelley retains his faculties, listens, learns, grows. I am like some recorder destined to bear witness. What exactly I'm supposed to see or do has been unclear for centuries. I have never tasted a McDonald's hamburger or Yoplait yogurt. I watch with longing as tourists knock back cold pilsners. I want to cry when I think how long it's been since I've had a glass of wine, but I can't make tears.

I have not been deprived of human desires. I simply no longer have the means to fulfill them. Nothing physical, I mean. I can't tell you how long I spent loitering in women's restrooms, watching ladies take down their pants to pee. That's pathetic, isn't it? Like I said, a man with a man's desires, trapped in the nothingness of my existence.

So, yeah. I get horny.

But since I am utterly deprived of physical sensation, it must all be in my mind, right? I spent a hundred years on that one.

Only recently have I detected some change, a shift in the nature of my own existence. Something is coming. Happening. And it's all tied up with Allen Cabbot and the strange adventure that he finds himself smack in the middle of at this very moment. But Allen can keep a moment.

First there is the matter of Dr. Dee and a very large pitcher of cheap wine.

FOURTEEN

Kelley and Dee sat at a rough wooden table in the corner of Kelley's favorite pub. It was a dark establishment, thick with the smoke of oil lamps and candles. Kelley could barely make out the faces of the other patrons. They'd gone through half a pitcher of wine, and Dee had loosened up a bit.

It helped that the doctor could not hold his liquor.

Kelley told a bawdy joke and Dee laughed. *Okay*, thought Kelley. *He's ready for more probing questions.*

Kelley tilted the pitcher, refilled Dee's goblet. "I can't help but wonder what all this secrecy is about, Dee. If I knew what was happening, I could help more."

Dee's frown was plain even in the dim candlelight. Instead of talking, he sipped wine.

"Is Rudolph impatient with us?" asked Kelley. "Are we not turning lead into gold fast enough for His Highness? Because I have to tell you, Dee, it's going to take years. Frankly, I don't think it's possible at all."

"Lower your voice." Dee looked from side to side, but nobody seemed interested in their conversation. "It's supposed to be a secret."

"*Supposed* to be," Kelley said, "but everyone knows. People whisper about it all the time, or they used to. It's sort of old news now, actually. Guess what they call the alleyway outside our workshop. The Golden Lane."

"I thought they called it that because the soldiers use it as a convenient place to urinate."

"There's that too."

Dee leaned across the table, motioned for Kelley to lean in also. Dee's hushed whisper was barely audible. "I can tell you this much. Transmuting lead into gold, all that nonsense, it's a cover story."

"Then why the hell have I been cleaning beakers and handling toxic chemicals for the past five months? And why the hell would we have a cover story and then act like it's a secret?"

"It's the oldest trick in the book," Dee said. "A couple of alchemists up to God knows what until all hours of the night. People are bound to be curious. They can't help themselves. So we make up a story and let people discover the secret. Once they think they know what's going on, they stop asking. The curiosity abates."

"What about *me*?" Kelley asked. "My curiosity hasn't abated."

"In time, Edward."

"And if we're not transmuting lead into gold, then what was all that talk about breaking a silver goblet into thousands of pieces until it's not silver anymore?"

"We're not transmuting lead into gold," Dee said. "But we are transmuting . . . something."

"Dee, you must confide in me."

"I've already said too much. This is a *dangerous* secret, Edward. Rudolph will have both our heads if it gets out, so please ask me no more."

"I'm just trying to help." Kelley sipped wine. "At least tell me when I might be able to know more. For pity's sake, throw me a bone."

"Rudolph's astrologers are the key," Dee said.

"I thought *we* were the key."

Dee cleared his throat. "Well, naturally. But next to us the as-trologers are the key. Soon they will bring us an object, and then, my dear Edward, then I will most certainly need your assistance. Until that time, I beg you to ask me no more."

Kelley sat back and nodded. Clearly he would get no more out of Dee until Dee was ready. "Our pitcher is empty. I'll get us more wine."

"Please no," Dee said. "My head is swimming. But I thank you for the drink. I've been working so hard lately, I feel like I might come apart."

Kelley smiled. "I know just the thing to ease your troubles, my friend."

Kelley's eyes creaked open at the first hint of sunlight. He sat up in bed, pushing the girl's naked leg off his chest. The rest of her was hidden beneath the bedcovers. Which one had he ended up with? The one with corn-yellow hair, he hoped. She had big tits. He couldn't tell from the leg.

He cast about, squinting his eyes, but didn't immediately see Dee and the other wench. Kelley's head throbbed. It tasted as if a small, oily creature had defecated in his mouth and then crawled down his throat and died. His skin felt slick and clammy. The first stirrings of something unpleasant were beginning in his belly. It seemed impossible that a man could feel this bad and still live. The entire chamber smelled of sweat and wine.

Kelley crawled out of bed. His legs felt like jelly. He went to the plush sofa and pulled back the heavy quilt. The naked girl underneath whined, curled into a fetal position, flinching from the light. It was the yellow-haired girl with the large breasts. Damn. That meant Kelley had been with the bucktoothed one. He shrugged. No matter.

Kelley found his breeches, slipped into them, and went downstairs.

There was a water trough in the courtyard directly across from the tower door. Dee was on his knees, his head dunked in the water. His white skin glowed a dirty orange in the rays of the rising sun. He wore only his underwear. He lifted his head out of the trough, water streaming and dripping from his hair and beard.

"You okay, Dee?"

"You did this to me, you evil bastard." Dee wiped water from his eyes. "What infernal scheme led man to invent wine?"

Kelley knelt next to Dee at the trough and splashed water into his face. "At least you hit it off well with Natasha."

"Who the hell is Natasha?"

"The young naked wench asleep in your chamber."

"Oh, God. My wife."

"She's back in England."

"Praise the Lord for small mercies." Dee suddenly grabbed his stomach, his pale skin fading to green. "Oh . . . no."

Kelley backed away.

Dee convulsed and heaved, spewed acidic, partly digested wine into a puddle to the side of the trough. "Oh, God." Dee shuddered and puked a second time.

"You should feel better now." Kelley didn't think Dee would recover quickly. With a little luck, the doctor would be out of commission all day and into the night.

Dee was stuck in a kneeling position, hunched over his own puddle of puke, a gooey strand of spittle still clinging to his beard. "I can't move. This is disgraceful. I have several experiments to see to today. I feel like there are tiny devils with pitchforks in my head, stabbing the backs of my eyes."

"I can't help but feel partly to blame," Kelley said.

"You are *entirely* to blame."

"I understand," Kelley said. "In that case, let me shoulder the burden today. You get back up to your bed and rest. I'll check in on the experiments."

Dee cast a sideways glance at Kelley. Kelley knew what the doctor was thinking. Did he really trust Kelley to handle his delicate experiments? In truth, nothing very important was happening in the laboratory, but Dee was obnoxiously fussy about his boiling pots and beakers.

"What will you tell people?" Dee asked.

"Anything you like."

"I command a certain amount of respect at court," Dee said, "and I would hate to see that respect tarnished."

"Of course."

"Tell everyone I've eaten bad goat cheese, and that I'm waiting for some digestion issues to resolve themselves."

"No problem."

Dee sighed. "Very well. Thank you, Edward. I think I will stay here and vomit a little more before crawling back up to bed."

"Take your time."

"One more favor, if you please," Dee said. "Can you please tell those women to leave? I don't think I can bring myself to look them in the eye, especially the blonde. Not after the unspeakable things I asked her to do."

Kelley didn't ask.

Kelley dressed and pulled himself together. Dee's shadowy, partial revelations had piqued his curiosity. Kelley shooed the wenches out of the White Tower, as he began to see his vague plan coming together. He needed Dee incapacitated and out of his hair for a day.

He looked briefly into Dee's laboratory. Nothing was exploding, so Kelley closed the door, locked it, and left for the main castle courtyard.

He made his way past the throngs of workers to the entranceway of St. Vitus Cathedral. As planned, he fell into a line of men pushing empty wheelbarrows. He'd intentionally worn his oldest, most threadbare clothing in an attempt to pass for one of the laborers. He still looked a little too clean, but nobody seemed to notice, so he pushed the wheelbarrow inside.

The interior of the cathedral was awe-inspiring, the ceiling arching high above him, dusty light spilling in through the elongated windows. Kelley had not attended mass regularly in years, but the presence of God never impressed him more than when he entered this cathedral. He felt dwarfed by the grandeur. The effect was spoiled somewhat by the line of sweaty men with wheelbarrows.

He dropped off the empty wheelbarrow and followed the line to a wheelbarrow full of dirt. He had only a split second to glance down the rough stone steps into the burial vault before he was swept toward the exit. A glance over his shoulder showed him grimy men coming up from the vault with buckets of earth, filling the empty wheelbarrows. He marched his new wheelbarrow outside, through the courtyard, and up a wooden ramp, where he dumped the dirt into the back of a wagon. Kelley presumed full wagons were driven someplace out of the way to dump the dirt, perhaps to farms that needed rich soil.

Dozens of men were participating in the dirt-moving endeavor. Kelley couldn't figure out a way to break the line and get down into the vault without drawing attention, so he plodded along, bringing back empty wheelbarrows, getting a load of dirt, dumping it into a wagon. Repeat. It was getting hot, and his hangover weighed him down.

Kelley was about to call it a day and slip away for a bath when a foreman shouted, "Water!"

A dozen boys toted water buckets hanging from ox yokes. The dirty men crowded around, dipping cups into the buckets. Kelley realized just how dry and dusty his mouth and throat were, but he saw his opportunity.

He went to one of the smaller boys, lifted the yoke off his shoulders. "Let me help you with that, little man. I'll take it inside for the others."

The flushed boy nodded. "Thank you, sir."

Kelley carried the water into the cathedral, set the buckets at the top of the steps that led down to the vault. He descended, and the temperature cooled. He was greeted by the moist smell of fresh earth.

"Water up top," Kelley shouted down the passage. "Take a break."

The clank and scrape of tools. Muttered voices. They came into view, about a dozen of them walking past him. They were caked with dirt from head to foot. They thanked him and trudged up the steps to the water buckets.

Kelley waited ten seconds, then went back down the passage.

He'd never been inside the vault beneath the cathedral, but he'd heard the same as everyone else, knew that dead rulers and bishops were entombed here. The most important figures had been granted tombs inscribed in Latin marking the brief history of the deceased. Lesser nobles had been given more modest accommodations. Skeletal remains, their hands folded over their chests, lined the broad shelves along the passage. Kelley paused to examine one of the hollow-eyed skulls and crossed himself.

He turned the corner and saw that the passage terminated with a hole in the masonry, about two feet wide and four feet tall. There were mounds of dirt on either side. They'd knocked a hole in the wall and had begun a new tunnel.

Kelley edged toward the hole and felt a cool, damp breeze on his face, less musty than among the tombs. He took a flickering torch from a nearby sconce and squeezed through the opening.

The tunnel was narrow; his shoulders scraped both sides in some places. He had to duck as he scooted through. Short beams had been installed haphazardly to discourage cave-ins. He sensed that the tunnel angled slightly downward, but maybe that was just his imagination.

The light from the vault faded behind him, and the darkness all but swallowed the orange light of the small torch. How far did this tunnel go? He was contemplating turning around when a rushing sound caught his attention. He cocked his head, listened a moment. He increased his pace forward, and the sound of rushing water grew with each step.

Abruptly the tunnel opened into a wide cavern. A light spray of cold water hit him suddenly. Kelley held the torch out before him, and the light was barely enough to give him the full picture. A small underground river rushed and foamed in front of him. He swung the torch one way, then another, trying to take in the whole scene.

The river flowed from left to right in front of him, angling down and swirling into a pool about forty feet across. Kelley lowered the torch and saw a muddy, narrow path in front of him, following the flow of the river down to the pool. There seemed to be some sort of construction on the far side of the pool, rough beams across the edge. He'd need to get closer to see.

Kelley put one foot on the muddy path. His foot slipped out from under him. He upended, landed hard on his butt, and began sliding, picking up speed and heading for the water. He dug a hand into the mud, felt rock beneath and felt a fingernail rip. But he halted his slide before tumbling into the river.

"Damn it."

He grunted, got to his feet carefully on the slippery path. His entire back and ass were caked with mud. He steadied himself, held the torch aloft.

He'd slid half the distance down the path and now stood at the pool's edge. There were beams and sandbags along the edge of the pool. It seemed the river had been dammed. Kelley held up the torch, looked across the pool, and saw a large passage. Not just dammed. Diverted. The small river rushed into the pool, swirled around, and emptied into the passage across the way. The path continued around the pool, narrow and muddy. Kelley had to put his back against the rough, wet stone to scoot sideways. The construction was more elaborate than it had first appeared. There was a drop of nearly twenty feet on the other side of the pool, and there was a sturdy ladder leading down to the floor of the cavern below.

The dam was large, with wooden beams holding rocks and sandbags in place. A lot of manpower had gone into diverting the river into the other passage. Kelley swung his leg over the edge, making sure to keep careful hold on the torch as he climbed down. The temperature dropped another few degrees. He shivered, wet and cold.

Kelley stepped off the last rung of the ladder and landed with a splash, the cold water coming halfway up his shin.

"Hell."

Kelley's feet were lumps of frozen meat in a matter of seconds.

He looked back up at the dam. The structure was not performing its task perfectly. Trickles of water spurted through here and there, so there was still a minor stream running along the river's old course.

Kelley trudged on.

The cavern was much bigger here. He held the torch as high as he could but still wasn't able to see the ceiling. He wondered why they'd want to dam the river. What was at the end of this passage?

Kelley's foot caught on something underwater, and he pitched forward. His hands flew out to break his fall, and he landed with a cold splash, the torch hissing out and plunging him into total darkness.

Muttering every curse he could think of, he sat up in the middle of the stream and blinked. *That's a lot of dark.*

He thought about feeling his way back up the stream, finding the ladder. If he was extremely careful, he could probably make his way back without falling in the river and drowning himself.

He was wet. He was cold. He was still hungover. This had been a terrible idea.

Kelley grunted, stood, and rubbed his backside where he'd landed on some rocks. Slowly his eyes adjusted. The darkness was not complete after all. Dimly he perceived the dull yellow flickering of torches at the far end of the cavern. There was light far ahead, around a corner.

He went forward, forcing himself to move slowly. This was no time for a sprained ankle. He stumbled a few times but managed to right himself without going into the water again, and soon he was at the bend in the cavern where it made a right turn. There was more light here, and Kelley picked up the pace. Soon the cavern turned again, and he saw a lot more flickering light.

He stood at the corner, peeked around the edge.

A handful of men milled around a construction site. One stood at a small wooden table, looking at an unrolled parchment. The large chamber was well lit by a number of torches and a large brazier. The echoes of a few men working with various tools mixed with the sound of rushing water coming from behind him. There wasn't much mud here, although the stream still ran through the center of the chamber and left again through a hole on the far side.

A giant waterwheel had been assembled, but they hadn't yet placed it in position. Kelley imagined the dam had been built to hold back the water for the construction and placement of the waterwheels. Presumably the water—or at least some of it— would be let loose again when the wheels were in place. But why? It was a hell of a place to grind flour.

The man standing over the parchment looked familiar. Yes, Kelley remembered him from the audience with Rudolph. Hans Vredeman de Vries. Rudolph had said something about the man's working with drainage.

Kelley couldn't stand it now. He had to find out what was going on. The curiosity burned a hole in his imagination. He waited until most of the workers were in another part of the chamber and the rest had their backs turned. He scooted fast around the edge of the cave, clinging to the shadows, and hunkered down behind a barrel and a pile of thick, coiled rope. He noticed a few narrow openings behind him, more natural tunnels.

There wasn't much to see from this vantage point, so Kelley moved stealthily toward a pile of lumber. He never made it.

Strong hands grabbed him from behind, one thick hand clapping over his mouth. He was dragged into a tunnel, backward into the long dark beneath the earth.

FIFTEEN

This isn't where I die.

I don't want to mislead you, so I thought it best to assure you now isn't when I meet my untimely demise. I mean, I'm a ghost, right? So something bad must have happened to put me in this circumstance. Yeah.

But not yet.

In the meantime, you're probably wondering what happened to Allen.

THE JESUIT SQUAD

SIXTEEN

After ten minutes, Father Paul began to wonder if Allen was coming back. When twenty minutes had passed, he knew something was wrong.

Father Paul touched the throat microphone hidden under his priest's collar. "Are you monitoring, Finnegan?"

"Right here, Boss," came the voice in his earpiece.

"I think I've lost Cabbot."

"Did he rabbit?"

"I don't think so. I think something happened."

The priest twiddled his thumbs a moment, smoked the remainder of his cigarette down to the butt. "Finnegan, how many can you round up without jeopardizing our surveillance?"

"Let me see." Ten seconds crawled by. "Five."

Father Paul thought about it quickly. Five was enough. "Where's the van?"

"Two blocks north of you."

"I'll see you in five minutes."

The priest pushed away from the table, made his way through the Globe's crowd and checked the restrooms. He circled the café once on the off chance that Allen had been caught in a conversation with some girl, but as suspected, Allen was nowhere to be found.

Father Paul went outside and turned north.

He stuck another cigarette in his mouth and considered. Somebody had gotten their hooks into the Cabbot boy. Father Paul thought he'd arrived early enough to preempt any sort of action by the opposition, and it irked him that he'd figured wrong. He'd planned to make Allen Cabbot his link to Evergreen. Father Paul could deal with Evergreen without the boy, but he didn't want to have to try. A lot of careful thought had gone into the plan.

The black van came into view, and Father Paul broke into a trot. It was a large, nondescript van, parked in an alley. The priest reached it and knocked on the back door. It opened, and he entered, pulling the door closed behind him.

The interior of the van hummed with electronic equipment. Father Flynn Finnegan was a giant pale Irish block of meat with a headset perched on his fat noggin. It looked like some children's toy headset. His black frock bulged with thick muscles. His red hair was growing gray at the temples. He nodded at Father Paul as he entered the van.

"Blake and Santana are on the way," Finnegan said. "What's the target?"

"Give me a quick rundown."

The big Irishman swiveled in his chair and tapped at a laptop. Pictures of buildings and houses flickered on various monitors. "Target zones alpha and beta are quiet," Finnegan reported. "But our people watching the house in Zizkov say a sedan pulled into the driveway six minutes ago. The lights are on, and there's activity."

"That's the one," Father Paul said. "Start the van."

"Right." Finnegan took off the headset, went to the front of the van, and squeezed into the driver's seat, cranking the engine.

Father Paul opened the weapons locker under one of the bench seats and withdrew a flak jacket. All the Battle Jesuit flak jackets had a small emblem over the heart—a golden cross, the bottom of the cross in the shape of a sword blade. He shrugged into it, looked at the other two young priests in the back of the van. They looked of the same mold: young, athletic, a steely-eyed appearance that seemed to indicate a cool, calculated readiness for action. He'd seen their files but had yet to speak with them in person.

He nodded at the tall black man sitting across from him. "Father Starkes?"

William Starkes shrugged into his own flak jacket. "Yes, sir."

"Good to meet you." According to Starkes's file, the man had served a hitch as an Army Ranger before earning a degree in religion from Princeton and then joining the seminary. Father Paul's outfit had only recruited and trained him three months ago. He was a good man on paper, but he looked nervous.

The priests strapped on nylon shoulder holsters, checked the magazines of their 9 mm Glocks. Finnegan punched in the security code on the gun locker's keypad and handed each priest a fully automatic H&K 9 mm submachine gun with laser sight and collapsible stock.

Father Paul shifted his attention to the short man sitting next to Starkes. Emile DeGaul had joined the French Foreign Legion at age seventeen and had already served eight years when his older brother—a priest—had been killed in an automobile accident. DeGaul had made some private deal with God that Father Paul didn't completely understand, and DeGaul had answered the calling a month later.

"Are you ready for this, DeGaul?"

"Absolutely!" His French accent was thick, but his English was good.

Father Paul saw that Finnegan was strapping on a flak jacket also. "Where do you think you're going, Monsignor?"

"You don't think you're going to keep an old warhorse like me out of this, do you, Father?"

"Didn't you just celebrate your fiftieth birthday, Finnegan?"

Finnegan flexed, and muscles rippled beneath his frock. A grin spread across his ruddy face. "Would you like to arm wrestle?"

A smile tugged at the corner of Father Paul's mouth. "No, I don't think I would. Call off Blake and Santana. I don't want to wait for them. Finnegan, take us to Zizkov."

"Right." The Irishman crammed himself into the driver's seat and drove toward the target house.

The three priests in the back of the van checked one another's equipment and made sure their gear was properly secured. They checked and rechecked their weapons. Father Paul handed out headsets. They put them on, plugged them into the compact radios on the shoulders of their flak jackets.

"Remember, this is an extraction," Father Paul said. "I want Cabbot secured and out of there as fast as possible. Let's try to keep casualties down. But never forget these are dangerous people. You see a threat, shoot to kill."

Grim faces nodded back at him.

"Shall we say a quick prayer?" DeGaul asked.

"Lord, aid us in Your work and help us to triumph over evil in Your name. Amen."

They all crossed themselves.

"How about grenades?" suggested DeGaul.

"Definitely not." Father Paul wanted to keep the number of things exploded to a minimum.

"There's a shoulder-based antitank missile in the storage compartment on top of the van," Starkes said.

"No!"

"We're a block away," Finnegan shouted from the front of the van.

"Put us someplace dark," Father Paul said.

"There's an alley up here. Give me two seconds."

Finnegan pulled in, the big van blocking the narrow alley. At this time of night, it probably wouldn't matter, and Father Paul didn't want to spend the time looking for a better parking spot. It would have to do.

"Stick to the shadows. Get into position. Wait for me to give the word. Go."

They spilled out of the back of the van, scattered, then ran in the shadows toward the target house. Finnegan and DeGaul broke off for a back alley to take them behind the house. Starkes trailed behind Father Paul. It was late at night in a quiet, residential section. So far nobody had seen them, but they couldn't count on luck for long. Best to get under cover as soon as possible.

Father Paul scooted under the low branches of a small tree in the front yard and signaled for Starkes to head down the narrow driveway to the side of the house. Father Paul then waited for everyone to get into position. The light was on in the front window. In a moment he'd need to creep forward and have a look.

"Where is everyone?" he asked in a low voice.

The earpiece crackled, and the priests reported in one at a time. Finnegan and DeGaul were in the rear, and Starkes was along the side. Father Paul covered the front. Nobody covered the other side because the target house was almost slap up against its neighbor.

"I want a quick scan. Tell me what you got."

"One window downstairs. Two up," Starkes reported. "All dark."

"The lights are on back here," Finnegan said. "Lots of movement. I see three people, no, make that four. Maybe they can— gun! I just spotted a weapon. They're definitely armed, boyo!"

"That decides it for me," Father Paul said. "We're going in hot, safeties off. Just watch out for Cabbot. Pick your entry points, and wait for my word. Finnegan, is that one with the weapon upstairs or downstairs?"

"Upstairs. There's a drainpipe. I can shinny up there, pop in, and handle the situation no problem."

"It's an old house, Finnegan, and you weigh ten tons. Send DeGaul up the drainpipe."

A slight pause. "Understood."

"Get into position and stand by."

Father Paul checked his weapons, then slowly approached the front window, crouched over. The first-floor window was big and low, very easy access. He looked inside, saw the back of a man's head, his chair back against the window. Beyond the man sat Allen Cabbot, looking tired and anxious. The priest wished he could get a better look at the other man. It was difficult to tell the exact situation. Father Paul had assumed that Allen had been abducted, but that wasn't necessarily the case. Maybe there was a more subtle way to handle this.

Father Paul saw Allen's eyes get big. Allen sat up in his chair, pointed at the window. The other man turned. There was a pistol in his hand.

Hell.

"Go!" Father Paul yelled into the headset's microphone. He took three steps back, then leaped through the big front window.

Glass shattered and rained, sparkling fragments spraying the man with the pistol. The priest tucked and rolled, came up in a shooter's stance.

The man with the pistol took a panicked step back and shouted, "Vatican thugs! Run!"

And then he pointed the pistol at Father Paul.

The submachine gun bucked in the priest's hands, sprayed the man with lead. Red blotches sprouting across his chest and belly. The man jerked and fell, a pile of dead meat. Father Paul was simultaneously aware of more gunplay elsewhere in the house. His team was in.

Allen was up and running out of the room. The priest couldn't blame him. People tended to flee from gunfire.

"Allen, wait!" Father Paul cried as he ran after him.

He ran into the kitchen, saw a young blond girl standing before Allen, her hand flung up in a *Halt!* gesture. Father Paul didn't halt; he charged at her, machine gun raised.

He stepped on something, his foot sliding along the linoleum floor and out from under him. He went into the air, drifting backward, the kitchen a spinning blur in front of his eyes. He landed on his back. Hard. The air went out of him with a *whuff*, and his mouth worked silently, trying to find breath.

He glimpsed Allen and the girl dashing out a side door into the night.

There was a long three seconds before Father Paul could catch his breath again. He groaned into a sitting position, then scanned the kitchen floor and saw a small, delicate teacup turned upside down. He'd stepped square on top of it, and instead of crushing the thing into dust, he'd slid across the floor on it, as if it had been an ice skate. His back ached in several places.

A bearded man in denim rushed into the kitchen, screaming, "Damn Papist!" He leveled a shotgun at the priest. The shotgun blast shook the room as Father Paul rolled to the side. Buckshot scored the cabinets behind him.

Father Paul flattened to his belly, swung the H&K, one-handed, out in front of him and squeezed off two quick bursts. A slug smacked into the attacker's shin, sprayed blood. He screamed, high-pitched and ragged, then collapsed on top of himself, the shotgun sliding out of reach.

"Oh, fucking shit. You shot my leg off. My fucking leg!" He writhed, tried to reach down and staunch the blood flow.

The priest lurched to his feet, went to the door, and looked outside. No sign of Cabbot or the girl.

"Damn."

He heard somebody come in behind him. He spun quickly, bringing the machine gun to bear.

"It's me." Finnegan held up his hands. "The rest of the

house is secure. Three more Society fanatics. They've been terminated."

"Vatican scum!" said the bleeding man on the floor.

"Put a sock in it, boyo. We'll get to you in a minute."

"Fuck you!"

"Did you get Cabbot?" Finnegan asked.

Father Paul sighed. "I missed him."

"He's out of your reach now," said the bearded man. "Kill me and ten more will rise to take my place."

"Then I suppose we'd better patch you up and keep you alive," Father Paul said. "I'd hate to have ten of you cluttering up the place. Plus it's damn difficult to interrogate you if you're dead."

"Tough shit, priest. You won't get anything out of me." He dipped a thumb and forefinger into his shirt pocket, came out with a pill, prepared to put it in his mouth.

"Suicide pill!" shouted Finnegan.

Father Paul and the big Irishman dove on the wounded man, grabbed his wrist as he strained to get the pill into his mouth.

"You can't stop me, you bastards!"

"No, you don't." Finnegan engulfed the man's fist with his own hammy hand and squeezed. The fingers popped open, and Finnegan grabbed the pill. "Got it."

"This is taking too long," Father Paul said. The local authorities would soon respond to the commotion. He touched his throat microphone. "Gather up the strays and meet back at the ranch. One minute."

"Hold on a second." Finnegan held the blue pill close to his eyes. "This is an Aleve."

"No, it's not," the fanatic said.

"The hell it isn't. I take them for my knees. It's an Aleve with the writing scratched off."

"It's a suicide pill. We've sworn not to be taken alive."

Finnegan grabbed the fanatic's face, squeezed until his mouth popped open, then shoved the pill inside. The fanatic squirmed, tried to spit it out, but the Irishman clapped a hand over his mouth. "Swallow it."

The fanatic swallowed it, and Finnegan removed his hand.

"You son of a bitch!" the fanatic shouted. "You've poisoned me."

"It's not poison, idiot. It'll probably make your leg feel better."

"That's enough," Father Paul said. "Finnegan, throw him over your shoulder. We'll fix his leg in the van. Let's move."

Somehow Father Paul would have to find the Cabbot boy. He was out there roaming Prague by night without the faintest notion of what was about to happen to him.

SEVENTEEN

Amy held his hand tight, pulling him along so fast that Allen almost tripped and fell flat on his face a dozen times. The *ra-ta-ta-tat* of distant machine-gun fire still followed them. Her blond braids streamed behind her. Allen huffed and went red in the face, a large quantity of pilsner sloshing in his stomach.

"I've got to stop," Allen said.

"Not yet. Keep running."

They ran through the residential area to a small park at the foot of a hill. Allen jerked his hand away from hers and threw himself on the first park bench they passed.

"Got to . . . stop, okay?" He gasped for breath. "I'm going to . . . puke."

She took his hand in both of hers and tried to pull him off the bench. "Come *on*! We can rest later. We've got to get under cover."

"Just one minute. I'm not kidding. I'm going to spew beer all over this fucking bench."

She sat next to him, put her hand on his forehead. Her palm was soft and cool. She smelled like cinnamon.

Both their heads jerked up at the sound of the sirens.

They saw the lights washing through the street a split second before the two police cars came into view, driving fast. Amy threw her arms around Allen and kissed him hard as the police cars sped past.

"What was that for?" A faint strawberry flavor lingered in his mouth from the kiss.

"Haven't you ever seen them do that in the movies?" she asked. "A man and woman trying to look inconspicuous when the cops go by?"

"I don't think it was necessary. They were probably too worried about the gunfight to care about a couple of people sitting on a park bench," Allen said. "Not that I minded."

She stood, grabbed his hand again. "Come on."

They headed for a narrow path on the other side of the park bench. It led uphill.

Allen groaned. "Can't we escape downhill?"

"We don't have to run," Amy said. "Just keep moving."

The narrow path zigzagged uphill and joined a wider path. It was steep enough going to wind Allen after five minutes. He got sweaty, puffed for air. The path led into a road, which they took to the top of the hill. A blocky gray building sat at the top.

"This is Zizkov Hill, isn't it?" Allen recalled the description in *The Rogue's Guide*. "The Monument."

"The National Monument, yes. We're approaching it from the back."

It looked like a big, squat concrete bunker. They circled around the side, then ducked into a breezeway that ran through the middle of the structure. The whole place was lit poorly by scattered streetlights. Amy stopped in front of a large, dark set of wood doors chained together with a thick brass padlock. She fished into her shirt and brought out a small key on a string, then unlocked the padlock and opened one of the doors just wide enough for both of them to slip inside. She closed it again, padlocked it on the inside.

The room was bare, gray stone, with a single Soviet-looking

lightbulb sticking out of a utilitarian fixture. A gray block humped up from the center of the floor—the tomb of the unknown soldier, which *The Rogue's Guide* said was now empty. There was nothing else in the chamber, and Allen was forced to wonder what they were doing here.

Amy reached around the side of the tomb, depressed a small square of stone. The tomb rumbled; the squeal and clink of chains, the hum of machinery. The top of the tomb slid halfway back. Allen stepped forward, looked inside.

A metal ladder descended into a tunnel below.

"We can lie low down here," Amy said. "Follow me."

She swung her leg over and into the tomb, went down the ladder.

Allen hesitated, then followed.

The bottom of the ladder let them off in an old service tunnel, where water pipes and other conduits ran along the floor and ceiling. The stone tunnel was barely four feet wide and less than six feet tall, again lit by low-watt bare bulbs every twenty feet. Allen had to bow his head slightly as he followed Amy.

Abruptly they came upon a man-sized hole in the side of the tunnel. They ducked inside.

The chamber, a large area full of pipes and valves, stretched ten feet high. The room was obviously some sort of central crossroads for all the plumbing and electrical wiring for the Monument and other buildings on the hill.

But the room had been recently altered.

Three double beds with matching pillows and comforters spread around the room. Beads and tapestries had been hung in an attempt to make the chamber seem livable. There was a desk with a computer. An easy chair with a lamp standing next to it. A few books on a footstool. A table set up with kitchen stuff, hot plate and microwave.

The Harry Potter poster over one of the beds just looked . . . wrong.

The girl on the bed with the camouflage comforter and matching pillowcases sat up, startled, setting aside a book she was reading. "What are you doing here? What's *he* doing here?"

It was one of the other girls from the Globe. The tough-looking one with black spiky hair and the heavy, dark eye makeup. She'd kicked off the combat boots and had put on torn jeans and a Clash T-shirt. The Clash? Was that some honest bit of retro or some kind of put-on? Allen's *mother* had listened to the Clash.

"Basil is dead, Clover," Amy said.

The Tough one—Clover—went blank, then her face slowly softened and her shoulders slumped. "Shit."

"I think they got the others too," Amy said. "I don't know what to do. Can we handle this, just the three of us?"

"To hell with that," Clover said. "I say we call for reinforcements. Get everyone in here, guns blazing, and put a lid on this fucking shit pronto."

"That would be rash."

Allen jumped at the new voice behind him. He stepped aside as she entered the room, the third one from the Globe. In the crowded café, Allen had only seen her sitting. Now he could see how tall she was—at least an inch taller than Allen, with a broad back, short hair, and tightly muscled arms, making her look like a cross between a phys ed teacher and a Navy SEAL. Her voice was deep and flinty.

"Sam!" Amy put a gentle hand on her arm. "Basil is dead."

"I know," Sam said. "I just came from there. The place is crawling with local fuzz."

Amy's eyes went glassy, on the verge of tears. "What do we do now?"

"Counterstrike," Clover said.

"That doesn't get us anywhere." Sam looked at Allen. "How far did Basil get with him?"

Amy opened her mouth, but Allen said, "Ask me, why don't you? I'm standing right here."

"Okay, sport. What did Basil tell you?"

"He didn't get very far," Allen said. "He started talking about alchemists."

"Did he tell you what Evergreen is doing?"

"No."

Sam nibbled her bottom lip in contemplation. "We need to call for help. They need to know back home what's happened to Basil."

"What about Allen?" asked Amy.

Clover scooted to the front of the bed, grabbed her combat boots, and jammed her feet into them. "Tie him up. Try the mind probe on him."

One of Allen's eyebrows went up. "Mind probe?"

"Do we have to? Allen's on our side now." Amy grabbed his arm. "Tell them, Allen."

"I'm not on *anybody's* side. I don't know what the hell is going on. I don't know who *you* are!"

"I'm Amy."

"This is ridiculous."

"We are The Three," Sam told him. "And we're members of the Society, an ancient order dedicated to preserving and protecting the balance of magic. The balance that Dr. Evergreen is about to throw completely out of whack."

Allen frowned.

"See how easy that was to explain?" Clover stuck a cigarette in her mouth. "Magic balance out of whack. Aren't you glad you asked?"

Allen could not think of anything he was glad about.

"Don't smoke," Amy said. "I hate it when you smoke."

Sam unwrapped a thin cigar, put it in her mouth, and lit it.

"You're doing that on purpose to irritate me. You know the smoke bothers my eyes."

"Clover's right." Sam inhaled, held it, then blew a long gray stream toward the ceiling. "We can't let you run to Evergreen and tip him off."

"It was the priests that broke in on us," Amy said. "They killed Basil. They tried to kill us. Allen saw them. He wouldn't be on their side. Not now. Would you, Allen?"

Allen opened his mouth. Shut it again. Amy had a point. It had been Father Paul. *With a machine gun.* Allen had seen his face clearly. On the other hand, Amy and this Basil guy had shoved him in the trunk of a car, had questioned him at gunpoint.

"Look, I don't know what to think. All I know is I don't want any trouble."

"Well, trouble is what you got," Clover sneered. "You're in this up to your ass, so deal with it."

"Leave him alone," Amy said. "He's overwhelmed."

"Boo-fucking-hoo."

"Enough." Sam puffed the cigar. "Let me think."

Allen pointed at the easy chair. "Can I sit there? I feel like I'm going to fall over."

Sam puffed the cigar, nodded.

"I'll get you a drink," Amy said. "Some water."

Allen collapsed into the chair. How long since he'd slept?

"Take this." Amy handed him a glass of water.

He drank, realized how parched he was, gulped it all down.

Sam stood next to his chair and placed a warm, calloused hand on his forehead. Blurry syllables spilled out of her mouth, too fast and strange to understand.

He blinked up at her. "What?"

"Nothing. Go to sleep if you're tired."

He put his head back. Maybe he'd close his eyes. Just for a minute. Just a . . . quick . . . forty . . . winks.

"Alllllleeeeeen."

Somebody was calling his name through the fog.

Cobblestones under his feet. Allen wore boots, high, hard, and black. Gray breeches and a ruffled, cream-colored shirt. Some kind of period costume.

Oh, hell. I'm in a Brontë novel.

The sound of rushing water came through the fog. Allen wasn't on a road. It was a bridge. He looked over the side, saw the Vltava flowing beneath him. He glanced back over his shoulder where Prague Castle would be on the hill, watching over the city below, but the thick fog obscured everything, blotted out the stars.

He jogged along the bridge, but it stretched on and on with no end in sight. The voice in the fog called his name again. *"Allen. Alllleeeeeen."*

"Who's there?"

She floated out of the fog like a ghost. Red velvet dress dragging the cobblestones, tight bodice pushing up white breasts. A black cloak with the hood thrown back revealed luxurious waves of dark hair.

"Allen."

Allen gulped. "Mrs. Evergreen?"

"This is a dream, Allen."

"I know."

"It's a dream, but it's real. I really am here in your mind. I'm inside you, Allen."

"Uh . . . thank you?"

"I'm calling to you, Allen."

"I'm flattered, but I'd like to wake up now."

She moved toward him, seeming to glide, as if there had been unseen roller skates beneath the billowing dress. She circled him as she spoke, trailing a delicate finger along his shoulders and back.

"My husband needs your help, Allen. He's been looking for you. Waiting for you."

"I was delayed." Allen felt guilty, ashamed. Like he'd disappointed her. "I've had some trouble with—"

"I know that you're with the witches," she said.

Witches?

Allen said, "There's a priest, too."

She hissed and stepped back from him. "How many?"

"I don't know."

She was suddenly in front of him again, blue eyes locked onto his. Allen stood paralyzed, a chill all over his body, a feeling like cold, stone hands holding his heart. He wanted to flee, yet he could not stand the idea of being away from her. He had to serve her. Please her.

"Tell me of this priest," she said.

Allen told her everything he knew. He reached into his ruffled shirt, pulled out the crucifix. "He gave me this."

Cassandra Evergreen flinched, took a step back. "It's not important. Put it away."

He put it away.

She forced a smile to her face, stepped close to Allen again, touched his cheek. The fog swirled in around them, clinging cold and damp.

"I will come to you again," she said.

"When?" The raw hunger in the single word embarrassed him.

But she was gone.

The ground left his feet. He was falling backward through the fog, a long, deep drop into nothing. Allen opened his mouth to scream.

"Knock it off."

Allen started, lifted his head, blinked.

The tough one stood over him. Clover.

"Where am I?" His voice was a hoarse croak. The easy chair in the witches' lair. He tried to lift his arms, found that his wrists had been duct-taped to the arm of the chair. More tape around his ankles.

"We'd prefer you stay put for a while," Clover said.

"Where's Amy?"

"Your little girlfriend's not here. And I don't trust you. Sorry if it's not comfortable. I think our Amy has a little-girl crush on you, so we thought it better if I stood guard."

"We don't even know each other."

Clover shrugged. "No, I guess not, but she's the nice one. She'd probably feel sorry for you, and we can't have you sweet-talking your way out of here right now. Not until we get further instructions from our people."

"What if I have to pee?"

"Hold it."

"Let me rephrase that. I have to pee."

There was no warmth in Clover's smile. She sucked hard on her cigarette, blew smoke into Allen's face. "What was all the noise about?"

"What noise?"

"You were sound asleep in the chair, and then suddenly you screamed." She blew more smoke at him.

"Could you fucking stop that please."

Clover smirked.

"It was just a bad dream," Allen said.

"No fucking shit, Sherlock. What was it about?"

Allen opened his mouth, closed it again. What *had* the dream been about? He strained to remember but couldn't. He couldn't recall a single detail; he retained only the vague feeling that there was something dreadfully important he was supposed to be doing. Being tied up only added to the sense of urgency.

And Dr. Evergreen. He and his wife would be wondering where the hell Allen was. Had they arrived in Prague yet? He needed to go to them, find them. It occurred to Allen he didn't know the time, how long he'd been sleeping. He didn't even know if it was day or night.

"Dreams can be dangerous things," Clover said. "Some must be taken very seriously. I don't mean the Freudian crap, or the ones where you show up to school in your underwear. The other dreams, the strangely vivid, disturbing ones. You need to be careful who and what you let into your mind."

She dropped the cigarette butt on the cement floor, smashed it out with the heel of her combat boot.

"I wish you'd dispose of those properly," Amy said from the doorway.

The grin on Clover's face was half snarl. "I was just chatting with your boyfriend."

"Stop saying that."

Clover made exaggerated kissing noises and flopped back down on her bed.

"I hate that you're so rude," Amy said.

"Better than being fake nice."

"It's, like, called courtesy, okay?"

Clover said, "Fake nice, courtesy. Just two ways to say the same thing."

"I really do have to pee," Allen said.

Clover grunted impatience. "Just spell him back to sleep."

"Spell?"

"Man, you really are slow on the uptake, aren't you?" Clover slid to the edge of the bed, a fresh cigarette between her fingers. "We're *witches*, man. Don't you get it?"

Witches. For some odd reason, this revelation didn't surprise Allen. It didn't even seem like a revelation.

"I went to sleep," Allen said slowly, "because I was exhausted. That's all."

"Wake up and smell the Ovaltine," Clover said.

"I also cast a spell to help us get away from the Vatican troops," Amy said. "Remember in the kitchen? When we were running from the priest? That was a hindrance spell."

Allen shook his head. "No, no, no, no. He tripped on

something. There was a cup on the floor, and he stepped on it. I *saw* it."

"Well, like yeah," Amy said. "Because I spelled him to do that."

"Oh, come on. He tripped, and we got away."

"Fuck him." Clover lit the fresh cigarette, puffed it hard. "He's just another nonbeliever."

"Remember when you came out to the alley and we put you in the trunk of the car?" Amy asked Allen. "The luring spell."

Allen rolled his eyes. "A gorgeous blonde asks me to meet her. Yeah, that's some complicated magic there."

Amy frowned. "You really don't believe us?"

"Don't waste your time with him," Clover said.

Amy pouted. Clover smoked. The silence stretched.

Allen cleared his throat. "Are you going to let me pee, or what?"

EIGHTEEN

Father Paul was not the sort of person who enjoyed throwing his weight around, but on the phone in the wee hours of the morning with an angry bishop, the priest had to remind the man how upset the Vatican might be if Father Paul was hindered in the pursuit of his important mission.

So the bishop pulled some strings and got Father Paul and his unit access to one of the interrogation rooms in a suburban precinct and a sympathetic police captain willing to lose the paperwork and look the other way. Finnegan escorted a bearded radical to the room, put him in a chair, and closed the door. They'd let him stew about a half hour while they watched him from behind a two-way mirror.

"A bit of a punk, isn't he?" Finnegan said.

"Still dangerous," Father Paul said absently. He watched the kid's knee bounce up and down. They'd had a doctor patch up the boy's shin after an X-ray had revealed that the bullet had only nicked the bone. Lots of bright red blood and screaming, but mostly sound and fury, signifying a fairly minor wound. The kid would limp for a while.

"We've sent his fingerprints through the system," Finnegan said. "We should have something back soon."

"We've let him twist long enough. I'm going to talk to him. You watch from here."

"Right."

Father Paul went into the interrogation room, the kid looking up with a start. Father Paul sat across from him, shook a cigarette loose from the pack. Lit it. Puffed. Sat back and smoked.

Give him a chance. See if he talks first.

"I don't know what you think you're going to get out of me."

The priest shrugged. "You want a smoke?" He held out the pack.

"Those things will kill you."

Father Paul put the pack away. "In my line of work . . . well, cancer sticks are pretty far down on the list. So, you're not European. No accent. What part of the States are you from?"

"Nice try, Priest. I'm not telling you dick."

"This is just routine, really. Small fry like you doesn't know much probably."

There it was. Just barely noticeable, a frown and a flinch. The kid wanted to think he was important. Not many revolutionaries aspire to be pawns.

"Let's just keep it simple," Father Paul said. "What's your name?"

"You can torture me all night, and I'll never tell you."

"We found your passport in your back pocket. Says you're Thomas Varley."

Varley looked away. "Shit."

"Where are you from?"

"You go to hell. I said I'm not talking."

"Your driver's license was in your wallet. Home address, Waco, Texas."

Varley slapped the table. "Damn it."

"Look," Father Paul said, "this'll all be a lot easier if we can just have a nice conversation."

Varley crossed his arms, sat back in his chair, his face stone.

"You put up quite a fight when we busted in on you," Father Paul said, putting a hint of grudging admiration in his voice. "Eight or ten of you guys were almost more than we could handle."

"Eight or ten? Man, there was only five of us. If we'd had ten guys, you Vatican motherfuckers would be toast."

Father Paul took a small notebook from his jacket pocket, scratched a brief note. "Five. Thanks for clarifying."

Varley slapped the table again. "Damn it!"

"Let's see." The priest tapped the pen against his chin. "Three dead, then you. That's four. Let's talk about number five."

"Let's not."

"A young lady. Blond and pretty. What's her name?"

"You're not tricking me into saying anything else, man," Varley said. "So just. Fuck. Off."

"I'm sorry to hear that." Father Paul turned to face the mirror. "Father Finnegan, I think we'll need to go to the next level of interrogation."

Ten seconds later Finnegan's enormous bulk squeezed into the interrogation room. He carried a little black bag in one fist. He set it on the table, opened it, and pulled out a syringe.

Varley's eyes went big. "No way, man. You're not doping me. To hell with that." He started to rise from the chair.

"Stay put." Finnegan took hold of Varley's shoulders and pushed him back into a sitting position, like a giant manhandling a ventriloquist's dummy. "It'll go easier if you hold still, lad."

"Oh, shit." Panic edged Varley's voice.

Father Paul filled the syringe with clear liquid from a small vial.

"I think this will pave the way for that nice, friendly conversation I was hoping for."

An hour later they put Varley on a cot in one of the holding cells and left him snoring there.

In the precinct break room, Father Paul and Finnegan hunched toward each other, discussing the interrogation in hushed tones. They each sipped tepid, bitter coffee from Styrofoam cups.

Father Paul would need sleep. He felt fatigue tugging hard at him around the edges. Somehow the big Irish slab of meat had the power to go on and on, but if Father Paul didn't find a bed soon, he'd simply keel over.

"He didn't know much, did he?" Finnegan said.

"Enough. A thread to pull. I want our people on this girl." Varley had known that her first name was Amy. It was a start.

Starkes entered the break room, put a short stack of papers on the table in front of Father Paul. "Just got these faxed. Not much on Varley. Pretty much stuff we know already."

"Thanks. Rotate those on surveillance. Everyone else should grab some shut-eye."

"Right." Starkes left.

Father Paul flipped through the faxed pages. Not much to work with. Varley was twenty-one years old, a college dropout. He'd drifted from one radical cause to another, looking to fit in someplace and stick it to the man. The definition of "The Man" seemed to shift as the wind blew. Corporations, the U.S. government, oil companies . . . and now the Vatican. Fighting the good fight against magical oppression. Didn't these people realize that Father Paul and his people fought twenty-four/seven to keep the world from plunging into chaos?

A simple thank-you would've been nice.

No. Stupid to think that. People like him and Finnegan and the rest labored in anonymity, and that's how it should be. The world didn't need to know what went bump in the night.

Something in Varley's file caught Father Paul's attention. The kid had dropped out of college right after a semester abroad in London. A transitional period, one cause to another. Father Paul sifted the information in front of him, but he couldn't find what he wanted, so he flipped open his cell phone and called the direct number to his support team back at headquarters. They said they'd have the additional information within thirty minutes. Father Paul sent Finnegan out to the van for his notebook computer. The big man brought it in, and Father Paul booted up. Twenty-three minutes later, he had the information he wanted.

Varley had attended university at a minor school in South London called St. Sebastian's. The school was unremarkable in every way except for a minor professor of folklore, who, unbeknownst to the rest of the faculty and student body, was high councilman of the Society.

So a young Varley had been recruited by Professor Jackson Fay, one of the most powerful warlocks in the past century.

Father Paul sighed, lit a cigarette. "Great."

Starkes stuck his head back into the break room. "Surveillance has picked up Cabbot. Location Beta."

Father Paul stood, gathered the loose papers quickly, and tucked them under his arms. "Find Finnegan and tell him to meet me at the van."

"You want me to gather everyone else?"

"No. Tell Finnegan if he's not in the van in ninety seconds, I'm leaving his ass here."

NINETEEN

Relief.

Allen stood pissing in the cramped bathroom. He wanted to weep, the relief was so profound. His hands had been taped together in front of him. His ankles were taped together as well. They'd let him hop in like that to use the toilet, but Clover had insisted on the precautions.

As he pissed, he glanced around the small bathroom. There had to be a way out of there. If he could cut himself loose, he might simply dash past them.

"Hurry up in there," called Clover.

Something. A nail file. Anything would do. Maybe he could chew through the tape.

He finished, zipped, and flushed.

He hopped back into the other room, flopped into the easy chair again.

"Feel better?" Clover asked.

"I'd feel better if you'd cut me loose and let me out of here."

"Tough shit."

Yeah.

"Why are you doing this?" Allen asked. "I just want to go home. I don't care what you people are doing."

"Well, you should care, man. That's the whole reason I'm hooked up with this outfit, right? Usually I'm kind of a loner."

"Really? Someone with your social skills?"

Clover went on like she hadn't heard him. "You might not care what's happening in the world, but a lot of us do. A lot of us want to do the right thing. Politics and world leaders and the United Nations and all that bullshit. That's nothing. Window dressing. If you knew the real forces tugging at the fabric of the universe, you'd shit your pants, man. So I *do* care, okay? I'm part of something bigger than myself, and I've never had that feeling before in my life and I'm not giving it up, okay? I'm one of the good guys, and what I do *matters*."

"That's a good speech. You rehearse that in front of a mirror?"

"You're kind of a smart-ass motherfucker, aren't you?"

"Spend enough time in duct tape, and the courtesy goes out the window."

"Yeah, well, we need you to stay put," Clover said. "If the bosses say you're valuable, then that's good enough for me."

"I'm flattered, but how could I possibly be valuable?"

"Standard Society MO," Clover said. "Get a guy on the inside. You're in with the Evergreens, and they're key to all this shit that's coming down."

"I really don't know anything about that."

"What you don't know could fill a fucking barn, dude."

"I'll make you a deal," Allen said. "I'll stop being a smart-ass if you stop being a bitch."

"No, I'll make you a deal. You shut the fuck up and I won't put out cigarettes on your scrotum."

The heavy door to the chamber swung open, and Amy rushed inside, flushed and panting. "We've got to go."

Clover leaped to her feet. "What is it?"

"They're coming."

"Shit." Clover grabbed a black backpack, started shoving in her possessions. "How many?"

"It wasn't clear," Amy said. "I think something's obscuring the magic. We've got to get out of here and then spread the word. This location is over. Nobody can come back here."

Clover slung the backpack over her shoulder, motioned at Allen with her chin. "What about him?"

"We've got to scatter. He'll come with me."

"Bullshit."

Amy spun, met Clover's hard gaze. "I said he comes with me."

Clover stepped back, nodded. "Okay."

Amy bent over Allen, touched his cheek softly. "The priests are on their way. You've got to trust me."

"Okay," Allen said.

She produced a switchblade, flicked it open in front of Allen's face. He flinched. She cut him out of the duct tape, then put the knife away. He rubbed the circulation back into his wrists.

"Clover, go out the front. Maybe you can lead them down the hill. They have a car, so stay off the road. You know the footpaths better than they do. Be well, sister."

"The Lady be with you, sister," Clover said.

They kissed quickly, brief and ceremonial.

Clover left.

"Come on." Amy took Allen by the hand, led him to another tunnel. No lights. Amy flicked on a flashlight. They jogged, the tunnel angled steadily downhill.

"Are we going deeper underground?" Allen asked.

"No. This leads to the bottom of the hill."

They jogged for three minutes, then slowed to a fast walk. The tunnel was narrow and dry, the floor covered with dust. The passage had clearly not been used in years.

"Do you know where we're going?"

"Theoretically," Amy said.

At last they came to a rusty iron ladder leading upward. They climbed, came up against a heavy metal manhole cover. Amy shoved against it without luck. "Help me."

"Move. Let me try."

They traded places on the ladder, and Allen heaved himself against the manhole cover. Just at the point he thought he might rupture himself, the lid lifted and he moved it to one side, spilling fresh air and weak daylight into the tunnel. He climbed out, sat panting on a cement slab surrounded by bushes. It was just daybreak. Amy climbed out behind him.

Allen glanced around. They were behind some building, a walking path visible through the bushes. "Where are we?"

"Bottom of Zizkov Hill, I think. The other side of where we climbed up."

A strange tour of Prague, Allen thought. He'd been all over the place and hadn't seen a damn thing.

Allen followed her around the corner of the building and came face-to-face with a large tank, the gun barrel aimed right at his nose.

"The military museum," Amy said. "Yes, this is where I thought we were."

Of course. Allen was losing his mind. The tank was old, a museum piece that clearly hadn't budged in decades.

"We need to get out of sight," Amy said. "We can head toward City Hall and blend in with the tourists, but we'll eventually need to lay low someplace, and I don't know which of the safe houses have been compromised."

Allen thought about it a moment, then said, "Follow me. I think I know a place."

Do you remember what Clover said about the MO of the Society, how they like to have a spy on the inside? She's right. Even hundreds of years ago. Hey, if it ain't broke, don't fix it.

1599

TWENTY

"Stop wiggling, little worm, or I'll conk you one on the noggin." British. Strong Yorkshire accent.

Edward Kelley stopped wiggling, let them carry him into the pitch black. Three minutes later, they set him gently on the rough cavern floor, the hand still over his mouth.

"How about a light, Edgar?" Another voice in English but a light Czech accent.

"Righto."

A spark and a flash. The man kneeling over him held a candle. A narrow passage, looked like a natural cavern. The man above him had an enormous brown beard, wore a dark green cloak with the hood up, black clothing beneath. Ruddy, full cheeks. A big man, broad through the chest.

The man behind him said, "I'm going to take my hand away from your mouth. Let's keep it quiet, eh?"

Kelley nodded.

The man with the Czech accent took his hand away, and Kelley turned to look at him. Bald. Gray beard. Big, alert eyes.

"We've been watching you, Edward Kelley."

Kelley smiled weakly. "How flattering."

"Let me show you something." The Yorkshireman—Edgar—handed the candle to the Czech. He rolled up his sleeve, showed a tattoo on his upper arm to Kelley. "Do you recognize that?"

Kelley squinted at the tattoo, immediately recognizing the square and compass formed into the shape of a quadrilateral. "Freemasons."

"Look closer."

Kelley leaned in to examine the tattoo in the dim candlelight. In the dead center of the quadrilateral was the sign of the pentagram. Kelley resisted the urge to genuflect.

"The square represents matter, the solid known tangible things of our world," Edgar said as he rolled his sleeve down again. "The compass stands for the spirit or mind."

"And the pentagram stands for evil," Kelley said.

A tolerant smile. "You know better than that. Alchemists are often accused of dark things, are they not?"

True enough. He'd seen some of the older, more superstitious serving women in the castle shy away whenever he or Dr. Dee passed. People feared the unknown. Peasants especially disliked change or anything strange. Kelley had known an old woman back in Ireland who hadn't come out of her cottage for a week because she'd seen a raven with a bit of string in its beak on a dead tree branch. She'd insisted the string had looked like a hangman's noose.

"The pentagram represents something in between mind and matter," Edgar explained. "Truths that are difficult to hold and know but nevertheless govern our universe. Powers that control a balance so precarious that the slightest cosmic sneeze could plunge us all into oblivion."

"I'd like to go home now, please," Kelley said.

"There are things afoot in Prague Castle that would chill you to the marrow if you knew their full extent," Edgar said. "We need your help."

"Me?"

"You."

"You want Dr. Dee. He's your man. To be honest, I'm not a very good alchemist. I can barely brew up a good laxative."

"Even now forces work to drive Dee away. He will flee Prague this very night. I have foreseen it."

"He didn't mention anything about leaving to me."

"This is perhaps not the best place for this discussion," the Czech said.

"Come." Edgar took Kelley's hand, pulled him to his feet. "This is a lot of strange news to drop on a man's head all at once. I know where we can talk, and there's a bottle of good brandy there." He slapped Kelley on the back. "Perhaps a drink would help fortify you, friend."

"Yes, please."

I can't possibly explain how time works for a ghost. Or, at the very least, how it works for this ghost. Sometimes I feel like I exist outside of time. Or perhaps I exist in all times at once. Or maybe I don't exist at all, and therefore time is meaningless. I'm not flowing in it, or maybe it doesn't flow around me. Are we each on a little raft, flowing in the river of time, or do we stand on the bank and watch it wind its way under our noses?

I've had nothing but time to think about it.

Intellectually, I know that the walk with Edgar through the tunnels beneath Prague Castle took perhaps twenty minutes, but in that deeper way we sense things, some peculiar machination of memory that mixes up duration and importance, the tunnels seemed like one lifetime. As I came out of the cave in the woods behind the castle, emerging into the daylight, I felt myself entering another lifetime.

I remembered the short hike to the little shepherd's shack not at all.

The brandy perhaps had something to do with this.

TWENTY-ONE

A rough wooden table, two chairs, a bedroll in the corner. A window. Thin beams of daylight slicing through the thatched roof. Dirt floor. Edgar built a fire in the small, stone fireplace in spite of the fact that it was damn hot enough already. All in all, the shack was a pretty miserable affair. Kelley had gotten used to life at the castle.

But the brandy was good. Edgar refilled the wooden cups again, and Kelley sipped. Very good indeed, better than Kelley could usually afford. It warmed his belly, made his head feel pleasantly light.

"Your friend doesn't want to join us?"

"He's keeping watch," Edgar said. "We should be safe here, but it pays to be careful."

Kelley paused, the cup halfway to his lips. "It has always been my impression that the Freemasons were influential people with powerful friends, yet I get the impression that you're hiding."

"Yes, I suppose I should explain," Edgar said. "Our Czech friend—never mind his name—is watching for Templars. The Society is, or was, a secret order of the Freemasons. We have broken from them, and now they hunt us. We have become an embarrassment to them, but they don't realize that only we stand between chaos and order. So we have been shunned and driven underground, but we hold fast to our mission still."

"How does your mission bring you to Prague?" Kelley gulped the brandy. The pleasure was almost sexual. The warmth spread to his limbs, the lingering remains of his hangover drifting away like smoke.

"Rudolph the Second." Edgar sipped at his own brandy more slowly. "The Holy Roman Emperor is delving into the arcane. Astrologers and wizards from the four corners of the earth have descended upon the emperor's court."

"And alchemists," Kelley hiccoughed.

"Indeed." Edgar topped off Kelley's cup. "Let me ask you this, Master Kelley. Can I call you Edward?"

"Please do."

"Let me ask you this, Edward. Would you take immortality if it were offered to you? Would you choose to live forever?"

"I suppose that might be useful."

"Would you trade your soul for this immortality?"

Kelley frowned, shook his head slowly. "No."

"Of course you wouldn't," Edgar said. "But that's what Rudolph would do. More than that, he'd trade the soul of the whole world. He thinks he can live forever, and he's not stopping to consider the power he will unleash in his blind quest to achieve his goals. That's why we of the Society must stand against such blind insanity. No one else can do it."

Kelley sipped the brandy and recalled his brief meeting with the emperor. The man had not been raving, had not outwardly seemed crazy. Kelley had to ask himself what was more likely. Was it reasonable to think the leader of the empire a lunatic bent on using arcane powers to achieve immortality? Or was it more likely that the man sitting across from him, in a shabby shack in the woods, who believed that only he and his Society could change the world, was in fact the one who might not be in full possession of his faculties?

On the other hand, Kelley could not deny the influx of strange scholars and astrologers into the castle. Dr. Dee himself had hinted at odd happenings at court. Kelley thought it quite possible that he had madmen on all sides of him. Maybe it wasn't too late for Sicily. Istanbul! Perhaps he could go east.

He saw that Edgar was awaiting some kind of response. He took one more sip of brandy to stall and gather himself. "What do you want from me?" The words were beginning to slur, but he didn't care. He held out the cup for more brandy.

Edgar filled it. "Information. You're on the inside. We need to know what's happening. Something is coming from the north. I have foreseen this as well, but the picture is unclear. You must tell us when things change. We must know when to move."

Kelley didn't want any part of this. He calculated a high probability of getting his ass thrown into the dungeon or getting his head chopped off or worse. He had a little money stashed away. He could buy a horse. Well, probably not a very good horse, but some nag to get him downriver and then maybe he'd trade the nag for passage on one of the boats. If he could get to the Mediterranean, the world would be open to him.

In the meantime, Edgar was watching him expectantly. Turning down the big man's request might have unfortunate consequences. Fanatics often seemed reasonable at first, but they could turn dangerous if thwarted. Best to play along.

"I suppose I can keep my ears and eyes open," Kelley said.

"Then you'll join our cause?"

"Yes." *And I'll unjoin two seconds after I leave town.*

A smile split Edgar's wide face. "Let's drink to it."

He filled both cups, and they drank. Kelley could really feel it now. He might need a quick nap before walking back to the castle. No, he'd stumbled home drunk before. He wasn't going to hang around with this man one second longer than necessary.

He'd bandy a few friendly words, make Edgar think he was enthusiastic about the cause, and then he'd leave this shack and get back to the castle as fast as possible.

Edgar smacked his lips and wiped his mouth with his sleeve. "This is a great day to welcome you into the Society, Edward Kelley. Now let us brand you to seal the deal and show your loyalty."

One of Kelley's eyebrows went up. "What?"

"I don't have the materials for a proper tattoo, but a brand is perfectly acceptable. Some of the younger men actually see it as a right of manhood, so you'll be able to brag about it to the ladies."

"I don't want a brand."

"Well, as I've told you, I don't have the ink for a tattoo. It'll have to be a brand. Don't worry—it only really hurts for a second."

Kelley stood, knees watery, pushed away from the table. "Uh . . . I think I'm going to go now."

"You're a member of the Society, Kelley." Edgar latched onto Kelley's arm with a meaty hand. "You've got to show it."

"No!"

Kelley tried to twist away, but Edgar pulled him across the table and turned him over. He pulled down Kelley's pants.

"What are you doing?" Kelley squirmed, but the big man held him easily.

Edgar reached for an iron that had apparently been in the fire the whole time. He brought out the branding iron, the square and compass symbol with the pentagram in the center glowing white hot. Kelley glanced over his shoulder, eyes shooting wide.

"No, wait," Kelley said. "Don't! Let's talk about—"

Edgar pressed the iron hard into Kelley's ass cheek. It sizzled and hissed. Kelley screamed. The smell of scorched hair and flesh. Edgar pulled the iron away, tossed it back into the fire.

"There," said the big man. "You're one of us now officially."

Kelley lay facedown on the table and groaned. "You son of a bitch." His ass throbbed fire.

"Now don't be that way," Edgar said. "We're brothers in the Society now."

"Sweet merciful God, that hurts. Why did you have to do that?"

"We prepared the branding iron ahead of time," Edgar admitted. "There is a spell binding you to the will of the Society. You cannot act against us now, and you will seek to keep our best interest at heart."

"That's some good crazy talk, but right now my ass is on fire. Hell and damnation." Kelley reached for the bottle of brandy, drained the last drop.

"I have a salve," Edgar said. "It'll soothe you somewhat and prevent infection."

A second later, Kelley felt Edgar smear something cool and greasy over his new brand. The hot sting subsided slightly. Kelley sighed. He slid off the table, pulled up his pants, not able to look Edgar in the eye.

"You should get back to the castle now," Edgar said. "We'll be in contact."

"Yeah. Okay." Kelley didn't need to be told twice.

He left the shack, limped along the narrow game trail back toward the castle, feeling vaguely ashamed.

TWENTY-TWO

Kelley went up to his room in the White Tower and flopped face-first onto the bed. The cool sheets soothed him. He let his eyes close. Yes, if sweet sleep would come to him, he could forget all about dark tunnels and secret societies and the deep burning throb in his backside. *Sleep, Edward Kelley. Sleep and dream of plump white serving wenches.*

"Oh, there you are, Edward," came Dee's voice from the doorway. "Come help me with something. There's a good fellow."

Kelley's eyes popped open. *Bastard.*

He pushed himself up from the bed, groaned. He followed Dr. Dee downstairs and out of the tower, to where a wagon waited in the lane. It was hitched to a tired-looking gray horse with drooping ears. Dee stood next to a stack of chests and trunks and other packages.

"Get on the other end of this, will you, Edward?" Dee bent, took one end of a long chest.

Kelley helped him slide it into the back of the wagon. He helped load the trunks and other items until the tiny wagon was overflowing. The effort made Kelley break out in a cold, slick sweat. Any good feeling he'd had from the brandy had faded. All he wanted to do was go back into the tower and flop into bed again.

"Thank you." Dee was panting too. "I had a young lad from the stables helping me, but the little scamp has run off."

"Listen, I'm not feeling all that well," Kelley said. "So if we're finished loading all of your worldly possessions, I'd like to get back to bed and—" Kelley blinked at the wagon as if seeing it for the first time. "Where are you going?"

"Didn't I tell you? I'm leaving. Back to England."

"You sure as hell did *not* tell me."

Dee wrung his hands, had trouble looking Kelley in the face. "Well, yes. I've . . . been recalled by the Queen . . . uh . . . yes. Some sort of trouble at court that . . . uh . . . requires my expertise."

"Oh, pig shit, Dee!" Kelley suddenly remembered Edgar saying he'd foreseen Dee's departure. "What's happened?"

Dee's eyes darted nervously up and down the quiet lane. "Happened? Whatever are you talking about?"

"Damn you, don't act stupid. Is it Rudolph? Has he done something insane?"

"Fool," hissed Dee. He stepped right up next to Kelley and whispered, "Do you want to put us on the chopping block? Keep your voice down."

"Talk to me, Dee."

"Okay," whispered Dee. "Okay, fine. Listen. There are strange things happening. Trust me, you don't want to be involved. If I were you, I'd pack and leave tonight."

"What strange things? Tell me."

Dee sighed, looked suddenly so weary. "Edward, I can't begin to explain. The complexities of—"

"Does Rudolph want to live forever?"

Dee froze, then slowly lifted his chin and looked Kelley square in the eye. "I don't know what you're talking about."

"Yes, you do."

Dee cursed, took Kelley by the elbow, and leaned in to whisper even more quietly into Kelley's ear. "The astrologers returned from their trip to the north. There were tales, villagers with wild stories about strange lights and the sky splitting open and the Heavens crumbling to earth. They found a village with a smoking crater in the center, every villager dead, their skin melted from their bodies."

Dee crossed himself, and Kelley resisted the urge to do the same.

"They brought something back in a large, iron box," Dee said. "They won't let anyone near it. I don't *want* to go near it. One of the astrologers told me that the three men who handled the object and loaded it into the iron box have taken violently ill. They are not expected to last through the night. All three are delusional and feverish."

Dear God. This time Kelley did cross himself.

Dee climbed onto the wagon and took the reins. "I'm getting the hell out of here. I'd do the same if I were you, Edward. Farewell." Dee flicked the reins, and the nag clopped down the lane.

Kelley raised a wan hand and waved, but Dee didn't look back. Kelley stood watching until the wagon turned a corner, the clip-clops fading away.

He stood long seconds in the empty lane. It had become eerily quiet—no sounds of workmen from the courtyard, no chatter from castle servants. He looked up. Even the wind had died. The flags and banners atop the castle walls hung limp. It was as if the entire world held its breath, waiting to see what doom would fall on top of Kelley's head.

To hell with this.

Kelley darted for the tower, took the stairs two at a time until he reached his living quarters. He grabbed his cloth bag, tossed in his clothes, a few books. He had a small bag of coins and hoped it would be enough to get him as far as a seaport. He should have lived more frugally these last months. He'd been too free with drink and women. No matter. If he could get to a port, he could work his passage if money ran short.

Kelley took his clothes from the cloth bag, and put them in the footlocker. He put the books back on the shelf over the bed. He was about to stash the cloth bag when he froze. He had just packed all that. What was he doing?

He stuffed the clothes back into the bag, took the books down from the shelf again. He was so rattled and nervous, that he didn't know what he was doing. He simply hadn't been paying attention. Really, the thought of all of one's skin melting off, well, that would distract anyone.

He put the books back on the shelf, looked at them, blinked. *What the hell?* He grabbed the books again, put the books in his bag. *Pay attention to what you're doing, idiot.* He packed his clothes again. He threw the bag over his shoulder, threw the door open, and headed down the stairs.

Kelley paused at Dee's room, then entered to see if the alchemist had left anything behind. Some of those potion ingredients could fetch pretty prices, especially certain herbs that might be out of season. He searched Dee's chambers but found nothing worth taking.

He went back upstairs to his room and dumped his clothes out on the bed.

He blinked at the clothes on the bed. *What. The. Fuck.*

This was ridiculous. Why couldn't he get his possessions packed and get the hell out of this place? He was suddenly, acutely aware of the pulsing dull pain in his ass. What had Edgar told him? The brand had been prepared with spells, magic to make sure Kelley stayed loyal to the Society.

No. It was all too far-fetched. He could walk away any time he wanted.

Kelley left the luggage, jogged down the stairs, and ran out of the tower. He made himself slow to a fast walk through the castle courtyard, kept up the pace toward the gate. He passed through the gate and left the castle behind. Soon he'd reach the Charles Bridge. Along the river he could catch a boat, or maybe he'd simply keep walking south. There was no particular hurry as long as he kept going away from the castle, away from Prague.

This would work. All Kelley needed to do was put one foot in front of the other. *Don't look back. Just keep walking. So long, assholes, you won't have Edward Kelley to kick around anymore.*

He passed back underneath the castle gates, passed through the courtyard. He stopped before entering the White Tower. How had he come back here? He could not remember turning around, returning to the castle.

He tried to leave again, walking fast, determined. He blinked, when he found himself back in his chambers in the White Tower.

"Son of a bitch!"

This time he ran, pumping his legs, his breath coming shallow. He ran and ran until a stitch burned in his side. He stopped, bent over, breathing heavily. He rubbed his side. His clothing was soaked with sweat. Kelley breathed deep, then stood straight.

He stood at the foot of the White Tower.

Kelley sank to his knees. "Oh, no no no no."

No matter what happened, he could not escape. It was as if his mind got distracted and his feet found their way back to Prague Castle and the White Tower.

Kelley ran in every direction. He walked, jogged, skipped. No matter what, somehow he ended up back at the White Tower.

The obvious fact that Kelley was now ruled by the Society's magic weighed on him with grim finality. He wasn't going anywhere. He was doomed to stay in Prague Castle and do the Society's bidding. He sighed, flopped into the chair at his small desk in his chamber. Edgar had made it clear that Kelley was to be the Society's eyes and ears inside. Perhaps that was the key. If Kelley fulfilled his obligation, maybe the spell would be broken. Maybe then he could leave.

That meant he'd have to find out what was in the iron box. Edward Kelley would have to confront the astrologers.

TWENTY-THREE

Kelley almost didn't make the final dozen steps. When he reached the top of the main tower of St. Vitus Cathedral, he collapsed on the stone landing, his chest heaving as he panted for breath. From the courtyard looking up, the tower had seemed only slightly taller than other towers he'd seen, but the arduous climb up the steep, spiral staircase had sapped the strength from his legs and stolen his wind. A sickly sweat broke out on his forehead and down his back. Kelley would have to start taking better care of himself. He drank too much.

"Who are you?"

Kelley rolled over on his back, looked up at the man in the robe. "I'm . . . looking for . . . Roderick." He paused, gulped breath. "I'm . . . Edward Kelley."

"I'm Roderick." The man was older than Kelley, even a few years older than Dee. He had a wild tangle of white hair that stuck out in every direction, a drawn face, and a nose like a beak; topped off by a white moustache and a beard with black streaks. "What do you want? I'm extremely busy." He had a thick German accent but spoke good English.

"I'm an alchemist at court," Kelley said. "I wanted to speak to you."

"One of Dee's cohorts," Roderick grunted. "I thought you'd gone."

"I understand you and your colleagues brought back something from the north. I'm interested to hear about it."

"Sorry to disappoint you, but it's none of your business," Roderick said, turning away from Kelley. "If you'll excuse me, I have work to do."

Kelley sat up, looked around the top of the tower. The construction was incomplete. At the moment, a crude wooden platform had been built around the stone landing. Roderick had some sort of strange device on top of a tripod. A stool stood right next to it.

"What are you doing up here?" Kelly asked.

"Waiting for sunset."

"What happens then?"

"The angle of the sun will be right to test this." Roderick indicated a wooden box at his feet.

Kelley went to the box and looked inside. Nestled in a bed of dry straw, a glass disc the size of a large serving plate glinted in the sun. Rainbow colors swirled in the glass, made Kelley's eyes cross. He reached for it. "May I?"

"You may *not*," snapped Roderick.

Kelley jerked his hands back.

"The finest glassblowers labored a year under the watchful eye of my best assistant to fashion that lens," Roderick said. "A single scratch ruins it. Even a greasy smudge from your finger will delay my experiment while the lens is painstakingly cleaned."

Roderick's head spun to the horizon as the sun rapidly sank. "Blast. It's almost time. Stand over there, Kelley. As long as you've disturbed my work, you might as well assist me. Over there. Stay still."

Kelley moved to the spot Roderick indicated, on the other side of the platform from the tripod. He stood still, watched the astrologer.

Roderick donned a pair of white gloves. They looked as if they'd been made of some soft material. Velvet? Very expensive and finely made. Roderick bent, took hold of the glass disc with utmost care, and lifted it slowly from its padded nest in the box. With exaggerated caution, Roderick took one deliberate step at a time. Kelley found he was holding his breath and let it out slowly.

Roderick mounted the lens in a frame atop the tripod, hurried to clamp it into place, twisting knobs and securing latches. He swiveled the lens on the tripod, pointed it at Kelley.

Kelley shuffled his feet. "Uh, what are you doing?"

"Keep still," ordered Roderick. "The sun is nearly at its optimal angle. This probably won't hurt at all. Much."

Kelley held up a finger. "You know, maybe this isn't such a good idea after all. I'm . . . uh . . . concerned that perhaps—"

The rays of the setting sun hit the lens. It flared a blinding blue, and Kelley flinched. It bathed him in soft cool light. Time seemed to slow. He saw the world creeping by, dust motes pausing in midflight. A bird over Roderick's shoulder wheeled with impossible slowness. His own heart beat a lazy *lub-thub*. He blinked his eyes, the eyelids falling as slowly as the setting sun itself, rising again like an old man in the morning.

Kelley's head grew light, his vision washing out in a hazy blue.

When his eyes popped open again, he was facedown on the platform, Roderick standing over him.

"So," Roderick began, "how do you feel?" Roderick held a quill poised over a piece of parchment.

Kelley felt strange, but also . . . rested? He stood. Yes. His aches and pains had vanished, as if he'd had a good night's sleep. As if he'd never been hungover in his life. He relayed this information to Roderick, who scribbled it on the parchment.

"Good, good." Roderick nodded, scribbled further notes. "This confirms what we suspected. Excellent."

"What did you do to me?"

"Nothing you shouldn't be thankful for, my good man. While you alchemists are mixing your little potions and bowel remedies, the Astrologers' and Wizards' Guild is harnessing the power of the cosmos."

"That's a good trick. Please explain."

"What do you know of sunlight?"

"It's warm and orange."

"Bah!" Roderick made an impatient face. "You call yourself a man of science. Very well, I'll try to keep this simple. When the sun comes up, you see its light shining down on the world. Seems simple, doesn't it? But you are, in fact, seeing millions of things happening at once. Countless elements all coming together in what seems to be the single phenomenon we call light. There are a number of waves, and they span a wide spectrum. But not just waves. Sunlight is actually composed—somewhat—of particles also, millions of them so small they are unobservable by the human eye. You're understanding all this?"

"Of course," said Kelley, who understood not one bit of it.

"I have spent a lifetime discovering these secrets and designing the lenses. By filtering out some waves and particles and allowing others to pass through, we can control . . . well . . . the full implications have yet to be fathomed. The sun is both the destroyer and creator of all life on Mother Earth. It is the Alpha and the Omega of all existence. Rudolph's generous support has allowed my work to reach fruition."

Kelley cleared his throat. "Yes, well, Rudolph has us working on an important project as well. The alchemists are divining the secret process of transmuting lead into gold."

Roderick paused, looked at Edward Kelley blankly, then burst into uncontrolled laughter. He stopped abruptly upon seeing Kelley's expression. "Oh, hell, you're serious, aren't you? Well . . . that's, you know, that's . . . uh . . . that's a good project too. Yeah."

Kelley sighed.

Upon seeing the alchemist unplacated, Roderick went on to say, "Listen, Kelley, you've been a good sport, letting me blast you with the lens and all. If you still want, I can probably arrange a quick glance at that iron box you're so curious about."

"That would be most gracious," Kelley said.

The brand on his ass stung briefly.

Roderick led him into the dungeons deep below the castle, past armed guards, through dim passageways illuminated by flickering torches. Kelley had not foreseen, nor desired, being underground again so quickly. He wondered if there were tunnels that connected the dungeons below the castle with the passages below St. Vitus Cathedral.

They finally arrived at a large set of thick, wooden double doors. Kelley counted a dozen guards in heavy armor standing in front of the doors and crowding the passage. They eyed Kelley with grim suspicion but parted to let Roderick enter. Kelley followed the astrologer into a large chamber with a vaulted ceiling. Braziers in each corner provided enough light for Kelley to clearly see an iron box on the far side of the room, a good hundred feet away.

Kelley also saw the dead bodies.

A half-dozen blackened corpses within ten feet of the iron box, all contorted in various stages of agony. Closer to Kelley were another three bodies, less charred but just as dead. Back another twenty feet was another dead man. The last body was maybe forty feet from where Kelley stood behind a rope that stretched the width of the chamber.

"We've been trying to determine the minimum safe distance for examining the object," Roderick explained. "We open the box and see if a man can live. If he doesn't, we move back ten or twenty feet and try again."

"You used live men for this?" Kelley swallowed hard, felt ill.

"Prisoners." Roderick pointed at the closest body. "That fellow was a horse thief, I think. The object emits some sort of invisible, destructive rays, not completely dissimilar to the sun waves I told you about earlier. Naturally, they called me in to lead the experiments. Rudolph is most excited by the find."

"This seems too dangerous to fool around with."

"There is always a certain amount of risk in discovery." Roderick reached for a thin rope dangling two feet away. "This line is attached to pulleys which will open the lid of the box if I pull on it. That's how we were able to safely open it when we sent the prisoners out. You can't see much from here, but would you like a look at the object?"

No. Kelley didn't want to see it. He wanted to run out as fast as he could, screaming all the way. His ass-brand flared a warning. Kelley winced and said, "Yes. Let me see it."

Roderick pulled the rope, and the iron box's lid creaked open.

A rock. That's all it was, a rock about the size of a dog's head. It did not glow or pulse. No screaming devils leaped from the box. A rock.

Then something. The room seemed to shimmer, like heat on summer cobblestones. A dark uneasiness crept into Kelley's gut, a sickly foreboding, the sudden acute certainty that sinister fingers probed him, reached inside his very soul. Any feeling of well-being left by Roderick's lens was utterly erased, leaving only the sour taste of decay.

"Close it," Kelley said. "Close it now, please."

Roderick released the rope, and the lid slammed shut. The sick feeling ceased immediately, like stepping away from a hot cook stove.

"Yes, best to keep it shut," said the astrologer. "We're at a safe distance, but better safe than sorry, eh?"

An acidic aftertaste lingered in Kelley's mouth. He turned away and spit. Rude. "Sorry about that."

"I did the same thing the first time," Roderick said.

"It's . . ." Kelley shivered. "Evil."

"Come, come, my good man, no, of course not. Let us conduct ourselves as men of science. Good. Evil. Terms peasants use for things beyond their understanding."

"Yes. Of course. I think I just need some air. Maybe we could go back now."

"Understandable. Yes, some fresh air will do you well, my good man."

Kelley followed Roderick back to the surface, memorizing every twist and turn in the dungeon. He would tell Edgar. The Society must know. This thing must be destroyed or hidden. Kelley was as sure of this as he was of his own existence.

Only a simple lump of rock, yet Kelley felt as if he'd looked into the eyes of hell itself.

TWENTY-FOUR

I didn't know at the time, but I was already dead. The dose of radiation I took would eat at me, and in a few short years that would be it. Like John Wayne and those other film stars, who got zapped in the desert without even knowing it, the whole time chasing stuntmen painted up to look like Red Indians.

Anyway, Allen is nearly naked and in the company of an attractive young lady. My guess is you'll find that much more interesting than my little tale of woe.

GIRL TROUBLE

TWENTY-FIVE

Allen stood in his dorm room, a white towel wrapped around him, pulling clean clothes out of his duffel bag. He felt nearly human again after the eternal night, a hot shower having washed away the stale beer and sweat and cigarette stink that had clung to him. He still needed sleep, but at least he didn't feel disgusting.

A second later the door opened and Amy slipped inside, shutting the door quickly behind her. "Nobody saw me."

The towel barely contained her. Amy's blond hair hung past her shoulders, a tight bundle from wringing it out. The smell of wet, freshly shampooed girl made things stir beneath Allen's own towel. He turned away, his cheeks going pink.

"We can't stay long," Amy said. "They'll think to look here sooner or later." She tossed her pink outfit onto the floor underneath the bunk bed. "And I'll need some clothes."

"I'm not sure what I have that will fit you," he replied, spilling the contents of the duffel onto the top bunk and sorting through the wrinkled, hastily packed clothing.

"We'll make it work." She stood right next to him and began to pick through the clothes.

Her bare shoulder brushed against his chest. It was so warm and soft that Allen thought he might faint. He moved away from her before he embarrassed himself. This was no time to be thinking of her tan skin and her red lips and how easily that towel could fall to the floor, revealing her ripe—

Stop it. Think of baseball.

Allen knew nothing of baseball.

Then think of Emily Brontë.

Somehow that was worse.

"I like that." Amy pointed at his chest.

Really? Allen had never considered himself a spectacular physical specimen. His chest was flat and hairless. He was, overall, a skinny, pale, and nerdy individual. Maybe Amy liked that sort of thing. Maybe she was a Ben Folds fan.

She reached out and took the crucifix in her hand, her fingers brushing against his chest where the cross dangled from the chain. "It's smart to wear it."

Allen shivered at the slight contact. He was making a tent in front of his towel. He turned away, and the crucifix slipped from Amy's hand. He sat on the bottom bunk, his back to her. "What's that on your shoulder?" he asked, referring to a tattoo about the size of a nickel.

"It's the Society's mark," Amy said. "It's the Freemason symbol, but with a pentagram in the middle instead of a G."

Allen lay his head on the pillow. "I think I just need a quick nap." A monster yawn swallowed his face.

"We can't stay here."

"Just five minutes." Allen closed his eyes. "I'm exhausted."

She sighed. "Me too."

The narrow bunk shifted with her weight as she scooted in next to him, her bare shoulder touching his back, her slender pink foot brushing his calf.

Are you kidding me? His erection was so full and painful that he thought he might need medical attention. He recalled a Viagra advertisement he'd seen on cable. *For erections lasting longer than four hours, please consult a physician.* This is how he would die, Allen thought. To come through a night of abductions and machine-gun·fire only to die of an excessive hard-on.

Amy yawned. "Just five minutes. Then we have to move."

"What if I went to Father Paul?" Allen said. "Explained that I have nothing to do with this. I could get on a plane, go straight back to the States."

"He wouldn't believe you, and besides, it isn't true. You're his link to Evergreen. The Vatican wants whatever Evergreen is after, that's for sure. I'm telling you, your best chance is to stick with me. We'll get word to a Society elder and get this all figured out. In the meantime, the only thing we can do is avoid being captured or killed."

They lapsed into silence. In thirty seconds, she snored lightly. A minute later she rolled over against him. He felt her chest rise and fall against his back with each breath.

Forget it. You barely even know her. Just go to sleep, idiot.

And somehow he did. Deep fatigue seeped into his bones, sapped him, pulled him into downy slumber.

"Allen. Alllleeeeeenn."

Oh, hell.

He wore the ruffled shirt again, found himself jogging through a green, misty forest. The voice kept calling his name. The fog swirled in so thick that it swallowed the trees around him. He glided through it, his boots touching down on cobblestone. The fog parted to reveal an iron gate and a stone wall, a graveyard beyond, large monuments as looming and eerie as a scene from a Hammer film.

Allen knew it was a dream. Or was it more? Some kind of visitation.

Cassandra stood at the gate, and Allen felt chilled to look upon her. She wore a bloodred dress, the half moons of her white breasts erupting from her bodice. This seemed less Brontë to Allen and more Harlequin. The entire scene seemed a bit off, in fact, fading in and out of focus as the fog ebbed and flowed.

"I can barely reach you, My Allen." Cassandra's voice sounded as if it came from the far end of a long tunnel. "This place." She gestured to the cemetery. "I cannot enter here. You must go. It is your task."

"Why?" Allen's own voice sounded too loud. "What's in there?"

"My life."

Cassandra slowly melted into transparency, blew away like smoke on the wind, melting into the fog.

"Wait!" shouted Allen. "What's in there?"

The fog closed in, and everything went gray.

Allen opened his eyes.

How long had it been? More than five minutes certainly. Amy still curled next to him, her warm breath on his neck. He checked himself and was never so happy to find himself flaccid. Now maybe he could get dressed with a minimum of embarrassment. He propped himself up on one elbow, prepared to nudge Amy awake.

A light knock at the door. "Allen? Are you in there?" It was a familiar voice.

The door opened slowly. A young woman stuck her head inside the dorm room. "Allen?"

Penny.

Allen pictured himself hovering over Amy, both of them in towels, and realized how it must have looked.

"Is that you, Allen?" Penny opened the door wider, allowing light from the hallway to stream in. "My flight got in yesterday late, so I waited until— Who the hell is *that*?"

Amy's eyes flickered open, and she saw Penny. "Hello."

Penny crossed her arms. "Hello yourself."

TWENTY-SIX

Amy slipped into a pair of Allen's gym shorts, then pulled them tight with the drawstring. She knotted the too-large, red T-shirt (which read CCCP in yellow letters) at the waist and somehow made the outfit work. Meanwhile, Allen turned his back to the girls and put on boxers, jeans, a dark green T-shirt, and socks and running shoes.

"I'm sorry," Amy said to Penny. "I know you came to visit your friend, but we have to leave now. This is extremely urgent."

"Yes, I saw how urgently you both occupied the bottom bunk without any clothing," Penny said. "Perhaps *urge* is the key element in the word '*urgent*' in this case."

"Damn it, Penny, you don't understand," Allen said, spraying deodorant under his shirt. "A lot has happened since I've arrived."

Penny's eyes shifted to Amy, then back to Allen. "Yes, I see you work fast."

"This is *serious*. I don't think Father Paul is the person you think he is."

Allen tried to explain the late-night firefight, the special-forces priests bursting in, the flight to the secret witches' lair beneath Zizkov, the story of the philosopher's stone. He tried to imagine how the story sounded.

It sounded like bullshit.

"I've known Father Paul a long time," Penny said. "There has to be a rational explanation."

"Maybe you didn't hear the part about the machine guns," Allen said. "He tried to kidnap me."

"Actually, it sounds like your girlfriend and her pals kidnapped you and Father Paul was trying to rescue you," Penny said.

Allen opened his mouth, paused, closed it again, and turned to Amy. "She has a point."

"The Society is only trying to *help*," Amy insisted. "We're the good guys here."

Penny scoffed. "That's debatable."

Allen shook his head. "I don't know what to think."

"Whatever you think, we can't stay *here*," Amy said. "Now let's move. Please."

"I have a place," Penny said.

Amy and Allen looked at each other.

"Well, they won't think you're with me, will they? We can go to my place and figure things out," Penny offered. "I'm sure you're wrong about Father Paul."

Amy chewed her thumbnail. "I don't know. You might not want to get involved with this."

"Listen to me, new girl." Penny jabbed a finger toward Amy. "I've know Allen a little longer than you have. I've invested a good bit of time in him, and I'm not ready to see him machine gunned or kidnapped. Let's get one thing straight right here and now. I'm on board for the party now, you get it? So if it's so damn important we get out of here before the sky falls, then let's shut up and get moving. Anyone got a problem with that?"

Allen blinked at her. "When did you get so assertive?"

Penny smiled, lips tight. "Get used to it."

They caught a tram a block from the university.

"You have metro passes, right?"

Amy and Allen both shook their heads.

Penny sighed. "They'll give you a ticket if they catch you riding the tram or subway without a pass. We'll have to risk it for now."

"Penny, this is dangerous," Allen said. "I don't think we should get you involved."

"Oh, just . . . shut up."

The tram took them over the Charles River and back past Letna Park. They entered a much less touristy part of the city, and Allen recognized the working-class suburb as Holešovice from *The Rogue's Guide.*

"The next stop is ours," Penny said.

The tram squealed to a stop, and they piled out with a dozen others, mostly Czechs scattering back to their homes. Penny led Allen and Amy down a side street. The neighborhood became residential. They stopped in front of a narrow, two-story house constructed of dull gray stone.

"Three of us went in on an apartment," Penny said. "We thought it would be more interesting and more comfortable than staying in the dorms. Come on, we're upstairs. An old couple live on the bottom."

They trudged up the stairs along the side of the house, and Penny unlocked the door and let them in.

Amy went ahead of them, peeking into every room. "Are we alone?"

Allen and Penny followed her. "I think," Penny said. "Blanche and Ian don't arrive until next week. I came over early to see *you*."

"Who's Ian?" Allen asked.

"Nobody that has anything to do with you," Penny said.

The apartment consisted of three bedrooms, a sitting area in the middle, and a kitchen with a small table.

"I call the furniture Commie Surplus," Penny said. "It all looks like drab leftovers from the fifties."

Allen dropped himself into a padded chair of faded orange. Some kind of fake leather. Amy helped herself to the narrow couch.

"There's nothing in the refrigerator, I'm afraid," Penny said. "I'd planned to hit the market later."

"Can I use your phone?" Amy asked. "I think I'd better get in contact with my people."

"There's no phone."

Amy nibbled her bottom lip, concern crossing her face. "They're going to be wondering about us." She looked at Allen. "About you. I've got to let them know we're okay and get instructions for what to do next."

"There's a pay phone near the tram stop," Penny offered.

"Wait a minute," Allen said. "I'm not interested in your calling your Society pals just so they can stuff me in a trunk again."

"We should get in touch with Father Paul," Penny insisted. "I'm telling you there's some kind of mistake. You're wrong about him."

"No!" Sudden heat in Amy's voice. "I need to get in touch with the Society. There are things happening, and we need to know. Come with me to the pay phone."

"To hell with that," Allen said.

"Then I'll go make the call myself," Amy said.

"If you do, I'll run out of here as fast as I can. As soon as you're out of sight, I'm gone," Allen warned. "Unless you promise not to tell them where we are."

She opened her mouth to object.

Allen cut her off. "Just tell them we're fine. Find out what's going on if you want to, but just give us some time to rest. Please."

Amy went a little pink in the face, clearly frustrated.

Too bad, Allen thought. *I'm tired of getting shoved around.*

"Okay," Amy said. "But you've got to promise to wait here until I get back. I could spell you, compel you to stay, but I don't want to do that."

Allen rolled his eyes. "Yes, fine. I promise. Please don't spell me."

"Okay. I'll be back."

She left. They listened to her footfalls fade down the outside stairs. The silence stretched a full minute.

"She's very attractive, Allen," Penny said. "I suppose I can understand why you'd be interested."

"Oh, just . . . we're not . . . I barely even know her and . . . what do you care, anyway?"

"Me?" Penny's hand went to her chest, her eyebrows arching in innocent surprise. "Oh, I don't care. None of my business. How you conduct yourself is of no concern to me." She made a low, disapproving noise in her throat, almost like a growl.

Allen sighed, then sank into the chair. "Don't be that way."

"What way?"

"*That* way."

"Okay, okay," Penny said. "It's just that we're close friends, and well, I don't know. I guess I feel a little proprietary about you or something, and it was just kind of sudden seeing you guys together in bed and, anyway, I don't even know what I'm saying so I'll just shut up."

Penny had always been there for him; she'd talked him back to sanity when he'd gone through the gut-wrenching breakup with Brenda. She'd been solid as a rock, a steadfast friend and classmate. Why was she so suddenly bent out of shape about a minor misunderstanding?

It was almost as if she was . . . jealous? She'd said she felt a little proprietary about him, but she'd meant like a sister. Right?

He rubbed his eyes with the heels of his hands. He couldn't think about this right now.

"My head is swimming," Allen said. "If I don't sleep soon, I'll drop dead."

Penny said, "Take my bed. The sheets are fresh. I should have offered sooner. Frankly, you look terrible."

He smiled weakly. "Thanks."

"I'll hit the market. You'll want something to eat sooner or later."

Allen pushed himself out of the chair and headed for Penny's bed.

"Allen?"

He paused in the doorway to her bedroom and looked back at her. "Yes?"

She smiled, warm, all earlier irritation gone from her face. "Never mind. I'll be back soon."

Allen crawled into Penny's bed and was asleep in less than ten seconds.

Father Paul and Finnegan stood in Allen's dorm room.

Finnegan poked through the random clothing spread out on the top bunk. "The boy's not much of a housekeeper, is he?"

"They left in a hurry." Father Paul's sharp eyes took in the small room quickly. "Just like in those chambers below Zizkov." He nudged a damp towel on the floor with his boot. "They showered and changed."

The big priest raised an eyebrow. "They?"

Father Paul pointed at the floor. "Two towels." Then he pointed at the pink wad in the corner. "Women's clothes. I saw her wearing them when we stormed the Society safe house. I think we fouled up, Finnegan. When we went in guns blazing to save Cabbot, it made us look like the bad guys, didn't it?"

"We'll set him straight, sir."

"We've been doing this all wrong," Father Paul said. "Instead of chasing after him, we need to get ahead, wait for him some-place down the line."

"Where?"

Father Paul stuck a cigarette into his mouth without lighting it. "What's the word on Evergreen's apartment?"

"About a block from here. We've got somebody watching," Finnegan said. "But intelligence still thinks it's a decoy. The pro-fessor has probably rented a place under a different name, maybe out in one of the suburbs."

Father Paul lit the cigarette, puffed. "Let's find out where."

Allen opened his eyes and looked at his watch. He'd slept three hours. He swung his feet over the side of the bed, felt fuzzy-headed. He shuffled into the tiny bathroom, splashed water in his face. The dim light over the sink buzzed. The face that looked back at him in the mirror had dark circles under the eyes.

Back in the sitting room, he spotted Amy on the couch, shoes off, breathing lightly. He tiptoed past her into the kitchen. Penny had left a note on the small table:

> Allen,
> There's food in the refrigerator. I'm going to let you and your Friend sleep. I can tell you've both had a tough time. I'll be back soon. Please wait for me.
> Penny

Allen built himself a salami sandwich on dark bread with some soft kind of orange cheese. A bottle of water. He sat at the small kitchen table, chewing and considering his situation.

Had Amy kept her promise to keep her Society friends at bay? He finished the sandwich, put the plate in the sink. And where had Penny gone? The sudden notion she'd gone to fetch Father Paul sent a shiver of anxiety up Allen's spine. Penny refused to believe the priest could possibly be one of the bad guys. She might be bringing him back here at this very minute in some misguided attempt to help Allen. Amy claimed to be one of the good guys too. Everyone said they wanted to help him.

So why did Allen feel like a rabbit with hounds on his heels?

He leaned against the doorframe between the kitchen and the sitting room, looked again at Amy curled on the couch. It could be a lot worse. He could be stuck with Clover. If he'd been on the run with the punk rock girl, he'd probably have been hog-tied with tape over his mouth, stashed in some closet.

Allen had to admit his time with Amy had not been entirely unpleasant. Perhaps that was why he'd felt slightly defensive with Penny earlier. He'd not been doing anything wrong with Amy when Penny had walked in on them—not that Allen would have refused any offers.

And yet . . . Penny. He was starting to see her in a way that hadn't occurred to him before. Or had it? Hadn't he always wondered about her? Just a little.

Okay, this was ridiculous. The completely gorgeous girl on the couch in front of him had been part of a plot to kidnap him. His close friend Penny was a devout Catholic who was likely on her way to a priest who seemed to favor automatic weapons over rosary beads.

Allen turned away from the sleeping girl and walked softly across the kitchen. He'd promised to wait until she returned. Well, she'd returned. Yeah, he was splitting hairs, but the fact was Allen had to figure things out, and Penny and Amy would only continue to cloud his thinking. He opened the door, stepped outside, and closed it quietly.

Allen needed answers. He walked quietly down the steps and headed toward the tram stop. The man who seemed to be at the core of this shit-storm would have those answers, Allen hoped.

Allen hopped the next tram headed toward Letna and Professor Evergreen's apartment.

TWENTY-SEVEN

Jackson Fay sat at the oversized wooden desk. It was too big for his small faculty office at St. Sebastian's College, but he liked the artificial sense of power it gave him, although he did not admit this to himself, not exactly in that way.

Power. It filled him yet left him hungry for more. The most powerful aphrodisiac he'd ever known, yet the climax never came. It was the curse of power that the more he had, the more he needed.

He looked out his dingy window. London was as drab and gray as his mood.

A knock, the one he'd been waiting for, sounded at his door. "Enter."

The door swung open and an old woman entered. She had steel-colored hair and deep lines at her eyes. She wore a black pantsuit, starched white blouse, and a bloodred brooch at the throat. An apple-cheeked man in a slightly garish pin-striped suit followed her, closing the door behind him. They stood crowded up against the desk.

"Professor Fay," the old woman said, nodding at him. Her companion nodded too.

"Margaret. Blake." He returned the nod.

"There is bad news out of Prague," the old woman reported. "Our people were hit hard, scattered. News trickles in, but we don't have the complete picture."

"The Vatican?"

Margaret nodded. "A crack squad of Battle Jesuits, if I'm reading the situation correctly. The cardinals are giving us top priority, it seems."

Fay steepled his fingers under his chin, sat back in the over-sized leather chair. He considered the bad news. Jackson Fay was a lean man, with straight shoulders and eyes so green it seemed as if someone had airbrushed them. He had thick black hair with streaks of white above each ear, and a sharp chin and cheekbones. He wore a tan tweed jacket and a muted red vest.

"We have perhaps overreached," Fay admitted. "What does the Council say about withdrawing our operation?"

"There's more," Margaret said. "Evergreen is apparently very close to the philosopher's stone."

"A little too damn close for comfort, if you ask me." Blake's voice had a mild Irish lilt.

Fay leaned forward and rested his elbows on the enormous desk. "That's not acceptable."

Margaret shook her head. "No."

"The stone in Evergreen's hands would be . . . problematic."

Margaret nodded. "Yes."

"Suggestions?"

Blake cleared his throat nervously. "We think our position toward Evergreen should . . . ah . . . be taken to the next level." He tugged at his tie, as if he was suddenly uncomfortable.

"We want him killed," Margaret clarified. "Before he gets the stone and uses it."

"That has already been attempted," Fay told them.

Margaret raised an eyebrow. Although the Society bylaws allowed the high councilman to take emergency actions without consulting the rest of the Council, the elimination of a rogue member would usually be seen as significant enough to call a meeting.

"And are we convinced he even knows how to use it?" Fay asked.

"The Council would prefer not to take that chance." Margaret shrugged, a slight movement.

"What if," posed Fay, "we let our Mr. Evergreen find the stone?"

Blake made a vague choking sound and tugged at his tie again.

Margaret asked, "To what end?"

"Finding it is the hard part," Fay said. "It would not be so difficult to then take it away from him."

The old woman considered, then said, "Naturally, if the stone were to come into our possession for safekeeping, that would be best. Perhaps our people could even divine a way to destroy the blasted thing."

"I suppose," Fay said. "But that's not precisely what I meant. What if we could find a way to use the stone ourselves?"

Blake went pale. Margaret frowned.

"This could be one of the most powerful arcane items in recorded history," Fay said. "Can we not harness its power, use it for our own purposes?"

Margaret and Blake looked at each other. Tension grew thick in the room.

"I would oppose such a scheme," Margaret said. "As I believe would the rest of the Council."

Blake nodded apologetically. "Yes, I'd quite have to agree, old chap. Just too damn risky, don't you see?"

Margaret's eyes were hard as granite. "I think our high councilman understands our feelings in this matter." Her gaze remained unwavering, locked on Fay.

Another long tense moment.

Fay sighed, relaxed back into his chair. "Naturally you're right, Margaret. You too, Blake."

The old woman's gaze softened microscopically. Blake actually laughed, wiped sweat from his forehead.

"As high councilman, it's my responsibility to consider all possibilities. I hope you can appreciate that. Still." He leaned forward, lowering his voice and encouraging the others to lean in to hear him. "There is one minor aspect of this situation you may have failed to consider fully." He reached for a small, wooden box at the corner of his desk and lifted the lid.

Margaret raised an eyebrow. "And what might that be?"

Fay reached into the box with thumb and forefinger, pinched out a small portion of the dull silver powder within. "This."

Fay blew the powder into her face, harsh syllables flying from his mouth immediately after.

The dust particles hardened to tiny diamond shards, blasting the old woman's face, shredding flesh and bone. Blood sprayed against the door and wall behind her. A scream began somewhere deep in her throat, but it was cut short as glittering death flayed her tongue, turned the back of her throat into hamburger. She dropped dead onto Fay's expensive Persian rug.

"Bastard." Blake looked appalled, confused, betrayed. Terrified. His hand glowed blue-green as he raised it toward Fay.

Fay was already out of his chair and across the desk. He grabbed Blake's wrist and twisted, the karma bolt discharging harmlessly into the ceiling.

With his other hand, Fay thrust a thin dagger into Blake's gut.

Blake grunted, eyes going wide. He looked down where Fay still held the blade in his belly. A silver skull at the end of the hilt grinned up at him. Blake's mouth tried to form words. Fay twisted the dagger, and Blake coughed blood.

"Anticlimactic, isn't it?" Fay said, acid in his voice. "All of the intricate and deadly magic at my disposal, yet you meet your end with a simple dagger thrust."

Fay jerked the blade out and thrust it home again. "Never underestimate the mundane." Blake twitched. Fay gave another stab to be sure, and Blake's eyes rolled up like cartoon window shades.

Fay let the man go, and Blake fell facedown across the desk, a pool of blood spreading to a stack of ungraded essays on King Arthur and the Holy Grail.

He looked from Blake's dead body to Margaret's ruined face. The sweet sensation of power still hummed along his bones. He'd been itching to try out the spell he'd used on the old woman. It had felt exactly as good as he'd anticipated. No heroine junky could know this feeling, no coke-head. And it was getting more difficult to reach this euphoria each time. Jackson Fay needed the philosopher's stone. He'd outgrown the Society, had long suspected his personal ambitions would have forced him to make some sort of decision like this sooner or later.

And he'd never liked Margaret anyway, possibly because he'd been able to tell she'd never really liked him. A shame about Blake, though. A nice enough fellow, eager to please, but ultimately useless and a bit weak.

Fay took a pocket handkerchief from his jacket, wiped the blood from his hands and dagger. Fay appraised the mess he'd just made. There was no time to deal with it now. A simpler aversion spell would keep people out of his office until he had time to tidy up. He really should try to discover a simple spell that made dead bodies disappear.

He picked up the phone and dialed the extension for his department's administrative assistant. "Edna, can you book me a flight to Prague? Right away, please."

TWENTY-EIGHT

Two hours later, Jackson Fay sat aboard a Virgin Airways flight to Prague, sipping a glass of Pinot Noir and contemplating the savage things he would do to Professor Evergreen to make him divulge the secrets of the philosopher's stone.

But a mere twenty minutes after Fay left the still warm bodies of his fellow Council members lying on his office floor, the red gem of Margaret's brooch began to glow at her throat, dully at first, then more brilliantly. A stranger walking his basset hound below Fay's office window paused to consider the sudden red glow, then shrugged and went about his business.

This is when Margaret joined me among the legions of the untimely dead. I wish I could have been there to show her the ropes. Still, she seemed to have a natural talent for it. In her own limited way, Margaret made a reasonably effective ghost.

TWENTY-NINE

The tram let Allen off at the edge of the residential neighborhood across from Letna Park. Had it really only been
twenty-four hours since Allen had been here to supervise Evergreen's strange delivery? It seemed a lifetime ago.

Now he would get answers. He would *make* Evergreen give
him answers. After all Allen had been through, he could not find
the brusque professor intimidating anymore. The guy owed him
an explanation.

He entered Evergreen's building and knocked on his apartment door. No answer. He knocked again. "Professor Evergreen?" He tried the knob. It was open.

He went inside.

"Professor?"

Allen noticed the suitcases straightaway, stacked in the entranceway next to an old-fashioned-looking steamer trunk. So
they'd arrived. Good. Allen stepped into the apartment. The
large crate Evergreen had been so concerned about was nowhere
in sight. In a swivel chair across the room, Evergreen sat at a desk
with his back to Allen.

"Professor Evergreen."

Evergreen didn't turn around.

Allen spotted the headphones, the wire leading to the MP3 player on the desk. Evergreen probably had the volume up to max and hadn't heard Allen knock or enter the apartment.

Okay, man. Time to do this.

Allen crossed the room, tapped the big man on the shoulder, raised his voice. "Professor Evergreen. We need to talk. A lot of strange fucking shit has happened since I got here and—"

Evergreen toppled over, slid from the chair, and landed at Allen's feet. His skin was as white as notebook paper. His eyes stared at the ceiling and his mouth hung open, tongue halfway out.

Allen hopped back. "Fuck!"

A ragged pink crater in the side of Evergreen's neck, like somebody had taken a giant bite of undercooked ham.

Allen swallowed hard. "Oh, man. That's not cool."

He backed to the center of the room, turned his head from side to side. What the fuck had happened here? Allen should call somebody. The local police, maybe. Or he could turn and haul ass. Why would anyone do this to the professor? Yeah, most of his students pretty much thought he was a dick . . . but this?

The light coming from the balcony dimmed, as if a dark cloud had passed in front of the sun. Allen went cold. The hair on his neck stood straight.

"Allen."

The voice so familiar it made Allen gasp. He stood frozen, wanting to back out of the room, but something sapped his will.

"Allen."

This time he turned his head, looked toward the half-open door of the apartment's master bedroom. The lights were off. A cold breeze picked up and came through the open balcony doors, tugged at Allen's hair and clothing. He thought he could just make out the shape of someone back in the dark bedroom.

"Who is it?" But Allen knew who it was.

"Allen, come in here, please."

Allen spoke slowly, like he was having trouble remembering how words worked. "Maybe you should come out here."

"I need you, Allen, need you to help me. Please. Come to me." There in the darkness. The eyes. They latched onto him. "Come to me, Allen."

He shook his head. "No." But he'd taken a step forward. His other foot moved. Another step.

He crossed into the darkness. Even with his head in a fog he noticed that the windows had all been covered with thick blankets. The room smelled of moist earth. She stood right in front of him now. The wind gusted behind him, and the bedroom door clicked shut.

"Allen," she said in a voice of clear crystal. "I need your help."

"Mrs. Evergreen, your husband is dead."

"Yes, Allen. I know. It was such a long trip, so hungry. I just couldn't wait. You must try to imagine how it was. You can imagine it, can't you? The longing and the need until nothing else matters. Nothing matters but satisfaction, and it burns, you need it so bad. Such a shame. So many plans. He'd brought me so far. I don't think he minded in the end. If it helps you to think of it like that, Allen, I don't think he minded at all."

"I don't know what you're talking about, Mrs. Evergreen."

"I want you to call me Cassandra."

Allen did not want to call her that. But he said it. "Cassandra." The word tasted good in his mouth, delicious and painful. Like Thai food.

She put a cool hand on his arm. Her eyes filled the room, the rest of her face and body only vague shapes in the darkness. "He can't help me anymore, Allen. I need you. I need you to go a place I can't go. You will do this for me."

No. He opened his mouth to deny her, but the words that came out were, "I will help you."

She was right up against him now. He felt her along the length of him, his breathing so shallow, head dizzy. He realized she was naked. Her hands roamed him. He stood still as a statue, afraid and enthralled and wanting her. She rubbed his erection, and her lips brushed his.

He felt faint. Felt like he was floating out of his own body. No. He *needed* his body. Wanted it to do things to *her* body.

Cassandra ripped off his shirt. She hissed and backed away, pointing at his chest. Anger flashed in her eyes. "Get rid of that!"

Allen's hand went to his chest, felt the cold metal of the crucifix hanging there. "This?"

"Throw it away."

Allen pulled it over his head, and cocked his arm to toss it out of the room. Hesitated. Something—faces flashing before his mind's eye—stopped him. Father Paul. Penny. He couldn't throw it away.

"Allen." Waves of pure sex radiated from Cassandra's naked body. "I'm waiting for you."

Allen tossed the crucifix over his shoulder, heard it rattle and clank somewhere out of the way.

What followed was a patchwork of sensations and memory. He was naked and on top of her, her back arched, mouth open, animal growls coming out of her. Long fingernails raked his back. Then she was on top. Had hours passed or minutes? The eyes. Always the eyes burning, branding her ownership of him onto his soul.

And there was pain.

Along his inner thigh, a white-hot intensity, her mouth on him.

But the pleasure flooded back again, arms and legs wrapping

him up, like she was trying to climb inside. A tangle of sheets. Relentless pleasure, sapping him, leaving him a spent husk. Exhausting, pulling him down.

Allen gave himself to exquisite oblivion.

He awoke to the night.

Allen sat up in bed, clueless where he was until patchy images clanged and tumbled through his brain. The windows had been thrown open, the curtains fluttering on a gentle breeze.

"Cassandra." He looked, but she wasn't there.

More memories, as they lay together in the darkness, her hot breath on his ear as she whispered his instructions. Somehow her words penetrated his fogged brain. He knew what he had to do to serve her.

He was way too naked. He saw his clothes on the floor and stood, winced at the slight pain in his thigh. He stood with legs apart, bent over to examine himself. Two dark punctures along his thigh about six inches from his scrotum.

He scratched his head, rubbed his eyes. *Where am I?*

He dressed himself. Every muscle ached. He grunted as he put on his shoes.

Back into the living room, and he saw The Professor's dead body still where it had fallen. *Oh, yeah. He's dead.* That fact no longer seemed very urgent.

Something cut through the haze of his programming, some prick of curiosity. Yes, he had his mission. He should get on with it, but he looked around the apartment, wondered. Where was the large wooden crate?

He headed for the second bedroom and walked into it. Completely dark. He felt along the wall for the light switch, found it, and flipped it on.

The room was barren of furnishings. There was only the crate in the dead center. The lid had been pried off and sat to one side. Allen approached, looked inside.

He saw an open casket with silk lining and a pillow for the comfort of the deceased. Between the crate and the casket, moist dark earth had been packed in tight, completely surrounding the outside of the casket. Allen's hand went to his throat. He stood there a moment, putting two and two together.

He ran out of the bedroom, darted into the bathroom, flipped on the light switch. He stood in front of the mirror, lifting his chin, feeling along his throat. Only smooth skin. He let his hand wander down to rub his thigh and considered the marks there.

He pictured the chunk that had been bitten out of Professor Evergreen's throat. He shivered. The man staring back at him in the mirror looked like a pale, shadow-eyed wraith. Some deranged derelict.

Allen left the bathroom, stumbled from the apartment, downstairs and into the street. The night was cool. Distantly he heard voices, somewhere a dog barking. He realized he was walking. Somehow his feet knew the right direction. South and west.

Strahov Monastery. The words had been put into his brain. So many words and images jumbling together, instructions and books and names and places all mixed up with a picture of himself, arms wrapped around Mrs. Evergreen—*Cassandra!*—her legs around him, heels digging into his ass, so many grunts and moans and just so much relentless *thrusting*.

He walked through the night, all of this information like a buzz in his brain growing louder and louder. Two words above all others throbbed within his cranium.

Edward Kelley.

THIRTY

"Wake up, bitch."

The girl on the couch blinked, rubbed her eyes, focused on the other girl standing over her, hands on hips. Penny was doing her best to sound simultaneously pissed and accusatory, with a hint of righteous indignation thrown in.

"What did you do with him?" Penny jabbed a finger at the witch. "And don't mess with me. I'm a lot tougher than I look."

Amy sat up, shook the cobwebs out of her head. "What?"

"Pay attention, blondie. Where's Allen?"

Amy stifled a yawn. "Is there any coffee?"

"This isn't fucking Denny's. I asked what you did with Allen."

It registered in Amy's eyes what Penny was asking. She sat straight, suddenly alert. "Allen's missing?"

"Duh."

"What happened to him?"

"That's what I'm asking you," Penny said. "I let you guys sleep because you were wiped out, but I just looked in on him and he's not there."

Amy stood, went to the bedroom, and looked inside. "No signs of a struggle. Did he leave a note?"

Penny frowned. "Are you trying to say you didn't have any-thing to do with his being gone?"

"Why would I still be sleeping on your couch if I'd called my people to come kidnap him?"

Penny shrugged. "Hey, I don't pretend to understand your cloak-and-dagger bullshit."

"You're coming off a bit hostile."

"Fuck you."

"See? That's what I mean."

"Two years!" Penny held up two fingers. "Two damn years I've been working on that boy. I nursed him back from the edge after he broke up with that Goth whore Brenda. Two damn years invested, and you come along with your blond hair and suntan and tight little ass and get your hooks into him in twenty-four hours."

"I do *not* know what you are talking about."

"The hell you don't." Penny folded her hands under her chin and batted her eyelashes. "Oh, my. I'm just so tired. Let me climb into this tiny narrow bunk next to you with nothing but a towel on."

Amy frowned. "Hey!"

"I'm not doing the soft sell anymore," Penny said. "Allen's mine, and that had better be crystal clear right now or some-body's going to get hurt. And I don't mean me."

"Is that a threat? Are you actually *threatening* me? Do you know who I am, what I can do to you?"

Penny's grin was pure wicked. "And you don't know anything about me either, blondie. I can turn your day real bad real quick."

Muscles tensed, both women looking like they might pounce at any second.

See, now this is where we should have a totally awesome cat-fight.

Have you ever seen two women go at it? I mean, two furious women with blood in their eyes, claws out, teeth bared? It's pretty hot. Lots of long hair thrashing around and clothes getting ripped off.

If I were in charge of such things, it would be catfight time. But I have no such power to manipulate the universe. Alas, my role has been relegated to that of observer. And reporter. The cosmos has put me into this position for the sake of posterity. It doesn't mean I don't enjoy the occasional naked catfight. Not this time.

Instead, this happened:

Amy held up her hands, took a step back, and exhaled. "Whoa. Hold on."

Penny eyed her with suspicion.

"I'm not after Allen," Amy said. "Not like that. Hey, I understand what it looked like. Sorry about that. But my only concern is keeping some very powerful magic out of the wrong hands. Nothing else."

"That's all Father Paul wants too," Penny insisted. "And he said he wants to keep Allen from getting hurt."

"Wait. Hold on. You *talked* to the priest."

"Uh . . ." Penny bit her bottom lip, looked away.

Amy backed away, tensed, glanced at the doors and windows. "Oh, my God. Are they coming here?"

"No!" Penny said quickly. "No, I . . . I didn't think Allen would want me to do that. As a matter of fact, I went in to wake him up so I could talk him into seeing Father Paul. I wanted to convince Allen he could help."

"Oh, yeah? Like your priest helped back at the safe house. With machine guns."

"They were trying to rescue Allen because *you* kidnapped him."

"This is getting us nowhere," Amy said. "Did you mean it when you said you didn't tell the priests Allen was here?"

"Yes."

"I haven't told my people either," Amy said. "So let's say we're both being fair and honest. Who does that leave to help Allen?"

Penny narrowed her eyes at the witch. "What do you mean?"

"I mean he's out there somewhere. If the Society didn't snatch him, and if the priests didn't take him, then where is he?"

Penny frowned. She was trying to think it through. "You think he left on his own."

"I don't know. Maybe he was trying to get away from me, or maybe he just didn't want to put you in danger. But right now we're the only people who can help him. Neither one of us wants to see him hurt. Let's put our heads together and go find him." Amy offered her hand. "How about it?"

Penny eyed the outstretched hand a little longer than was probably polite. She took it, and they shook.

"I'm going to need a cup of coffee," Amy said.

"There's a place down the street," Penny told her. "Let's move."

THIRTY-ONE

Allen glided through nighttime Prague as if on autopilot.
He passed the dark and empty Sparta Stadium, crossed
Milady Harakove, and entered the western reaches of Letna Park,
where the bike paths and walking trails crisscrossed through the
trees. Allen never lost his way. One foot plodded in front of the
other. The small chunk of his brain that was still thinking in-
dependently fretted over Cassandra Evergreen. Had he made a
covenant with evil? Would he contract some kind of unholy ve-
nereal disease?

Must . . . obey.

Trees closed in around him, and the complete darkness was
terrifying and comforting. He trudged on. An owl hooted, and
Allen froze. Eyes in the night. *Never mind. Keep going.*

The trees opened suddenly, and there was Prague Castle before him, sprawling and magnificent, high walls and towers lit for
the tourists. Even compelled as he was to move on, Allen made
himself pause a moment to take in the view, to gaze upon the
onetime seat of the Holy Roman Empire.

Then the urge to obey grew uncomfortable enough to spur
him on. He passed Sternberg Palace on the north side. Schwarn-

bersky Palace came into view soon after. The whole area was lousy with historical crap.

He cut through another thin patch of forest and found the old monastery at the foot of Petrin Hill. *The Rogue's Guide* entry to Strahov Monastery read like this:

Old libraries. No action.

Allen crossed the rambling cobblestone courtyard to the wide, wooden front-entrance double doors. He read the hours posted on the front door. The place opened for tourists at eight in the morning. Allen looked at his wristwatch.

1:36 a.m.

Stupid arbitrary half-assed vampire hypnotism bullshit.

A nudge in his ribs. Somebody was yammering foreign talk at him.

Allen blinked his eyes open, then looked up into the bored face of a uniformed man. Badge. Gun. Cop. The inside of Allen's mouth tasted like old cabbage and feet. He sat up, his back, shoulders, and neck aching from six hours of sleeping on a stone bench.

The cop jabbered in Czech.

"I'm sorry." Allen rubbed his neck, stretched. "I'm waiting for the monastery to open."

Already a small crowd of tourists gathered at the front entrance, cameras around necks, khaki shorts and hats, T-shirts with the Czech flag on the front.

The cop sighed. "American."

"Yes."

"Okay." He pointed to the big double doors. "Over there. Almost open." He tapped his wristwatch.

"Thanks."

Allen fell in with the rest of the tourists and waited. It opened, and he soon found out there was a separate entrance fee for the libraries and the picture galleries. It was eighty Czech crowns to tour the libraries, but they told him university students could get in for fifty, about the price of a cup of coffee. He paid and shuffled inside with the others.

He paid another forty crowns for a guidebook in English. The two libraries were known as the Philosophical Hall and the Theological Hall. The guide described the Theological Hall as housing the collection of ancient arcane learning. Allen went there first.

The hall was impressive, and Allen stood a moment at the entrance, taking it all in. The ceiling vaulted overhead like a barrel, giving the place a feeling of space, rich stucco, paintings. Globes and lecterns with books on display lined the walls, bookcases at least a dozen feet high. It was immediately clear one could not simply approach the shelves and start pulling off books as in a normal library. The guide said there was a reading room with specific hours that didn't start until later, and all handling of the books was carefully supervised.

Allen left this library and found the Philosophical Hall.

This library was even more impressive than the last.

The bookshelves rose fifty feet high on both sides, all the way up to a richly detailed ceiling painted—according to the guide—by Franz Anton Maulbertsch, depicting scenes showing mankind's search for ultimate wisdom. The shelves towered over Allen, made him feel like a spec.

Books. Lots and lots and lots of books.

This wasn't going to be easy.

Allen was considered by his professors to be an outstanding researcher. He could walk into any university library back in America, plop himself in front of a computer terminal, spend an hour getting the hang of the system, initiate a search, and walk out with anything he needed. The dust on these books was older than any library in America. Nothing appeared to be computerized, at least not at first glance.

Okay. Stop. Think. What's the smart way to do this?

He went back outside, found a cart selling hot coffee, sat down with the guidebook. He devoured a brief history of the monastery. It had been founded in 1143, had been burned to the ground in the 1200s, and had survived Hussites and Communists. Allen paged through again, tried to find passages that involved the relevant time frame.

There wasn't enough here. He needed a computer.

He finished the coffee and began asking directions. The same cop who'd hustled him off the bench pointed him toward an internet café. Allen thanked him and started walking.

Allen realized it was no longer Cassandra's control that compelled him. It was his own curiosity. Whatever the vampire had done, it must have worn off with time and distance. He still felt the urge to investigate, the need to get to the bottom of . . . of whatever the hell it was that had taken over his life. Or maybe he was kidding himself. Maybe it was part of her spell that made it seem like it was Allen's own will that propelled him forward.

It didn't matter. He was going to solve this. He was going to get answers.

He circled the base of Petrin Hill to the east and veered south until he ran into a busy street and a cluster of shops, cafés, and other businesses. He followed the boulevard about five minutes until he found the internet café more or less where the cop had indicated. He ordered another cup of strong, black coffee and paid for an hour of web time. At the end of the hour he paid for two more and switched to espresso.

The monastery had its own website; it must have been a popular attraction, because there was an English-language option. Allen steadily worked his way through a more detailed history of the place. He borrowed a pen and jotted notes on a paper napkin.

He was narrowing it down, getting a workable plan together for finding his prize.

A man named Jan Lohel was abbot at Strahov from 1586 to 1612, which covered the time period in question. Perhaps they organized their materials according to the time at which they were acquired. Some collections might be attributed to particular abbots. Allen made a note.

It would likely be a handwritten manuscript, and in English. Narrowing it to works in English would help a lot. There! What was that? He hit the Back button and read more carefully. There was a special treasury room that housed rare volumes and fragile manuscripts. Any handwritten originals would be there. He was certain of it. Allen was a step closer.

He guzzled espresso, the excitement of impending discovery fueled by caffeine.

Allen poured over detailed summaries of a dozen historical anecdotes that seemed pertinent at first, but ultimately he scrolled on.

And then he had it. By 1603, a number of longtime residents of Prague Castle had left for good, including astrologers and alchemists. Many personal effects and written documents had been sent to storage in Strahov Monastery.

Allen knew the room he had to search, and he'd narrowed it down to the exact year.

Very soon he would be reading the last written words of Holy Roman Alchemist Edward Kelley.

1599

THIRTY-TWO

This astrologer fellow is a complete ass, Kelley wrote in his journal. *He's almost as bad as Doctor Dee.*

At least Roderick seemed to know his business better than that old fraud Dee had. For six weeks, Kelley had assisted the astrologer, working with the lenses and examining the stone from a safe distance, observing various experiments, many of which had been gruesome and dangerous. In no time at all, Kelley had been relegated to his typical duties of fetch and carry. Just like working for Dee all over again.

Except now Kelley felt he served two masters. Edgar sent his Society agents at least twice a week for progress reports. They frowned and crossed themselves upon hearing the details of Roderick's vile experiments. Only occasionally did Edgar come himself, warning that soon the Society would need to make its move.

Kelley simultaneously dreaded and welcomed whatever the Society planned. On the one hand, he wanted this over, to be free of Prague Castle so he could leave and never look back. On the other hand, Edgar's vague hints implied that the Society's scheme involved sudden, blinding violence. Kelley was sure to be caught in the middle.

In the meantime, he kept the journal, partly so he could offer a detailed report when the Society agents checked up on him, but also because he thought somebody somewhere would need to know what had happened here. Anyway, his writings would probably be disregarded as delusional fantasy. Why bother? But he scribbled in the journal every day.

Kelley finished his morning entry, then slid the journal into its hiding place under his clothes chest at the foot of his bed. He walked the short journey through the castle courtyard, into the castle, and down the dark twisting steps to the dungeon, where he found Roderick.

Emperor Rudolph was there.

Kelley froze and began to back out of the chamber when Roderick looked up and spotted him.

"Ah, there you are, Kelley. Fetch a couple of bodies from the corpse room, will you? There's a good man. Relatively fresh ones, please."

Kelley's shoulders slumped. "Okay. Give me a minute."

He trudged the corridor, grumbling under his breath, until he arrived at a thick wooden door. He pulled it open on creaking hinges and went inside. Dark, only the flickering torchlight from the hall behind casting its dim orange light on the pile of dead bodies. The ones on top would most likely be the freshest. He grabbed a man that looked a bit on the thin side—easier to carry—and took him back to the stone chamber, passing under the sharp eyes of Roderick and the emperor. He arranged the man in a wooden chair ten feet from the iron box, then went back to fetch the next body.

A young girl with a good volume of red hair. Slight. She looked easy to carry too. He bent, grunted as he heaved her over his shoulder and lugged her back. As he arranged her in the chair, he froze, going cold, heart skipping a beat. He knew that face.

Oh, God. Bianca.

He had finally remembered her name. The young serving

girl who had warmed his bed so many times. He hadn't seen her in a couple of weeks, and the kitchen staff had told him she'd come down with fever. Bianca.

Kelley stood, backed away from Bianca, feeling leaden, like his skin was made of ice. He went back to Roderick, indicated the bodies were in position.

"What's the matter with you, Kelley? You look as if you've seen a ghost."

"It's just . . . nothing."

"Well, pay attention. His Highness has asked for a demonstration, and I mean to oblige him." Roderick turned to the emperor. "Highness, there is still much work to be done before we reach our ultimate goal, but I believe you'll be impressed with our progress thus far."

Roderick entered the stone chamber, motioned for Kelley to follow him. "Help me position the lenses."

Kelley had watched the elaborate construction process as a dozen men had labored to install the apparatus. The machine consisted of a series of round frames into which the lenses were slid into place. There were eight sets of lenses, with three lenses in each set. Pulleys and levers had been rigged to raise or lower the lenses into place, and there were multiple permutations of ways the lenses could be arranged. Roderick and Kelley lowered the apparatus until the lenses encircled the iron box.

"I want the middle lenses only," Roderick said.

Kelley turned screws, loosening the middle lenses in their brackets, lowering them into place, then tightening the screws again.

"Okay," Roderick said. "Out of the room."

They retreated back into the hall and shut the iron door with a clang. A window about the size of a serving tray had been cut into the door, thick and obscenely expensive glass separating the observers from the goings-on within. After having conducted several experiments, Roderick had described the additional precautions as likely unnecessary but prudent nonetheless.

Roderick stood close to the door and peered through the window at the iron box and lenses, with the corpses sitting limply by. He signaled Kelley.

Kelley went to the big crank on the wall, grabbed the handle with both hands, grunted, put his back into it, and started turning. He picked up speed. The crank turned a shaft that connected to gears on the other side of the wall that connected to another shaft, which ran along the ceiling to more gears that turned the apparatus.

The lenses began to spin around the iron box, slowly at first. They picked up speed until they were a shimmering glass blur surrounding the box. Sweat broke out on Kelley's forehead and under his arms, but he kept up the pace.

When Roderick judged the speed sufficient, he pulled the lever that opened the iron box. The stone glowed a deep red, lighting up the lenses with almost blinding intensity. Kelley had seen it before and had thought, at first, that the light show had actually been quite beautiful.

Until he'd seen the result.

Roderick motioned Rudolph to the window. "Come witness, Your Highness."

The emperor paused. "Is it safe?"

"Quite safe behind the protective barrier, I assure you." Roderick knocked on the iron door to indicate its sturdiness. "Come see. The effects will soon make themselves evident."

Rudolph approached the window tentatively until he was standing shoulder to shoulder with the astrologer, his nose a half inch from the window glass. The Holy Roman Emperor was obviously curious. Years of planning and a small fortune had gone into his scheme. Just as obvious was the fact that he was a little nervous. Even emperors reported to a higher power.

The interior of the chamber was awash in bloodred light, pulsing as the stone emanated its rays.

"Observe, Highness." Roderick pointed. "Like our sun in the sky, the stone emits a spectrum of rays with a variety of properties. I believe the stone is attuned with the very fabric of reality, the same force that controls the tides and the seasons. The special lenses filter out the properties we don't want or need while allowing the beneficial properties to continue on. By controlling these rays we can achieve different effects. There! It begins."

Nothing happened at first. The emperor watched, unblinking, through the window, holding his breath. Then there was movement so slight it seemed a mirage at first. But when Rudolph gasped, Kelley knew the emperor had seen it.

A flutter of a single finger to start off. The male corpse lifted his head first, lurched out of the chair to stand on wobbling legs, head lolling like a dead chicken's. It opened its mouth, and a sort of choking cry erupted from its gob.

Rudolph crossed himself, a gesture Kelley had never seen the emperor make.

"You've brought him back to life," Rudolph said with awe.

"Er, well, not quite, Highness," Roderick admitted. "They are merely animated—undead, if you will."

"Undead?"

"Yes, a sort of state between life and death," Roderick said.

"And that's what you think I wanted?" The emperor's stare was as hard and flat as the iron door.

"No!" Roderick's eyes went wide. "Of course not, Highness. My goodness, no. I'm merely pointing out that we've taken such a big stride. Not immortality, not yet, but not death either. We haven't quite conquered death, but we've given it a good kick in the family jewels."

Rudolph nodded toward the shambling corpse. "Death would seem a preferable state to *that*."

"You're right of course, Highness." Roderick bowed formally. "Still, they are rather durable. We've made a dozen or so the past week, and they're damn hard to get rid of. Chop off an arm or a leg and they keep going, eh? Might actually be a little more like immortality than we thought." Roderick chuckled.

Rudolph did not laugh. At all.

Roderick cleared his throat. He wiped sweat from the back of his neck. "Your Highness is rightfully concerned. I simply wanted to demonstrate that we're doing some amazing things. I feel certain it's a matter of time before we find the right combination, filtering out the bad properties and allowing only select ones to bathe the subject. Life, Highness. It is within our grasp. I know it."

The emperor looked back at the zombie, which was now clawing uselessly at the wall. "Immortal life. Is science the answer, Roderick, or are we damning ourselves?"

"Highness, if there is a God, then surely He has given man dominion over all the earth. This stone may be from the heavens, but it fell to earth. Surely God has sent it to us, perhaps even as a test. I think it's our lot to push our intellects to the breaking point, to divine that which our Lord has sent us. Maybe He's testing us. Perhaps it's the ultimate test."

"Perhaps," Rudolph said quietly.

Roderick signaled Kelley to cease cranking. He pulled the lever to close the iron box. Kelley rubbed his shoulders. He'd worked up a good sweat.

Rudolph put his hand against the glass, looking into the chamber, as if mesmerized. "What about the other one?"

"Highness?"

"The other dead body. The young girl. She . . . it . . . isn't moving."

"Not uncommon, Highness. Sometimes the procedure fails to yield results. Perhaps certain bodies are not receptive." A shrug. "It's one of the mysteries that make our research so fascinating."

"Yes. Fascinating." The emperor's face remained blank. "I must think on this. Thank you, gentlemen, for the demonstration." He turned and left, a shadow seeming to hang over him.

"That's damned peculiar," Roderick said after Rudolph had gone. "I thought he would be more enthusiastic." He scratched at his beard, contemplating.

"Maybe he was ashamed," Kelley muttered.

"Eh?" Roderick lifted his head. "What was that?"

"Nothing. What should I do with it?" He indicated the zombie.

The astrologer looked up and down the hall. "Damn. All the soldiers have gone. It usually takes three or four each to hack them down safely. Can you let him chase you into the storage room we set up, Kelley?"

"They bite."

"Yes, but they're so slow. They just sort of shuffle along, don't they?"

Kelley sighed. "That worked fine when the room was empty, but now I'll run straight into a mob of them if I lead the new ones inside. It's getting crowded in there."

"Hmmmm, we'll need to devise some new way to dispose of them, I suppose. Maybe we can burn them all when the room is full."

Kelley pictured it, his gut lurching at the thought.

"We can leave them for tonight. Get some sleep, and we'll figure it out in the morning."

Kelley nodded, looked one more time at the back of her head, all that red hair.

He was glad he couldn't see her face.

Kelley returned to his room in the White Tower, and lay down, exhausted, in bed. Sleep would not come. Part of him was appalled at the crimes against nature he'd witnessed in the past few weeks, and another part of him was ashamed by the fact that these scenes were a little less appalling to him each passing day. He even found himself occasionally sharing Roderick's scientific enthusiasm, wondering how a particular experiment would turn out. Could a man get used to such things? He hated the thought of it. Seeing Bianca's dead face had shaken him, had yanked him back to the reality of what they were doing.

He tossed and turned, tangled the blankets, every muscle in his body aching for the sleep that wouldn't come.

He lay a long time, then he heard the door to his chamber open on rusty hinges. Kelley turned his head, saw the darkened figure enter.

"Who is it?"

No answer. Kelley held his breath.

The figure approached, and the bed sagged as it climbed on. Kelley's pulse clicked up a notch.

The figure crawled on top of him and Kelley trembled. He opened his mouth to scream but couldn't find the breath for it. The figure leaned forward, her face coming into the moonlight, her nose an inch from Kelley's. Bianca was ghost pale, her lips black, eyes red, teeth sharp and yellow.

"Take me, Edward, my love. Put yourself inside me."

And then Kelley did scream.

He thrashed, bucked the zombie off of him, kicked her away, rolled off the bed and hit the floor hard, tangling himself further into the bedclothes. He . . .

. . . opened his eyes.

He stood, panting, his heart racing. The yellow rays of dawn crept over the trees beyond his window. He looked around the room frantically, little panicked noises leaking out of him. A dream. Bianca. Just a dream.

He knelt to retrieve his journal from its hiding place beneath the chest. He took it to his desk and dipped his quill in ink, but he couldn't write. His hands shook. He filled a cup with cheap, dark wine, spilling some. He drank, letting it burn down to his belly, then took up the quill again.

> I can no longer be part of this abomination. Edgar must
> be contacted. It's time. The Stone must be destroyed
> or hidden. It stops now.

Kelley poured another cup of wine. He drank and wept.

THIRTY-THREE

"**I**t has to be now," Kelley said heatedly. "I'm cracking up."

Edgar shushed him. "Keep your voice down."

They knelt next to each other on the cold stone floor of St. Vitus Cathedral, hands clasped in prayer. Edgar had snuck in dressed as one of the workers, although there were fewer workers now. In the castle, there was a strange tension, a growing, unspoken sense that something portentous was coming to fruition. There had been fewer and fewer casual visitors to court, little sign of foreign dignitaries and the normal activity of state, almost as if Prague Castle had been quarantined. As if the city held its breath, waiting for something dire and long-anticipated to finally drop its turd of doom right into the soup.

"We're not ready," Edgar whispered. "We're still gathering strength."

"I'm not doing this anymore." Kelley said it with authority. He was putting his foot down. "Do it now, or I quit."

"Are you forgetting?" Edgar asked. "You've sworn allegiance to the Society."

Did the brand on Kelley's ass flare slightly, or was it his imagination?

"I might not be able to escape, but I'll kill myself. I'll drink poison or throw myself off the top of the White Tower. Then you can find yourself another dupe."

"Pull yourself together, Kelley. My God, you're a wreck. I can smell the wine on your breath. It's seven in the morning." He eyed Kelley, a hard appraisal. "You'd do it, wouldn't you? You'd kill yourself."

Probably not. Kelley was too much a coward. "I can't stand the constant horror anymore." This, at least, was the honest truth.

Edgar sighed. "Two days. Give us two more days."

Kelley closed his eyes tight and bowed his head. He couldn't remember how a prayer went, couldn't think of anything that didn't sound like whining, couldn't think of anything to ask that he deserved. To Edgar he said, "Two days. No more."

"We'll need your help from the inside."

"Just tell me what you want."

Roderick had set up a small antechamber near the entrance to the dungeon as a personal study. That's where Kelley found the astrologer, hunched over a table littered with documents and diagrams, small models of the machines and gadgets he'd designed in service of the emperor's mad project.

Roderick muttered to himself. There were bags under his eyes. Kelley thought the man had been looking more fatigued these past few days. They'd all been pushing themselves, but until now, the old man had seemed inexhaustible, buoyed and driven by his singular purpose.

Kelley cleared his throat, not sure if he should enter.

Roderick looked up from some obscure parchment, allowing a moment for his eyes to focus. "Oh, it's you, Kelley. Come in if you like. Have a seat."

Kelley lowered himself into the rickety wooden chair opposite

Roderick. He noticed the cup of wine at the astrologer's elbow and could not remember ever seeing the man drink before.

"I'm at an impasse," Roderick said. His voice sounded so tired that Kelley wondered if he might be ill.

Kelley leaned forward, elbows on the table, hands folded. "Oh?"

"We can make a corpse almost alive," Roderick said. "Almost alive. What the hell good is that? It is merely walking death. But we're so close, Kelley. I know it."

"I thought it was just a matter of finding the right combination of lenses," Kelley said.

Roderick frowned. "I suppose. I mean, that's part of it, certainly." He shook his head and *tsk*ed. "I may not have been entirely honest with the emperor. Yes, the lenses. Of course. But so much more. We could experiment for a hundred years, fill the dungeon with zombies and still not stumble upon the exact answer."

He reached below the table, came up with a jug, filled his cup with more wine. He held the jug out to Kelley. "Can I offer you a drink?"

Kelley grinned. "I never touch the stuff."

Roderick sputtered laughter. "Good one." He filled another cup, passed it to Kelley. "The duration we expose our subjects to the stone is likely one of the problems. It's possible we simply haven't allowed the process to complete."

Kelley sipped wine. "Then you're going to have to find somebody bigger and stronger than me to turn that damn crank. I'm wearing myself out. My heart might explode."

"Fret not. We're already in the process of constructing a much more elaborate version of the device we've been using. You won't kill yourself cranking."

Kelley recalled the dammed river and the waterwheel in the caverns beneath St. Vitus Cathedral. He almost commented but remembered he wasn't supposed to know about that. Instead he said, "Is it really corpses you want to bring to life anyway? I thought the emperor's goal was immortality."

"A fair point." Roderick sipped wine, smacked his lips. "There are two ways to go about this. The emperor and I spoke at length about it in the early days of the project. The first option." Roderick held up a finger. "We fashion a device that confers immortality upon the subject. But how would we know if it worked or not? Expose a living man to immortality rays, and what's the difference? Alive is alive."

Kelley admitted he hadn't thought about it like that.

"But the difference between *dead* and alive—now, that's measurable. This brings us to option number two." Another finger. "We create a device which brings the dead back to life. The emperor could die an infinite number of times, and always he could be brought back. In theory." He sighed, sipped more wine.

Kelley thought about this. "What if he breaks his neck?"

Roderick looked up from his wine. "Eh? What was that?"

"If Rudolph dies from a broken neck, and you bring him back to life, then . . . what? He's alive with a broken neck?"

"Oh." Roderick scratched his beard. "Yes, I see what you mean."

"Or if he dies of old age," Kelley said. "You might bring him to life and then he just dies again five minutes later because he's so old."

"Uh-huh."

"Then you have to consider that maybe nobody will *want* to bring him back," Kelley said. "I mean, his heirs might want the throne someday, and if the man is dead, he won't be able to bring himself back, will he?"

"Okay, now you're just being annoying," Roderick said. "I admit there are some minor details to work out."

A protracted moment of silence, both men sipping wine.

"I wasn't trying to be negative," Kelley finally said.

"Never mind," Roderick said.

"You know, you could probably make a fortune curing hang-overs," Kelley said.

Roderick said nothing, looked at Kelley as if he'd been examining a dog or an especially stupid child.

"That first day I met you," Kelley explained, "you zapped me with that sunbeam through the lens. I never felt better in my life. You could go from tavern to tavern. Charge a copper a piece to put all the drunks back into shape. Probably better money than the immortality racket."

Roderick sat straight in his chair, his eyes round and suddenly alert. "What did you say?"

"I said you could probably make better money than—"

Roderick stood abruptly, walked quickly from the room.

Kelley frowned. "Well, what the hell?"

When the astrologer failed to return, Kelley finished the jug of wine.

Kelley shrugged into his clothes the next morning and slouched toward the dungeon entrance. What would Roderick have for him today? No doubt something menial or horrifying.

Inside the castle, Kelley ran smack into a crowd of gawkers, all looking up at one of the big windows. Roderick was there, directing two workmen who stood in the window's frame, trying to put one of the astrologer's big lenses into place.

"Be careful, damn you!" shouted Roderick. "Put even a scratch on that, and I'll see you hung from Powder Tower."

"What's all this?" Kelley gawked with the rest of them.

"I've been at it since dawn, Kelley," said Roderick. "All thanks to you, don't you know?"

"Me?"

"You reminded me about the power of sunlight," Roderick said. "I'd been operating under the misapprehension that the stone was a chunk of the same cosmic stuff as our sun. Not at all! It is the opposite. A reflection almost."

"I don't understand."

"I think we can use the stone and the sun together." The excitement in the astrologer's voice was barely contained. "We have to bring yin and yang together."

"I still don't understand."

"Notions I brought back with me from my travels in the east," Roderick said. "The upshot is that two sources of contradicting— yet complementary—energies must collide to create the effect we're after. Some say the origins of the universe were created through such an act of creative violence."

Kelley tried to keep his face neutral. "I thought God created the universe."

Roderick cleared his throat. "Yes, of course." He looked back up at the workmen standing in the big window. "Be ready with that lens. The sun will be right soon." He gave Kelley a friendly slap on the shoulder. "Follow me, and I'll demonstrate what I've been telling you."

Kelley followed Roderick down the stairs into the dungeon. At the bottom of the stairs, another lens with a highly polished mirror behind it stood on an iron stand. Down the corridor where they turned the corner was yet another lens.

"These have all been placed at just the right angle," Roderick explained.

They passed three more lenses before arriving at the room that housed the stone. A few more of Roderick's assistants stood waiting for him, one holding a small wicker cage with a small bird flitting around inside.

Roderick took the cage, reached inside, and brought out the bird. It looked small and fragile in his fist. He handed the cage back to his assistant, then closed his other hand over the bird's head. The bird began to twitch, its wings flailing.

Kelley flinched. "What are you doing?"

"A quick suffocation does the least damage to the body."

At last the bird went still. Roderick took it into the stone chamber, placed it on a stool near the closed iron box. He returned, told his other assistants to get back down the hall and prepare to relay his commands. They left at a jog.

"I'll need you on the crank, Kelley."

Kelley pointed. "But the door's still open."

"Never mind that," Roderick said. "Just make sure not to stand directly in front of the doorway. You won't get any direct rays if you're off to the side."

Kelley remained dubious, but he manned the crank and waited for Roderick's command. Nervous.

"Angle the sun lens!" Roderick shouted.

The command was relayed back down the line, loud voices echoing in the dungeon halls. There was a long pause, and then the hallway filled with light. A blue-white beam flashed past and into the chamber room. Kelley yelled and jumped back.

"Back on the crank, Kelley," Roderick shouted. "Get to it."

Kelley cranked, the lenses spinning within the chamber. Roderick pulled the lever, opening the iron box. An electrical crack deafened Kelley. He winced but kept cranking. Rainbow lights washed through the hall, blinked and shimmered. Kelley felt nauseous and dizzy. His teeth hummed with a sharp vibration. The dungeon had become a blinding, deafening hell.

Kelley screamed but kept cranking.

Roderick pulled the lever again to close the box. He shouted back up the hall. "Finished!"

The sunbeam cut off. The hall went dead silent.

Kelley fell backward, landed hard on his ass. He was drenched in his own sweat, panting.

"Stay here," the astrologer said.

Roderick entered the chamber. He didn't come back right away. Kelley stayed on the floor. His shoulders ached from cranking at such high speed. He wished somebody bright and young and pretty would rub his shoulders. He wished he was back in Ireland, wished he'd never met Dee or Roderick or come to this place. How might his life have been different if he'd really studied the sciences, gone to the university? Instead he'd picked up dribs and drabs of knowledge, bits of science and the occult. This is where it had landed him. A sad little con man turning a crank for lunatics.

Roderick emerged from the chamber, cradled something in his hands. He stood without moving, his head upturned toward the ceiling, eyes closed. A wan smile played over his face. He stayed like that for such a long time that Kelley thought there might be something wrong with him.

Roderick turned his head slowly, smiled at Kelley. He walked to the alchemist, paused a second, then sat down on the floor across from him.

"What happened?" Kelley asked.

"Look." Roderick opened his hands.

The bird bounced into Kelley's lap, its head twitching from side to side. It peeped, flapped its wings. Kelley looked closely. It was not a zombie. It was a live, normal bird. Kelley reached for it, but the bird spread its wings, then darted into the air and into the depths of the dungeon. Kelley looked after it, mouth agape.

Roderick the astrologer had done it. He'd taken death and had turned it into life. Impossibly. Against the laws of man and God. The astrologer had done it.

And Kelley was terrified.

THIRTY-FOUR

The daily routine and attention to security within Prague Castle were obnoxiously irregular. On any given day, five guards in light armor might patrol the dungeons, or there might be twenty, depending on whether the emperor was scheduled for an inspection or if additional troops were needed to dispatch a fresh batch of zombies.

There were seven guards on duty the morning of the assault. The one constant was the guard at the main entrance of the dungeon whose job it was to lift the bar from the inside and allow entrance to anyone who spoke the proper password. This guard was Kelley's responsibility.

The guard sat on a stool and watched Kelley approach. Kelley smiled, held up a tankard of mead. He'd stashed a dagger at the small of his back under his clothes, and he shuddered at the thought of using it. Hoped it wouldn't be necessary. Couldn't stand the thought he might have to jam it into this young fellow's throat. Kelley didn't want to kill anyone.

"Looks like a dull job." Kelley had picked up more than enough Czech for casual conversation. "How about some refreshment?" He offered the tankard. *Please take it.*

The guard smiled crookedly, a tooth missing up front. He was maybe eighteen years old. "Much obliged." He drank, slurped, drained the mug, looked at Kelley with appreciation.

Kelley chatted with him another two minutes. Soon the guard began to sway on the stool. His eyes rolled up and he fell backward, chain mail clinking on the stone floor.

Kelley took some mild satisfaction from knowing that his alchemy skills had not completely atrophied. He could still whip up a sleeping draught from basic ingredients.

He lifted the bar of the door and pulled the iron ring. The heavy door swung inward.

Edgar and a dozen hard-looking men crowded into the dungeon entrance, all carrying short, thick swords and hand axes. They were prepared to hack through chain mail. The men were dressed in the coarse brown clothing of laborers, but they had the broad, powerful builds of fighting men, steely eyes seeking opponents.

"Good work, Kelley." Edgar handed him a sword. "Let's go."

Kelley looked at the blade in his hand. "I don't want this!"

"No time to be squeamish, man. The bloody deeds are at hand!"

"I opened the door. Bloody deeds are your department."

Two more guards appeared at the end of the hall. They drew swords. "Halt!"

"Have at them!" Edgar yelled.

Edgar's mob collided with the guards, blades flashing, axes rising and falling, biting through chain mail. Blood spurted. Screams! An empty helmet flew through the air and clattered at Kelley's feet. The guards were dead meat by the time Kelley caught up.

"There are only three more," Kelley told them. "And Roderick the astrologer. He's an old man, and I don't think he's armed."

"Let's go, then," Edgar said.

"Wait." Kelley grabbed Edgar's tunic. "Don't open the box. Take it out of here. Hide it far away. I don't even want to know where. But *don't* open it."

"You've told us already," Edgar said. "Now man up, Kelley. Bring that blade and let's finish this."

Kelley sighed. Okay, he could trail behind. No problem, bring the sword and jog along after them. He could hang back and not fight. "Lead on, then. I'll follow."

"Right. Let's go!" Edgar raised his sword. "No prisoners!"

The mob cheered, followed Edgar. Kelley tried to jog after them.

Something tugged at his ankle.

Kelley looked down. One of the hacked guards was not quite dead, and he had latched onto Kelley's ankle.

"Knock it off." Kelley tried to kick free. "Stop that."

The guard spit blood, lay on his back, one eye gouged out, the other fixed on Kelley. He coughed and wheezed, more blood foaming over his lips, but the hold on Kelley's ankle was like iron.

"You've done your part, okay? The fight is over." Kelley lifted the sword. "You want me to hack that hand off?"

No reply. From another part of the dungeon the sound of clashing steel reached him.

"Damn it." He knelt, tried to pry the fingers loose, but they were locked on.

The guard croaked, spit more blood.

"Oh, shut up." Kelley rapped the knuckles with the flat of the sword blade. Hard. He kept hitting until the hand let go. "Finally."

He ran after Edgar's mob and found three more dead guards. One of Edgar's men lay dead as well. Kelley kept running, gripping the sword hilt firmly. He didn't want any part of the violence, but he was determined to be ready.

A dozen steps from the Stone chamber and—

—an explosion.

Fire belched from the chamber, scorched bodies flying out, tumbling against the stone walls like dice.

The dungeon shook. The stone floor came up and smacked Kelley in the face, his sword clattering away, ringing in his ears, dust and screams and the smell of burnt fresh. He blinked his eyes, tried to see. Smoke filled the hall, crumpled blackened bodies, clothes still aflame.

Kelley forced himself to his feet, then shook his head and picked up his sword. He staggered into the stone chamber.

Roderick stood tall and straight in the center of the large room, a semicircle of blackened bodies in front of him. Edgar stood ten feet from Roderick, his face half bloody and charred, anger and pain alive in his one good eye. He lifted his sword, yelled, and charged the astrologer.

Roderick stretched out a hand, harsh words flying from his mouth. Jagged blue bolts left his fingers and slammed into Edgar's body. He shook and twitched as the blue lightning coursed through his body. His eyeballs popped. Bile boiled from his mouth.

Roderick released him, and Edgar collapsed into a smoking pile.

Kelley blinked at the scene, mouth agape. *Oh. My. God.*

Roderick poked at Edgar's body with a toe, satisfying himself that the man was gone. "Society do-gooders. I'd expected to see them long before now, I must admit. Fools."

Roderick looked up at Kelley, spotted the sword in his hand. "I appreciate your coming to my rescue, Kelley, but as you can see, I've handled the situation."

"Um . . . okay."

Roderick went from body to body, examining each one. "Help me get these corpses into a pile, will you, Kelley? They're a bit crispy, but they'll make for an interesting experiment when we zombie-fy the next batch."

THIRTY-FIVE

Three months passed like an eye blink. Even after the success with the bird, Roderick insisted on more odd experiments.

Kelley let himself go numb. He plodded through his daily routine with Roderick, adjusting lenses, lugging corpses, finding corners of the dungeon to fill with writhing zombies until they could be burned or hacked apart by castle guards. For about a week, Roderick called upon Kelley's skills as an alchemist to concoct a series of potions. It was hoped injecting the corpses with these potions might promote various effects when they were exposed to the stone's rays, but the astrologer soon grew tired of this avenue of experimentation.

They tried animals for a while. The dungeons echoed with the sound of fluttering wings as zombie pigeons filled the air, until their wings decayed and their feathers fell out and they could no longer stay aloft. The pigeons then scooted along the floor, flapping skeletal wings and going nowhere.

Zombie goats tried to butt Kelley, but there was no passion in it. They'd simply put their horns against Kelley's leg and lean into him without zeal.

Zombie chickens, zombie pigs, zombie ducks, zombie fish,

zombie cats. One incident with a zombie bear that left two guards dead.

The pathetic sight of a zombie puppy made Kelley weep openly, and he was forced to retire to the White Tower for the rest of the day, where he drained a jug of wine. Maybe breaking down like that was good. Maybe it showed he yet retained some shred of humanity. Or maybe he was just that much closer to madness.

On his way into the dungeon the next morning, Kelley met Roderick on his way out. The astrologer carried an armload of diagrams and parchments. He looked happy and excited.

"Just in time, Kelley. Follow me."

"What's going on?" Kelley asked.

"No more cranking those lenses by hand, my good man. I think you'll be impressed. Come see."

Kelley followed the astrologer out of the castle to St. Vitus Cathedral. Halfway there he guessed where they were going. It had been a long time since Kelley had first encountered Edgar and seen the underground river in the caves beneath the cathedral. He tried to act surprised when Roderick led him down and through the vault.

Where there had been a ragged hole knocked into the wall, there was now a proper archway. The stonemasons had done their jobs. The tunnel beyond that was smoother and wider. When they reached the river, Kelley observed a row of wooden posts with thick rope strung between for safety.

"As you can see, we've diverted this underground river to open up the chamber beyond," Roderick explained. "We've cleared a number of areas for different purposes, but what I want to show you is just up ahead. Be careful going down the ladder."

The ladder had now been anchored more securely, and Kelley followed Roderick down to the trickle of a stream where the underground river had once flowed freely. Flickering lamps hung from hooks, illuminating the path—a flagstone walkway that now paralleled the water all the way into the main chamber with the waterwheel.

Kelley noticed that the trench had been deepened to allow a greater flow of water to the wheel. The wheel wasn't turning at the moment. Workers were busy installing a larger version of the apparatus from the dungeon, with more lenses, gears, levers, shafts—all of the astrologer's bright playthings. The money and man hours already put into the project must have been staggering. Kelley could only guess.

Roderick was showing off, gesturing grandly at the wheel. He dove into a tedious and protracted explanation of the machine's workings, the colossal efforts needed to divert the river and expand the chamber, the exact calculations to place the reflecting mirrors. Kelley let the information wash over him, the technical details becoming white noise in his ears.

He belched and tasted last night's wine.

Kelley realized he was killing himself. He'd fallen into a deep depression; drank himself to sleep every night and ate barely enough to sustain himself. For his health and his sanity, Kelley had to escape this place. As the astrologer droned on, Kelley thought how he could do it.

Kelley felt confident the spell on his ass-brand had been broken when Edgar had been killed, so there was no magical restraint on him now. But security in and around the castle was tighter than ever. People who knew the secrets of the castle dungeons—people like Kelley—were especially kept under lock and key. The emperor didn't want tales of the walking dead to spread throughout the city. The peasants were already wary enough of the strange goings-on at court, with rumors of alchemists and magicians. Turning lead into gold was one thing, but trespassing against the laws of God and nature was something else entirely.

He considered the tunnels. When Kelley had first encountered Edgar, the man had taken him through a twisting tunnel that had let out in the woods beyond the castle. It had been months, but could Kelley perhaps find that same passage, use it to escape? He looked about the chamber and spotted a number of caves leading off in various directions. He'd probably get lost, and anyway, there was an armed man at every entrance.

Never mind. He would escape or die trying. Kelley would form some kind of plan, and he would leave.

Kelley spent the rest of the day hauling items from Roderick's antechamber near the dungeon down to a workspace beneath the cathedral. There were some delicate instruments that needed careful handling, and the astrologer didn't trust the common laborers to take proper care.

That night Kelley lay awake in the White Tower. He'd already written the day's events into his journal, but he did not crawl into a wine jug as usual. Saving himself was his new purpose. That he might not deserve saving didn't enter the equation. He'd earn it later.

Perhaps he could get Roderick to send him on some important errand in town. He'd simply not return to the castle. Or maybe in the general work and confusion beneath the cathedral, he could find Edgar's tunnel and escape that way. He wouldn't be able to take much. Luggage would naturally draw suspicion.

A knock at his chamber door startled him. Nobody ever visited him in the White Tower. Ever. Not since Dee had gone.

He sat up in bed, hesitated. "Come in."

Roderick entered. "Good. You're awake. I took a chance." He glanced around Kelley's room. "Your accommodations seem adequate."

"I'm comfortable."

Roderick nodded, toyed with a rolled-up piece of parchment in his hands. He seemed to be considering it. Finally, he stepped forward, handed it to Kelley. "I need you to memorize this then return it to me in the morning."

"What is it?"

"Oh . . ." Roderick shrugged. "It's the final sequence. Instructions for the machine."

"What?" Kelley stood, unrolled the parchment. He looked over it quickly, trying to take it all in at once. "It's finished?"

"Fully assembled."

As much as he hated the machine, hated what it did, Kelley could not help but feel awe. Such an undertaking. Finished at last. What would it mean to the world?

"Why give me the instructions?"

"I just thought somebody else should know how to operate it," Roderick said. "It occurred to me only just an hour ago that I'm the only man alive that knows completely how the contraption works." He chuckled.

"Are you going somewhere?" Kelley asked.

"No, no. Nothing like that." Roderick waved the notion away. "Just a precaution, you know. What if I choke on a chicken bone or something? Wouldn't that give the emperor fits? It's simple common sense. Somebody else should know. But that's the master copy. Memorize it and give it back to me in the morning. There's a good fellow."

"Okay."

"Sorry to disturb you, Kelley." He flicked a wave. "Good night." The astrologer let himself out.

Kelley examined the intricate instructions, complete with diagram. Roderick must have been drunk or out of his mind. If Kelley had a year, he'd never be able to memorize all this. He took out his journal and began to copy the information. It took him two hours. He checked the information three times to make sure he'd duplicated it perfectly.

He had.

He laughed. So much time and effort. Who would ever read it?

UNDERSTANDING LYCANTHROPY

THIRTY-SIX

Ten minutes to closing, and Allen figured they would probably check the restrooms.

He'd spent the last hour scouting possibilities. Hiding in the reading room was his best option, since there was only one door between the reading room and the special collections, where they kept the handwritten manuscripts. At least, that's where Allen *hoped* they would be.

The reading room: Six rows of five desks each. A service window at the far end of the room where patrons checked out reading material. Enormous Czech flags on poles stood in each corner of the room, and various framed maps and portraits hung on the walls. Allen stood with his hands clasped behind his back and pretended to examine one of the maps. The monastery had almost completely drained itself of tourists and other patrons. Soon they would shoo out the stragglers. There was only one other patron in the reading room—a middle-aged man with a sizable pile of books.

Come on, dude. They're going to close soon.

Three minutes to closing, the man finally stood and began to gather the books. He took them to the window, and Allen held his breath, as he edged toward the corner of the room. The man at the window took the materials from the middle-aged patron, turned his back.

Now!

Allen leaped into the corner of the room, grabbed the corner of the big Czech flag, and spun twice, completely wrapping himself within the smooth fabric. He stood perfectly still next to the flagpole, only the bottoms of his shoes showing. Hopefully nobody would notice.

He stood there like a flag mummy, wrapped up, the fabric tight on his face. Within three minutes he was hot, and it was hard to breathe. Allen thought maybe the flag was some synthetic fabric that didn't breathe well. Sweat fell from his neck and down his back, but he didn't budge. He developed an itch at the very top of his ass-crack.

No. Put it out of your mind. Don't move.

He finally heard footsteps, the jingle of keys. Allen held his breath. A bead of sweat trickled down his back. He wanted to swipe at it, squirm. The sound of a door opening. The lights went out. The door closed again, the sound of locks tumbling. Footsteps fading away.

Allen stood perfectly still another five minutes, then slowly unwrapped himself from the flag. The room was nearly pitch black, a feeble glow of light from beneath the door. He felt his way forward and tried to recall the layout of the place from the guidebook. The special treasure room was beyond the service window and down a short hall.

His knee smacked sharply into a desk, and Allen swallowed an expletive.

Any cartoon cat burglar would have invested in a flashlight. But Allen was a grad student specializing in the Brontës. *How incredibly useless.* He bumped his other knee into a different desk.

"Fuck!"

He clapped his hand over his mouth, held his breath, listening. No security guards. No blaring alarms.

This is stupid. He went to the wall, felt along until his hand passed over the light switch. He flipped it on. No windows. Nobody would see the light.

He went to the door next to the service window and tried the knob. Locked. He yanked on it, nudged his shoulder against the door experimentally. Very locked.

Okay. An experienced cat burglar would have had a flashlight *and* some tools. Maybe he could look around the room, find something to jimmy the lock. The hinges. Maybe he could knock them out somehow, take the whole door off. He was an intelligent guy. He just needed to figure this out. He glanced at the service window.

It was open.

He hopped up on the counter, swung his legs around, and dropped into the little room beyond.

A chair, a desk, a phone. A small TV with a cold-war antenna. Something that looked like a card catalog, but it was in Czech. Only one other door, so that had to be it. He tried the knob. Locked. No surprise.

He searched the desk, then the shelves. He ran his fingers along the ledge above the door and hit something metallic; he knocked it off, and it clanged on the tile. He got on his hands and knees, searching, crawling under the desk until he found it—a dull copper key.

Allen unlocked the door and entered a short hall. This cat burglar stuff was child's play. He found another door, open this time. He pushed it open, and its hinges squealed with ancient rust. He entered. This time it was a little harder to find the light switch—a black push button installed sometime between Hitler and Khrushchev. He pushed it, and dim lightbulbs in wire cages overhead spread halfhearted illumination through the long room.

Imagine any old university library, with shelves floor to ceiling. Now imagine nobody had dusted the place since moveable type had been invented. Add a sort of musty basement smell. Now pile old papers on all these shelves. Label everything in Czech.

Might as well be looking for the fucking Holy Grail.

Okay. Where to start. Find a system. Maybe not *the* system, but something to get walking in the right direction. That was the key. Even the most half-assed library has some kind of order, even if it's something that evolved by accident. He couldn't read Czech, but names and dates would be recognizable. He picked up the first stack of papers he could reach.

They fell apart in his hands.

I hope that wasn't important.

The conditions here were appalling. Allen considered his library experience quite good; he'd always admired the ones that had taken special care to restore and preserve their special collections. The items in here seemed to have been dumped in any old manner, happily forgotten. Allen supposed that since material in here dated back to before the first library in America had even been built, he could maybe cut them a little slack. Much of this material had been low priority during the Soviet occupation, and it was only in the past decade that professionals had begun to sort through it all.

Okay, find something less fragile. Get your bearings.

He scanned the shelves, found something bound in leather, lifted it carefully and opened it in the middle, to find pages filled with tiny, uneven scrawl. He presumed it was in Czech, but it might have been some other language. He searched for a date, turned each page with care. Finally he found it, at the top of a page—1897. He replaced the manuscript, continued a few paces down the aisle. He repeated the procedure, paged through eight manuscripts until he found the next date: 1765. Was he going in the right direction, or was it arbitrary? He checked two more manuscripts ten feet down the aisle—1760 and 1746. He jogged farther down. False starts ate away the time. So many manuscripts were illegible. Slowly he marched backward through the centuries.

1701.

1640.

1598.

He'd arrived. Could it really be this easy? Allen indeed had a knack for research, an almost preternatural talent most of his professors envied. His eyes seemed to gravitate to the right passage. An instinct for cross-referencing. Imagine a superhero whose mutant power was prying out a library's secrets. Perhaps in his youth he'd been bitten by a radioactive librarian. That was Allen. He should have worn a cape.

He needed to give himself a ten-year margin of error in each direction. He sorted through the stacks, looking for anything in English. His heart leaped when he found something in his own language, and he rapidly consumed each line with his eyes until he discovered it was the log of a stained-glass-window maker who'd come to trade techniques with the glassblowers of Prague. He almost replaced the manuscript on the shelf, but some instinct urged him to keep reading. A clue. The window maker had been staying at Rudolph's court. If this log had been among the materials transferred to the monastery from Prague Castle, then Allen might be close.

More manuscripts, accounting ledgers, private journals, letters. Very few manuscripts in English. His eyes blazed over words, phrases, diagrams, dates, a maddening blur of script. The dust sent him into fits of sneezing on multiple occasions. He wiped sweat from his brow, smearing himself with dust and grime.

Some luck! He found a number of manuscripts in English and pored over them.

. . . should get a new shipment of fruit as soon as . . .

. . . My Darling, how I miss you. I should be home in spring . . .

. . . Roderick's experiments continue to worry me . . .

. . . The German ambassador was a delightful fellow, but his pig-faced wife . . .

Wait.

Allen backed up to the previous manuscript. The handwriting was ugly and slanted, just barely legible. He read with growing excitement. Yes! This was it, the alchemist's journal. The diary of Edward Kelley. Allen Cabbot held it in his hands, the account of the alchemist who'd helped discover the philosopher's stone. It had been here in the monastery the whole time, hidden for more than four centuries.

It had taken Allen just over three hours to find it.

THIRTY-SEVEN

"This is getting us nowhere," Penny said. "We can't just keep wandering aimlessly through Prague."

They walked along one of the city's small parks, their footfalls echoing along the cobblestones. The street was deserted.

"I thought he might go back to the Globe," Amy said. "He can send email there. He hasn't been in the city long enough to know any other places. And he didn't go back to his dorm room."

"He's not that stupid," Penny said. "Anyone looking for him will check the dorm. He knows that."

"I'm out of ideas. If you'd just let me contact my people, they could help search for him. We have resources."

"Not any more than you'll let me contact Father Paul. We had a deal. Can't you cast a spell to find him?"

Amy shook her head. "It's not as easy as it sounds, you know? Casting a spell isn't like wiggling my nose on *Bewitched*. I need materials, a safe and quiet place to cast. Witchcraft is a subtle and complex art."

"I think Allen was right," Penny said. "I don't think you really have any powers at all."

"Don't start!"

Penny sighed. "Listen, I think I can do something that will help, but you've got to promise not to freak out."

"Why would I freak out?"

Penny took Amy's hand, led her behind a row of thick hedges, out of sight of the street or any houses. "Sometimes people freak out."

"I'm in the Society," Amy said. "Freaky stuff is my business."

"Just don't freak out."

"Stop saying that!"

Penny began to unbutton her shirt. Amy raised an eyebrow. Penny took off the shirt, gooseflesh rising on her white skin. She reached back to unclasp her bra.

"Okay," Amy said. "Now you're freaking me out."

"Just watch for anyone coming." Penny took off the bra, her small, pert breasts bouncing into view. She bent, pushed her skirt down, kicked off her shoes.

"Is this a sex thing?" Amy asked. "Because I don't go that way."

"Last warning," Penny said. "Don't freak out."

Jackson Fay emerged from the terminal with his carry-on bag slung over his shoulder. He immediately spotted the two girls waiting for him on the other side of customs.

He approached them, smiled. "Hello, Clover. Sam."

"We got your message," Clover said. "There's a taxi waiting outside."

"Well done," he said. "I'll have questions."

"We'll fill you in."

Fay looked around. "Where's Amy?"

"We had to scatter," Clover told him. "We think she's with Cabbot. She checked in to say she was safe but refused to give her whereabouts. She said the situation was awkward. It's . . . suspicious."

"Yes." Fay scratched his chin, wondered what the girl could be up to, where she might be. He wasn't in the mood for complications.

"We attempted a tracking spell," Sam said, "but they must be blocking us somehow."

Yeah, right.

"I'll need a hotel," Fay said. "Let's go."

Father Paul stood next to Finnegan. They looked down at Evergreen's pale, lifeless body, the fleshy pink gash in his throat garish and horrible.

Father Paul sighed, stuck a cigarette in his mouth. "You got a light?"

"I don't smoke," Finnegan said.

"Really? Since when?"

"About a week. Ten days maybe. It'll kill ya."

"I'll quit after this job."

"You said that before."

"Well, I'm saying it now."

Finnegan nudged the body with his foot. "What about him?"

"If she doesn't need Evergreen anymore, then she's got her hooks into somebody else," Father Paul said.

"The Cabbot boy?"

"What do you think?"

"Yeah." Finnegan rubbed the stubble on his jaw. They both needed sleep. "And Penny wouldn't say?"

"Poor girl's in love."

"Damn," Finnegan said. "Maybe we can still get through this without love fucking it up."

"From your lips to God's ears, Father Finnegan."

THIRTY-EIGHT

Back at the service window, Allen rifled the small desk, looking for what he needed. He wrapped the fragile manuscript in a triple layer of old newspapers and tied up the whole thing with brown twine. When he got someplace safe, he'd open it and take a closer look.

He climbed back through the window, went through the reading room, and let himself into the hallway beyond. He wove his way through back offices and storage rooms until he found the doorway out, an exit labeled in Czech, German, and English.

No alarms sounded. Nobody came after him.

Which way?

He headed up Petrin Hill. He remembered from the map in *The Rogue's Guide* that numerous paths crisscrossed the hill. He could lose himself up there in case someone followed, emerge on the other side. Some paths were well lit, others not. *The Rogue's Guide* had also mentioned the fact that hookers used the shrubbery as convenient hideaways for quickies. Interesting information but not particularly useful at the moment.

At first Allen stuck to the main path, which was well lit and smoothly paved. He kept heading up. He passed a young couple strolling arm in arm. Harmless, but they could still talk to the police. *Have you seen a young man with a stolen alchemist diary? Which way did he go?*

He turned onto a gravel path, narrow and dark, but still heading for the top of the hill. From there he could survey his surroundings and decide where to go next.

Next. Yes, that would be tricky. It was not safe to go back to his dorm; it had been foolish to go there the first time, in fact. Too easy for people to find him. And he didn't relish returning to Penny's apartment and having to explain why he'd gone off without her. There would be some hurt feelings there, but time to apologize later. Right now he needed a quiet place to examine Kelley's journal. A well-lit desk and nobody trying to kidnap, seduce, or kill him.

And while seduction was admittedly the least appalling of the options, the sudden thought of Cassandra both terrified and excited Allen, sending conflicting sensations coursing through his body.

No. Don't think about it.

He trudged up the path, gravel crunching. He panted with the exertion. Allen wasn't in bad shape, but the hill went up and up. He'd left the well-lit path far behind now, and the darkness closed in on him. He stepped off the path a few times, had to reorient himself by moonlight.

Allen heard something and froze. Had he heard footsteps, or was it just himself he'd heard? His own panting was loud in his ears. Something rustled in the bushes far back down the path. Bird? Rabbit?

Vampire?

He began walking again, took another dozen steps and stopped. Okay, he definitely *did* hear something. Something too large to be a bird or rabbit rustled the bushes. Allen strained his ears, heard a sniffing sound, or maybe it was heavy breathing. There! A dark shape slunk from the bushes, pausing in the middle of the path. Allen's heart picked up speed. He didn't move, held his breath. Maybe it would go away.

It moved, turning toward him. Glowing eyes stabbed him from the darkness.

It came toward him.

"Fuck!"

Allen clutched the manuscript to his chest and ran.

He ran straight up the path at first, but when he heard the rapid footfalls behind him, he realized his pursuer would overtake him quickly. He took a sharp right turn into the woods, where he dodged among the trees and low branches, stumbling over roots. How did he think getting lost in the woods would help? A sort of strange clarity told him he was panicking. Branches slapped at his face, tugged at his clothing.

The thing plunged into the woods behind him, pulling closer.

Oh, God, I'm going to die I'm going to die I'm going to die I'm going to—

His feet flew along the easiest path, turning downhill. He stumbled, and his hands flew out to grab a tree trunk. The manuscript flew away.

"Shit!"

He didn't pause, didn't even think of stopping to pick it up. He ran so hard that he thought his heart would explode. Sweat drenched him.

A howl split the night—a single note, deep and clear, rising above the hill.

Allen went cold.

He entered a small clearing, knew he couldn't run anymore. He would collapse any minute. He picked up a fallen branch and turned, backed up to the other side of the clearing, the branch held feebly in front of him.

Allen waited.

He saw the eyes first. It stepped into the clearing, moonlight giving it shape. An enormous dog. No. A wolf. Reddish-brown fur. Allen blinked. It was the same animal he'd seen so many months ago in the woods behind Professor Evergreen's house.

That's. Fucking. Impossible.

It took a step toward him, and Allen raised the branch.

The wolf threw its head back and howled again. Allen trembled. Allen waited to die as he imagined fangs tearing out his throat.

The wolf didn't budge. A moment stretched. It howled again.

Allen sensed movement down the hill, heard somebody clumsily trudging through the bushes. Allen opened his mouth to yell for help, but his voice caught, fear choking him to silence.

The wolf howled again.

Distantly, a woman's voice whined, "Okay. I heard you, for Christ's sake. I'm coming."

The wolf nodded its head, pawed at the air.

Bushes rustled to Allen's left, startling him. A woman stumbled into the clearing.

Allen's eyes popped. "Amy!"

Amy panted, held an armload of clothes. "Uphill? Is this revenge for dragging you up Zizkov?"

"Amy, stop. There's a wolf." He pointed with the branch.

"Yeah." She plopped butt first onto the grass, still out of breath. "Try not to freak out."

"What?"

Amy pointed at the wolf. "Look."

The animal began to shake, going into rapid convulsions. It made pained sounds, whined and growled. Its back arched. Limbs began to stretch and elongate horribly, its muzzle distorting and flattening into a face.

Allen could not imagine a more horrifying sight than this creature melting and deforming, redefining itself, fur melting into flesh, this monster growing more familiar by the second. A scream. Human.

She lay momentarily in a fetal position, then stood on shaky legs, hands going to mussed hair.

"Penny," breathed Allen. "Oh, my God."

Allen's world tilted dramatically. So many questions.

Penny stood naked, white and curved in the radiant moonlight.

THIRTY-NINE

Jackson Fay checked himself and the girls into a suite at the opulent Carlo IV hotel. He would plan his next move in comfort. He would need to locate Evergreen. He would need to determine if the man was a threat or not, prepare both defensive and offensive spells. Better to be over-prepared than under.

But at the moment, he was famished. Room service brought three carts of food and two chilled buckets of champagne. Fay had been embezzling from the Society for three years in preparation for his break with them.

Clover gulped a glass of champagne like it was ginger ale. "This beats the hell out of the service tunnels underneath Zizkov."

Sam reached for a shrimp cocktail. "Yeah."

"I could get used to this." Clover stuck a cigarette into her mouth, flipped open her Zippo.

"Don't smoke," Fay said.

Clover froze, the flame halfway to her cigarette. "Sorry?"

"I don't like the smell," Fay said. "You have your own room. Smoke in there."

She shrugged. "Right. Okay. I'll suck a quick one. Back in a minute." She went into her room and closed the door.

"She smokes too much." Sam popped a shrimp into her mouth, chewed as she refilled her champagne glass. "Is there a spell for lung cancer?"

"Maybe we should discover one." Fay sat back in his chair, looked at Sam. Long legs, tan. Athletic. Not very feminine in T-shirt, denim shorts, and hiking boots, but he could tell there was a good figure under there, and now that he'd eaten, Fay contemplated satisfying other needs.

He stood and plucked the rose from the vase on one of the serving trays. Classy place. Fay would never live in middle-class mediocrity again. He would always have just exactly whatever he wanted. This he vowed to himself.

Fay used the rose thorn to prick his finger, raising a drop of blood. He peeled off one of the rose petals, mashed it between his thumb and forefinger, then mixed the blood with it until it turned into a pink paste. Sam saw none of this as she hovered over a dish of caviar.

"Let me refill your glass." Fay took it from her, slipped the paste into it, then poured champagne on top, muttering words under his breath. He handed it back to her. "Drink up."

She smiled. "Thanks." She sipped, smacked her lips.

Immediately her eyelids grew heavy and a dreamy smile spread across her face. She took a step closer to Fay, a soft purr coming out of her.

"I think you should take off your clothes," Fay said.

She nodded, set her champagne glass aside. She pulled off her shirt, to reveal heavy breasts held back by a sports bra. She unclasped it, let them fall. Brown nipples poked out like pencil erasers.

"Very nice," Fay whispered.

She smiled, unzipped her shorts and let them fall, stepped out of them and peeled her white cotton panties down over her hiking boots. Her pubic hair had been cut into a narrow line.

He cupped a breast, ran a thumb over a nipple. Sam gasped

pleasure. He reached down to her seam, and she closed her eyes, moaned.

Fay thrilled at the moist warmth. Being the most powerful wizard on the planet was going to work out just fine.

Clover threw open a window, puffed the cigarette as she gazed upon Prague from her third-story window. Not a lot of traffic this time of night, but this part of the city never did shut down entirely. It was actually a pretty neat town, she thought. If she hadn't been here on Society business, she would probably have found a number of ways to amuse herself. Maybe catch the night scene, scope out a few bands.

But then again, she wouldn't have been here in the first place if it hadn't been for the Society. She'd jumped at the opportunity. What in the hell would she have done with her life back in Evansville, Indiana? Jesus.

It was the Society that allowed her to go places, do things, be part of something. She couldn't help thinking she'd bungled things with Allen Cabbot. She puffed, frowned, promised herself she'd do something to make up for it. Prove to Fay and the rest of the Council she wasn't a fuckup.

Wouldn't it be kick-ass to get promoted, learn some of the big spells, get in on the real secrets? Damn right. That would be cool.

She should probably get back to Fay. She didn't want to seem ungrateful. But the bed looked so comfortable. It would be easy just to fall into cool sheets, catch a few hours of shut-eye. She'd been awake nearly the entire time since fleeing Zizkov, only stealing a quick catnap here and there.

Clover went to the vanity mirror and looked closely at her face. There were dark circles under her eyes, and not the cool kind she did herself with makeup sometimes. Real dark circles. She thought her face suddenly looked ashen too. As a matter of fact, it was getting paler by the second, and wrinkles were forming. What the hell?

An old woman's face replaced her own, emerged from the mirror.

"Motherfucker!" Clover stumbled back, fell onto the bed, and scooted back all the way to the headboard, her arms flung up to fend off the apparition.

"It's me, Clover," the old woman said. "Do not be alarmed."

Clover blinked, looked more closely at the pale figure, who hovered, mostly transparent, the rest of the room visible behind her. Wait. Clover knew this lady. "Margaret?"

"Yes, child. Where are the others?"

"Sam is here," Clover said. "We can't find Amy. Where are you?"

"I've gone beyond," Margaret said. "But I managed one last spell, something I set up ahead of time just in case. You must listen to me, Clover. Jackson Fay is a traitor. He has betrayed the Council. He murdered Blake and me."

"That's impossible."

"Why else would I appear to you in this fashion?" asked the ghost. "Fay has betrayed us."

"But he's in the other room right now. With Sam."

"Flee, child. Go while you can."

"But Sam."

The ghost began to fade. "I must warn others. My time is limited. It's . . . difficult to judge time where I am. I think I've only been this way a few short hours, but another part of me feels as if I've always been here. So gray and silent. I must go."

And she was gone.

Clover sat on the bed, stunned.

Sam. Clover could not—*would* not—leave without Sam. She went to her backpack to search for something she'd prepared several weeks ago, a spell she'd been afraid to try. Now was the time.

She found the plastic baggy, opened it, put the contents into her pocket. Ash. It seemed only like simple ash, but it had been prepared, with so many ingredients—herbs, a goat's heart, and the crushed bones of a cripple. She'd had to do a little grave robbing for that one. It had all been mixed and blasted in an iron furnace. If she could catch Fay by surprise, fling it in his eyes and say the words—yes, it might work. He'd be paralyzed for several hours—or maybe only seconds. The old book hadn't been clear. It was suicide to go against a wizard like Fay toe to toe, but that's not what she had in mind. She just wanted to slow him down, give herself and Sam a chance to get the hell out of there.

She went to her bedroom door, put her ear against it but heard nothing. She turned the knob quietly and pushed the door open barely a sliver so she could take a peek.

She clapped her hand over her own mouth to stifle a surprised gasp.

Sam reclined naked on the couch, arms and legs spread, a clear invitation. Fay approached her. He was naked too, his erection pulsing at Sam, bobbing as he stepped closer to mount her.

Clover backed away from the door, searched the room with her eyes, and saw a large ceramic vase. She grabbed it, hit the door at full speed on the way into the next room. Fay looked up, startled, then backed away from Sam, his eyes momentarily showing surprise, then narrowing to anger. Clover raised the vase over her head with both hands, grunted, and heaved. It flew.

And cracked square against the center of Fay's forehead, ceramic shards flying in every direction.

Fay cursed, stumbled back over a coffee table, and crashed into the room service carts. A tumult of dishes and silverware. Fay lay groaning, tangled in the tablecloth.

Clover was at Sam's side in a second, grabbed her arm, yanked. "Come on!"

Sam only looked up at her, that dreamy expression on her face.

"Damn it!" Clover grabbed the closest ice bucket and dumped it on Sam's head. "Snap out of it."

Sam screamed, sputtered. "What the f-fuck?" She looked down, saw herself naked, and yelped.

Fay lurched to his feet, a gash on his forehead bleeding freely. He wiped the blood out of his eyes and glared rage at Clover. "Bitch!"

Clover shoved Sam. "Run!"

Sam jumped up from the couch, sprinted for the door.

"I don't think so." Lightning leaped from Fay's outstretched fingertips, crackled and struck Sam in the back. She froze for a split-second as the entire room went white. Then she collapsed, eyes rolled back, mouth hanging open, smoke rising from her dead body.

"You son of a bitch." Clover spun on Fay. She reached into her pocket, came out with a handful of ash, and flung it into his eyes, the long-memorized command words tumbling from her mouth.

Nothing happened.

Fay bent down, grabbed a napkin from the wrecked room service cart, and wiped the ash from his face. Then he began to laugh.

No. Clover shook her head, couldn't believe it. *I did everything right. I know I did. It should have worked.*

"Surprised?" Fay asked. "Poor little girl can't make her magic work."

Tears welled in her eyes. No. There had been a mistake. This wasn't right. Sam. Was Sam really dead?

Clover turned, ran for the door.

Fay cut her off, grabbed an arm, twisted it behind her back. Pain lanced up through her shoulder, and she went rigid. Suddenly there was a blade at her throat. She wept, fat tears rolling down her cheeks.

"You spoiled the party," Fay said. "Now, why would you do that?"

"I . . . I . . ." What could she say? Oh, Sam. Poor Sam.

"I would have let you join in," Fay said. "Would that have been so bad? All I needed was a ride from the airport, and if you're not going to provide me with any entertainment, then I'm afraid you're no longer of any use, young lady."

Clover drew a breath for a scream, but nobody ever heard it. Fay's blade bit quick and deep.

FORTY

Allen got on his hands and knees, and peered under a thorny bush. "I mean, Jesus. You know? What am I supposed to think? It's like I don't even know you."

Penny followed behind him, still buttoning her shirt. "It's not an easy thing to tell somebody, okay? I mean, hell, remember Jenny Mackenzie from Victorian lit last semester? She got the clap over the summer and *still* hasn't told her boyfriend."

"This is different."

"Of course it's different. It's always different."

"But you're very *very* different."

"You don't have to treat me any different," Penny insisted. "I don't need your . . . your racism."

"Racism? It's not like you're Chinese."

"Animalism then," Penny said. "Whatever."

"I mean, you're a . . . a—"

"Don't say it!"

"Say what?"

"Werewolf," Penny said. "We hate that word."

Allen walked in a widening circle, bent over, scanning the ground. The first rays of dawn helped only a little. "What's the right word?"

"Lycanthrope."

"Lycan-what?"

"Lycanthropy is a disorder," Penny said. "A rare virus in conjunction with an even rarer genetic predisposition. The Third Vatican Council ruled it as a medical condition. As opposed to the work of Satan."

"I've never heard of a Third Vatican Council."

"You're not supposed to have." Penny scanned the ground now too. "Where did you drop it?"

"I don't know," Allen said. "I was slightly terrified at the time."

"Following your scent was the only way I could think to find you, and I can only do that in wolf form. How many times do I have to say I'm sorry?"

Allen sighed. "I just need to let this sink in. It's been a strange couple of days."

"For me too," Penny said. "That's not really how I wanted you to see me naked for the first time."

"Over here!" Amy's voice came from forty yards away, through more thick bushes.

Allen and Penny found Amy. She handed him the manuscript, still bound up with twine and newspaper. There were leaves in Amy's hair, grass stains on her shorts.

"It seems okay."

"Open it," Penny said. "I want to see."

"Not here." Allen clutched the manuscript to his chest. "It's too old."

"I don't even know what it is," Penny said.

"I told you. It's Edward Kelley's diary. The alchemist."

"Back to my apartment," Penny said.

"No," Amy said quickly. "They'll think to look there."

"I told you I didn't tell Father Paul where we were," Penny said.

"I don't trust you."

Penny sputtered. "You don't . . . after I let you see me . . . Oh, my God. You suck."

"I'm not saying your motives are bad," Amy said. "I just won't risk it."

"Oh, you so very much suck."

"I just need a table and someplace quiet," Allen said. "Preferably not too crowded."

"Like a library?" Amy said.

"Been there. Done that."

"I know a place," Penny said, "but it won't be open yet."

"Okay then," Amy said. "Breakfast."

They walked back through Mala Strana in no particular hurry. The city was waking, the morning cool and dewy. They circled Prague Castle on the north side, pausing to gander at the walls and towers.

"In there." Allen tapped the Kelley diary. "That's where he wrote it."

They continued on, back through Letna Park. In the light of day it was pleasant, trees arching in a canopy over the path. Allen pictured himself here with Penny under other circumstances, walking hand in hand, on the way for a cup of coffee. Two healthy young people in an exotic foreign country. Why couldn't it be that simple?

They reached the Holešovice suburb and found a hip little café that was just opening, serving eggs, toast, sausage heavy enough to sink a naval destroyer, and coffee so strong it could eat the paint off the wall.

"Push the dishes aside," Penny said. "Let's see the diary."

Allen shook his head. "No way. Spill some of that coffee on it, and the whole thing will disintegrate."

"I'm so curious, I can't stand it," she said. "How did you even know to look for it?"

Allen went a little pale remembering his encounter with Cassandra. He couldn't quite bring himself to relate that experience to Penny just yet. Then he remembered there was something else he hadn't told her.

"Penny, Professor Evergreen is dead."

"What?"

Allen related the story to the girls, how he'd found the professor dead, the chunk bitten out of his throat.

"Oh, my God," Penny whispered.

Amy said, "Good."

Penny's eyes went big. "Did you just say '*good*'?"

"I'm sorry. I don't mean I hope he suffered or anything like that. It's just good he's out of the way. He was a traitor to the Society. We were all pretty worried he'd get a hold of the philosopher's stone and do something really fucked up with it. His wife's a vampire, you know."

Penny sputtered coffee. "A what?"

"Vampire."

"Unbelievable," Penny said.

Amy pointed a finger at her. "*You're* a werewolf."

"Lycanthrope!"

Amy narrowed her eyes, turned back to Allen. "How did you know about the diary? How did you know to look in the monastery?"

Allen opened his mouth to tell them. Of course he would tell them. Time to come clean. These people were on his side. So why wouldn't the words come out? He suddenly felt Cassandra's cold touch and shivered. He realized with acute dread that whatever spell the vampire had put on him had not completely evaporated.

He held up his hand for the waitress. "Check, please."

Penny said she'd found the place her first day, tired and jet lagged but too excited to sleep. She'd strolled the streets of

Holešovice and stumbled upon the Veletrzni Palace—the Trade Fair Palace.

A gleaming example of modern architecture, the Trade Fair Palace housed Prague's collection of twentieth-century art and was one of the main reasons tourists made it out to the suburb. The four floors of paintings and sculptures attracted groups of students on the weekends, but on an early weekday morning, the small café in the lobby was utterly deserted. All very modern, sharp angles and white plastic, metal chairs that looked uncomfortable but weren't.

"They have a couple of Picassos here," Penny said.

Allen held up his copy of *The Rogue's Guide*. "This place isn't even in here. All this book tells you is where to get drunk and laid."

Penny laughed. "You're not actually using that to get around Prague, are you? That was a gag gift."

They picked the table farthest from the entrance, and Allen untied the twine, peeled away the newspaper.

Amy and Penny crowded in on either side of him.

"I can't do this with you reading over my shoulder," he said. "You're making me anxious."

"We're curious too," Penny said.

Amy crossed her arms. "Yeah."

"Okay, just wait. Hold on." Allen pointed at the café counter. "I need napkins and plastic coffee stirs."

"One second." Penny went to fetch them.

"I'll bite," Amy said. "Napkins and coffee stirs?"

"These old manuscripts damage easily." Allen ran his hand lightly over the leather cover. "Watch and learn."

Penny returned with the napkins and stirs, gave them to Allen.

"Okay." Allen pointed to the chairs on the opposite side of the table. "Both of you sit over there."

The girls looked at each other and frowned, but they took their seats without complaint.

Allen took the cracked and worn leather cover between thumb and forefinger, and opened the manuscript with utmost care. Edward Kelley's erratic scrawl was faded but legible. Allen began to read, skimming, slowing down occasionally to determine if a particular passage was pertinent. He used the plastic coffee stirs like surgical instruments to carefully turn the pages, sneaking a stir under an edge, lifting it carefully, catching the page with the other stir and letting it down again delicately. When he came to some caked-on dust, he dabbed at it with one of the napkins.

"Are you going to read some of that to us?" Penny asked. "Or do we just sit here watching you turn those pages with plastic sticks?"

"It's not all relevant, okay?" Allen gestured at the thick manuscript. "This thing looks like it covers months and months. Maybe more. Probably what we want is toward the end, but I don't know. I don't know anything. I have to go through all this, and I'm trying to do it fast, but I don't know what I'm going to find or when."

"Read us something," Amy pleaded. "We can't stand it."

"Fine," Allen said. "Here's a sample." He read the following passage out loud:

> This serving maid is unquenchable. Last night she used her mouth on me in ways that surely are sins in the eyes of the Church. She begged me to return the favor. Unfortunately, I do not believe she had bathed in several days and—

"Never mind," Penny said. "We'll do it your way." She nudged Amy. "You want some coffee?"

Amy grimaced. "No way. The last cup almost ate through my stomach. Some tea?"

"Be right back." Penny left for the café counter.

Amy waited until Penny was out of earshot, then said, "You're holding back something about the vampire."

"No, I'm not."

"I could tell. Back at breakfast."

"No."

"How did you know where to look for the diary?"

Allen hesitated. "Dr. Evergreen told me."

"You said he was dead."

"He . . . told me before he died."

"You're a terrible liar, Allen."

"Okay, yes. It was Cassandra. She made me fetch the diary from the monastery."

"She 'made' you?"

Allen sighed. "It's sort of . . . complicated."

"Allen, if she sent you for it, then she'll want it. When night hits, she'll come, and then we'll have a vampire on our hands. The Society thought Evergreen had something bad planned for the philosopher's stone, but it was Cassandra all along, wasn't it? She needs it for something."

"She didn't tell me for what," Allen said. "But I plan to find out. She may have sent me to find the diary, but I didn't take it to her, did I? I'm going to get to the bottom of this, but I'll need your help, okay? I just . . . I don't want to say anything to Penny about Cassandra. It's embarrassing."

"Embarrassing? But why would—" Amy's eyes went big, comprehension dawning in her expression. "Oh, my God. Did she do that vampire hypnotism thing on you? Did she *seduce* you?"

"Keep your voice down." He felt himself turn red.

"She *did*, didn't she?"

Allen saw Penny returning with tea and coffee. "*Shush.*"

"That's hot," Amy said.

Allen glared her into silence just as Penny sat down and passed a mug of tea to Amy.

"Did I miss anything?"

"Nope." Allen kept his eyes fixed on the manuscript, deliberately not looking at either of the girls.

He focused on passages, trying to find something important. Kelley went on and on about life at the castle, lengthy tirades against somebody named Dee. He skipped ahead, feeling a little more urgency to get to the meat of the matter. Amy and Penny lapsed into a conversation about shoes, then poetry, then where Amy had attended college. Allen tuned them out, focusing on Kelley's words.

At last he found something, but he reread it again to be sure.

Allen cleared his throat. "Ladies, I think you might want to hear this."

PRAGUE CASTLE

1601

FORTY-ONE

Kelley entered the castle but turned away from the dungeon. He hadn't been there in nearly two years, not since operations had moved entirely to the caverns beneath St. Vitus Cathedral. Instead he turned toward the castle infirmary, going in quietly so as not to disturb the few lingering patients—soldiers who'd injured each other during sword practice, stable hands kicked by horses, and other minor injuries.

He paused near an old nun who wrapped a bandage around a soldier's shoulder. "How is he today?" Kelley asked.

She shrugged. "No better. No worse."

"He's still by the window?"

The nun nodded.

Kelley walked past the beds to the end of the long room and around a silk screen that had been erected to allow the man in the final bed some privacy. Sun streamed in the window, its warm rays illuminating the floating dust motes.

Roderick lay under a thin sheet, perfectly still, arms folded across his chest, his face like chalk. His chest did not noticeably rise and fall with breath; nothing animated any of his features. Kelley thought he might already be dead, but the old man's eyelids lifted slowly.

"Hello, Kelley." Roderick's voice was a weak croak. "I said you didn't have to visit me anymore. It must be terribly depressing."

"I can make you some more of that tea if you like," Kelley offered. "To calm your stomach. If I can find the right tree bark and some other ingredients."

"No more of your alchemy. It doesn't help anymore," the astrologer said. "There is only dying left to do, and that will be that."

During those early months, Roderick had seemed only slightly ill or, perhaps, malnourished, given his long hours trying to complete the project for the emperor. The astrologer was an old man, after all, and while Kelley's first impression of him had been of a tireless force of manic energy, certainly a man of his age could only go for so long without an extended rest.

But Roderick's health had grown steadily worse. He'd faded to skin and bone, hadn't been able to keep food down. His teeth had rotted and fallen out. Finally, he hadn't been able to walk anymore and had been confined to bed for the past two months, where he'd continued to wither.

Kelley sat in silence on the windowsill, looking at his shoes, not saying anything.

"I was arrogant," Roderick said at last.

Kelley looked up. "What?"

"Arrogant and foolish," Roderick said. "I've toyed with powers that have killed me. We have all damned ourselves. Why don't you go home?"

"Rudolph won't let me," Kelley said. "With you about to . . . die . . . I'm the only one that knows what to do with the machine."

"Yes, I suppose that's true. I'm no longer needed, am I?"

"I know how to position the lenses and activate the machine, but I have no idea how or why it all works," Kelley said. "If something breaks, I wouldn't know where to start."

"Just remember never to open the box," Roderick said.

"Never. I transferred the stone to a lead box. Did I tell you that? It protects better."

"You told me last time."

"Did I? How long ago was that? Never mind. My mind is going, Kelley. It won't be long now. You have to keep the lenses clean. There are maintenance spells to ward off casual dust and rot, but anything done by you the spells will interpret as an intentional alteration. The lenses must be spotless before use. If something warps the light flow, it might alter the effects."

"You told me."

"You should escape, Kelley. For God's sake, don't you have a family?"

Kelley said nothing. He had no family. But really, where else was there to go? He felt branded, like an outcast. He felt it so strongly in his heart that surely it must show on his face. Where could he go where decent people would look him in the eye and not know he'd spit in the face of God? No, Kelley was doomed to live out his days in Prague Castle, a sinner hiding among other sinners, a madman in a city of madmen.

"The dreams are the worst," Roderick said. "It is always early in the morning, on the verge of waking. I'm dead and my soul travels into a deepening gray, no color, no light, just on and on into eternal gray, a vast nothingness."

"It's just a dream."

Roderick erupted into a spasm of coughing that startled Kelley.

The astrologer gestured to a white cloth on the stand next to his bed, and Kelley handed it to him, jumping back when the coughing was renewed with double the force. Roderick coughed into the cloth, his body shaking violently. The cloth came away bright red.

Roderick sank back into his pillow. He seemed to deflate right before Kelley's eyes, as if the life force fled from the old man's decaying body.

The astrologer closed his eyes. "Don't let this happen to you. Edward, listen. Don't let it happen. Go now. There's nothing you can do here but watch me die."

Kelley opened his mouth, could not think of one comforting thing to say, no words of hope or wisdom, nothing to acknowledge anything other than death. He said nothing, walked away from Roderick's bed, walked out of the infirmary, didn't look back. His mind's eye saw again the blood so red on the white cloth.

Kelley went back to his room in the White Tower and uncorked a fresh jug of wine. He drank and drank, but nothing would wash away his sins.

The sun shimmered orange on the horizon when Kelley heard the bells. Something was happening. He rose from his chair, stumbled, realized he hadn't moved in hours. He'd sat staring out the open window, slowly making the jug of wine disappear. He righted himself, went to the window ledge.

People ran across the courtyard below. One came toward the White Tower.

Kelley flopped back into the chair, closed his eyes, and waited. Soon he heard the footfalls on the stairs. A second later, there was a knock at the door.

Go away.

The lock came louder, a voice shouting on the other side of the door, "Master Kelley!"

He stood reluctantly, went to the door, and opened it a crack to see a teenager on the other side, with a dirty face, greasy hair. Some random lackey from the stables or kitchens.

"Master Kelley?"

"What is it?"

"Word's all over that he's dead, sir. The emperor has everyone running every which way. Said to come fetch the alchemist. I've got to get back, but the emperor wants you right away and no mistake!" Breathless. He dashed away before Kelley could ask him anything.

He went downstairs and out of the tower, paused to dunk his head in the water trough, where he drank handfuls of water. Damn, he was still half drunk.

He was halfway to the castle when he was intercepted by one of the emperor's robed advisors. He recognized the man's face but couldn't come up with a name.

"Is it true he's dead?" Kelley asked.

"I'm afraid so," the advisor said. "Naturally, the emperor wants to . . . ah . . . take the opportunity to test the device." The advisor quickly looked around to make sure no one had overheard him.

Kelley shook his head. What would Roderick think about being brought back to life by his own invention? "Where is he?"

"They're putting him into dry clothes now," the advisor said.

Kelley stopped walking, then looked at the advisor, confusion on his face. "Dry clothes?"

"I thought you'd heard. He drowned in the Charles River. It happened just an hour ago."

"Wait. What was he doing in the Charles River?"

"That's hardly relevant." Haughty. Impatient.

"But I just . . . how did he get to the river?"

"The emperor's cousin was boating with a couple of young ladies. He fell in and drowned. It's hardly—"

"Hold on. Who? The emperor's cousin?"

"Who do you *think* we've been talking about?"

"I just . . ." The emperor's cousin. Not Roderick. "I was confused for a moment. Never mind. Lead on."

Kelley followed the advisor to St. Vitus Cathedral, past a brace of guards keeping out casual worshippers, and into the vault leading to the caverns below. The paths had been completed and roped off for safety; the entire underground complex had been completed. Even the ladder that led down the front of the dam had been replaced by narrow stone steps along the cavern wall.

It had been explained to Kelley that the caverns would be the most well kept of state secrets, the legacy of the Holy Roman Emperors. That was one of the reasons a dead peasant had not been brought in previously to test the machine on a human. If the peasant was brought back to life, then he would need to be killed again to keep the secret, and not even Rudolph could bring himself to be that bloody. Only the emperor and the royal family and his heirs would have access to immortality.

Laborers who'd worked in the caverns had been pressed into the army and sent to faraway campaigns. Soldiers standing outside the cathedral had no idea what they were guarding. Of course, rumors spread of the strange activities in and under the castle, but the emperor's spies continued to spread the tale that the alchemists were transmuting lead into gold. (A rumor that also helped explain why so much lead was being sent to the castle.) It was a cover story that would hold for centuries.

They entered the waterwheel chamber, where Holy Roman Emperor Rudolph II waited with more advisors and captains, the most powerful and influential people at court. They watched him expectantly as he approached. Kelley stood before the emperor and bowed his head just enough to show respect. He'd been through too much to grovel. He no longer cared what happened to him.

Rudolph looked him up and down. "Kelley, isn't it?"

"Yes, Highness."

"And you can operate this machine? Roderick has shown you?"

"Yes, Highness."

The emperor stepped aside, gesturing to the table on the stone dais. A man lay stretched out on the table. A circle of lenses hung from a thick chain above, with a prism and another, larger lens in the middle of the circle.

"My cousin," Rudolph said.

Kelley nodded, climbed the steps of the dais, looked down at the young man on the table. Fair hair, still slightly damp, clean bright skin. He'd been put into a dry robe of plain, white cloth. Bare feet. He didn't look dead at all. He looked like he was sleeping, dreaming of something far away. Kelley put his hand on the man's chest. No heartbeat.

"Can you do it?" Rudolph called from below.

Kelley pointed at a wall of lead a dozen feet wide and seven feet tall. It had been erected as protection from the machine's rays. "You'll be safe behind there."

The emperor and his advisors looked at one another a moment, then scurried behind the wall.

Kelley looked at the cousin's smooth face again. Had he deserved to die so young? Was he a good person? Kelley had never met him in life. Maybe God had selected him for death. Perhaps he was wicked and cruel, and it was a kindness to the world to be rid of him. Who was Kelley to decide his life or death? Kelley tried to convince himself he wasn't deciding anything. Roderick had built the machine. Rudolph had given the orders.

Kelley was simply pulling the levers.

"What's happening over there?" Rudolph called from behind the wall.

Kelley frowned, ignored the emperor.

The alchemist circled to the other side of the dais, where a row of twenty levers connected to gears and pulleys and flywheels. He pulled the first lever, and the sound of rushing water filled the cavern. The waterwheel turned, slowly at first, then more rapidly. The other levers determined the order of the lenses, the flow of light, lowering the whole apparatus. It all had to be done in the exact order. Kelley had been over the scribbled instructions in his journal a thousand times. He knew the procedure by heart.

"Do you hear me?" shouted the emperor. "What's happening?"

Shut up, you lunatic. I'm working.

Kelley began to pull levers. The lenses lowered, surrounded the table. Overhead, gears meshed. Powered by the waterwheel, they began to spin. The big lens in the middle lowered until it was directly over the emperor's cousin, three feet from his chest. Portals opened overhead. Sunlight from above, reflected and re-reflected through lenses and mirrors, poured through the shafts, struck the lenses brilliantly white.

Kelley had expected it, but he flinched anyway.

Rudolph stuck his head around the corner, squinted into the light. "Damn you, alchemist. Don't you hear me talking to you?"

"If you want to live, Highness, get back behind the protective barrier."

Rudolph frowned but ducked back behind the lead wall.

Hatred and resentment swelled within Kelley. Who was this insane ruler to defy the will of God, to squander the resources of an empire for his mad schemes? How many had died and suffered for Rudolph's vanity? Kelley's need to defy the emperor compelled him at that moment like no other force on earth, his need to rebel palpable.

Since the emperor and his men were behind the lead wall, nobody saw the terrible thing Kelley did next.

When his act of defiance had been completed, he pulled another lever, rechecked the lenses, and retreated back behind the lead wall with the others. Here there was a final lever. He pulled it. Gears spun overhead. He could not see, but he knew what was happening. The lead box opened, and the stone's rays flooded the prism beneath it. The rays emerged from the other side of the prism and struck the lens directly above the emperor's cousin. The ceiling of the cavern jerked and danced with colored lights. Rudolph and his men cowered. A few crossed themselves.

The final lens bathed the emperor's cousin in warm red light. The waterwheel spun. A crack like thunder.

Kelley shoved the lever back into place, closing the lead box. He rushed up the dais, shut off the waterwheel. He pushed another lever, and the lenses encircling the dais retreated back to the ceiling.

He glanced at the table, jumped back, startled, eyes wide.

The emperor's cousin was up on one elbow. He glanced around the cavern. "Am I in hell?"

"Yes," Kelley said.

Rudolph and his men rushed up to the dais. "Cousin!"

"I remember the river," the cousin said. "What happened?"

"Resurrection!" Rudolph said. "Nothing less than resurrection."

Kelley studied the cousin's face. Warm and alive. It had worked.

They crowded around the young man, slapped him on the back. The mood in the cavern became boisterous and celebratory. They escorted the cousin out, talk of a banquet leading the way.

Rudolph looked back at Kelley over his shoulder. "Good work, alchemist. Secure things here before you come up."

And they were gone.

Kelley blew out a sigh, then sat down on the steps up to the dais. The only sound in the cavern was the flowing water, which had slowed again to a trickle.

He sat awhile.

Then he stood, again pulling the lever that lowered the apparatus with the circle of lenses, prism, and lead box. He climbed up on the table and unfastened the lead box from its place. He was surprised by its sudden weight and almost dropped it. He carried it down the steps to the bottom of the dais, then set it down hard, breathing heavily.

The morbid need to open the box and look inside nearly overwhelmed him, but the urge passed quickly.

He picked up the box again, grunted, and began the long climb back to the surface.

On his way back to the White Tower, he met the old nun who worked in the infirmary. She told Kelley that Roderick the astrologer had died.

CALLING ALL
DEAD PEOPLE

FORTY-TWO

Allen flipped another page carefully with the plastic stirs. "According to this, Edward Kelley was the only one to attend Roderick's funeral. Not even a priest."

"How awful," Penny said.

"Oh, no." Allen looked at the page, flipped back, read again.

"What is it?" Amy asked.

"Kelley put the philosopher's stone in the grave with Roderick," Allen said. "He said it seemed fitting. And he wanted to keep it hidden from Rudolph. A final act of defiance."

"Wow," Amy said. "And it's still there?"

"I don't know." Allen flipped another page, kept reading.

"Then we're good, right?" Penny said. "I mean, that solves the problem, doesn't it? The stone is buried. Nobody evil gets it. All is right with the world."

"It's not that simple," Amy said. "There's the Kelley diary, for one thing."

"Destroy it," Penny said. "Burn it."

"It's too late for that. We all know about it. The right spells would make us talk, even good old-fashioned rubber hoses and bamboo under the fingernails." Amy turned to Allen. "We've got to call the Society."

Penny frowned. "How the hell would that help?"

"If they have the stone for safekeeping, then Allen's out of danger. Making him talk won't matter."

"Then let's call in the Vatican," Penny said. "They can protect it better than your people."

"You're still forgetting I don't trust either of those organizations," Allen said. "We've come this far. I say we get the stone ourselves."

"Dammit," Amy said. "That's exactly what Cassandra *wants* you to do."

"Except I won't be fetching it for her," Allen said. "Ladies, I'm getting to the bottom of this. Are you with me or not?"

"You're Indiana Jones all of a sudden?" Penny said. "I'm not sure I like this side of you." A pause. "Or maybe I do."

"We don't even know what cemetery this astrologer guy is buried in," Amy pointed out.

Allen shook his head. "I know. I can't find anywhere in the manuscript where Kelley mentions the cemetery by name, and—" Allen sat up, eyes going unfocused, a strange expression on his face. "Cemetery."

Penny reached for him, stopped short. "What is it?"

"In my dreams," Allen said. "I've been seeing images of a cemetery."

Amy asked, "Would you recognize it if you saw it?"

"I don't know."

"Let's make that our priority," Penny said. "We'll put his name into Google and find out where he's buried. There's an internet café upstairs."

"And after we find out, then what?"

"Isn't it obvious?" A mischievous smile spread over Penny's face. "We go grave robbing."

Ninety minutes later they had nothing. None of the popular historical websites or Wikipedia mentioned Roderick by name, although accounts of alchemists and astrologers and other occult figures at court were plentiful. Amy brought up pictures of various graveyards around Prague, but Allen could not say for sure that any one of them matched his dream images.

"And the diary doesn't say either," Allen said. "Kelley says Roderick was entombed, and that he put the stone in with him. And he calls Rudolph a madman. But nothing about the name of the cemetery."

Penny turned away from the computer screen, rubbed her eyes. "This is useless."

"If I had all the time in the world, I could find it," Allen said. "But if I have to dig up a grave, I'd like to be in and out of the cemetery before nightfall."

"Why before nightfall?" Penny asked.

Amy put her fingers up to her mouth and mimed a set of fangs.

Penny blanched. "Oh, yeah." Amy's recent revelation still troubled her.

The three of them sat there. A minute passed.

"There might be somebody who can help," Amy said.

Penny crossed her arms. "If you say somebody from your precious Society, I'll scream."

"No. Somebody freelance. The Society puts him on specialized errands from time to time."

"This person is safe?" Allen asked.

"He can keep his mouth shut, if that's what you mean."

"Call him."

Amy and Allen stood in the doorway of the two-story brick building in the old Jewish Quarter. The Quarter—*Josefov*—had an almost claustrophobic feel, the old buildings crowding the narrow, cobblestone street, souvenir kiosks hogging much of the sidewalk. To Allen, the Quarter felt old, with so much more history then the Letna area and the younger Holešovice suburb.

Amy raised her hand to knock but cast a sideways glance at Allen. "You sure about this?"

"There's no time for anything else."

It was already late afternoon. It had taken hours to track down Amy's contact, and Allen felt more and more nervous every minute they inched toward nightfall. Allen worried with growing apprehension that there were still bits of Cassandra's vampiric hypnotism lingering in his subconscious, and he couldn't be sure how he would react if he saw her again.

Amy knocked. They waited.

Somewhere nearby Penny had installed herself at a café or coffeehouse. She didn't tell them where in case Allen and Amy were interrogated, but she was close at hand in case she needed to effect some kind of rescue or, at the very least, call in the cavalry. Penny had raised holy hell about being left out, but she could see the wisdom of the maneuver.

Amy was about to knock again, when the door opened.

"Abraham Zabel?" Amy asked.

The man looked from Amy to Allen and back again. "You're the one who called earlier?"

"Yes."

He nodded. "I'm Abraham Zabel. Please come in."

Allen thought Zabel did not look anything like he imagined a wizard should look. Maybe he was thinking too much of Gandalf. Zabel looked like Allen's dentist. Allen hated his dentist.

Zabel led them into a small sitting room. The furnishings were old—not Commie surplus, but not quite antiques either. Threadbare chairs, a table that needed polishing, tall shelves filled with books, a small Persian rug, also threadbare.

Zabel didn't sit, didn't offer chairs to Amy or Allen. "So what can I do for you?"

"We need to speak with a dead man," Amy told him.

Zabel nodded. "Uh-huh. Who's paying for this?"

"I'm with the Society. I know you've done jobs for us before, and I was hoping our credit was good. It's sort of a rush job."

Zabel frowned, eyes darting around the room. "What do you know about my work for the Society?"

"No details," Amy said. "I heard your name, knew you were in Prague. I'm not even sure you have a spell for what we need, but we had to try something."

He seemed to relax, scratched his chin. "I have a spell. How long?"

"What?"

"The person you want to speak with," Zabel said. "How long's he been dead?"

"A little over four hundred years," Allen said.

Zabel laughed. "Who do you want, Rudolph the Second himself?"

"Edward Kelley."

Zabel stopped laughing. "Who sent you here? Somebody's playing a joke on you. Or on me."

"Please," Amy said. "We think the philosopher's stone is—"

"The philosopher's stone?" Now Zabel laughed again. "Now I know you're jerking me. Save it for the tourists, okay? We've all heard the legends. I don't have time for jokes."

"This isn't a joke," Amy said.

"It doesn't matter," Zabel said. "You expect me to pluck a four-hundred-year-old ghost from the cosmos and bring him here so you can play twenty questions. Spells like that are complex. I'd need a lock of his hair or some clothing, something to help focus the spell. Otherwise it's pointless."

"What about this?" Allen held out the manuscript. "It's Edward Kelley's diary."

This caught Zabel by surprise. He looked at the manuscript. "His what?"

"I found it in Strahov Monastery," Allen said. "It's handwritten."

Zabel reached for the manuscript, and took it carefully. "This has to be some kind of hoax."

Allen shook his head. "It was kept in the library's special collection. It was among the items relocated from the castle."

"The philosopher's stone." A hint of reverence crept into Zabel's voice. He ran his hand over the cracked leather. "Lead into gold. It's nonsense."

"I don't think it has anything to do with gold," Amy said. "The stone represents a kind of power. Something never seen before."

They stood in a small circle, nobody speaking. Zabel had a faraway look in his eyes. He bit his thumbnail in thought while he held the manuscript in his other hand.

"I think," Zabel said, "that you've piqued my curiosity. Wait here."

Zabel left and returned two minutes later with a black leather bag, the Kelley diary tucked under one arm. He motioned for Amy and Allen to follow him.

Amy asked, "Where are we going?"

"To the roof," Zabel said.

They followed him up to the second floor, down a hall and into a small bedroom, up a tight spiral staircase to a trapdoor in the ceiling. Zabel slid back an iron bolt, threw the hatch open. Daylight flooded in.

They climbed out onto the roof. There was a clean breeze, a good view of the castle beyond the river. Zabel pulled over a small table, placed the diary in the center. He opened his black bag and began to fish around for items. He came out with a squat, black candle, lit it from a book of matches, and set it next to the diary. Allen squirmed at the sight of the open flame near the old manuscript but said nothing.

Zabel measured various powders into a mortar and pestle, crushed some dried leaves and other ingredients into the mix. He mumbled words that danced just at the edge of Allen's comprehension.

"Can I help with something?" Amy asked.

"Just stay out of the way." Businesslike. No time for chitchat.

When he'd crushed and mixed the powder to his satisfaction, he took a handful, flung it at the candle flame with a few harsh syllables.

A purple gout of flame erupted from the candle, engulfed the entire rooftop. Allen and Amy flinched, but the flame was cool, didn't burn. The purple light continued to shimmer around them, turned the world beyond the rooftop into a hazy blur, like they were looking at Prague through the bottom of a bottle of grape soda.

"Damn," Amy whispered.

Allen agreed. Damn.

"This is a particularly potent casting," Zabel said. "Usually I do this for people who've lost a loved one, six months dead or a year. I thought I'd better crank up the power for what we need. I hope I haven't overdone it. I wouldn't want this to turn into a cattle call."

"What's that?" Amy asked.

"Sometimes the summoning catches other spirits. Not all ghosts are at the same level of self-awareness. A powerful spell like this . . . moths to a flame. Even when it's not meant for them, they often come anyway."

"That doesn't sound very useful," Allen said. "Do we have to wait very long or—shit!"

Allen jumped back, bumped into Amy. A glowing apparition hovered in front of him. A young girl, a ragged slice across her throat. Her eyes were hollow, her mouth open, a vague moan.

"That's just Bethany," Zabel said. "She haunts the building next door, so she didn't have far to come. Murdered, I think, but I don't know the whole story."

"Great." Allen tried to sound sarcastic, but it came out slightly frightened. "How many more of these things?"

Zabel grinned. "Wait and see."

FORTY-THREE

As wizards go, Zabel is a better technician than he is a scholar. You can see he has little interest in reading my diary. To him it's more useful as a component for his spell. But he knows about the philosopher's stone—the legends, anyway. The notion that the stone holds some secret power appeals to his natural wizardly greed for power.

I suppose it's possible that—

Did you feel that? No? Okay, sorry. Got distracted. As I was saying—

There it is again!

Don't tell me you didn't feel that.

I feel it tugging me so hard that I dig in my heels. Not actually my heels, of course. That's just the outside manifestation of my resistance. If you were able to see me being dragged along the halls of Prague Castle, you'd see my heels digging in, my hands grabbing at doorknobs and window ledges, like a doomed astronaut trying to keep from being blown out an airlock. That's what it looks like, but it's with my mind that I resist.

I don't fight it too long. Too strong. Some mighty hand that has reached for me, grabbed me.

I go with the flow and start to fly, sailing over the castle walls and toward the river. I haven't been this far in decades. I stop wondering what's happening to me, such is the awe of seeing this part of Prague again for the first time in so very long. I'm over the river now, a tour barge below me, young couples sipping wine. I am equal parts blue sky and wind.

The far bank comes into view, crowded *Josefov* beyond that. I have not seen the Jewish Quarter in three hundred years. I glance to the right and to the left. A half-dozen glowing streaks in the sky, ghosts like me. We converge on the same place.

A pulsing purple beacon on a *Josefov* rooftop. I feel like a kite being reeled in, right toward the rooftop. People standing there I recognize. I already know them, yet I've never met them before. Time works so strange here.

I land on the rooftop. Zabel is there, sending away other ghosts, lost souls. Confused. I don't want this. I try to blend in, hide toward the back of the crowd. Zabel spots me over the shoulder of another ghost, and I look away.

Come here.

I shake my head no.

Yes.

I resist, but it's no use. I float toward him. He has me now. The other ghosts fade, dissolve, dismissed. They evaporate to whatever perpetual doom they call home. It's only me and Amy and Allen and Zabel holding my leash.

You are Edward Kelley?

I say nothing. My ghost teeth bite my ghost tongue. The pain is real.

ARE YOU EDWARD KELLEY?

Yes.

Zabel pauses to say something to Allen and Amy, but I can't hear it. It's as if a translucent, purple curtain hangs between us. Zabel turns back to me.

Tell me about the philosopher's stone.

I say nothing.

Tell me.

No.

Now Zabel gets tough. I feel something, like he's reaching inside me, strong-arming. It feels like cold iron fingers in my chest, getting a hold of my soul, squeezing it like a physical thing. I scream, and nobody hears it. I cry. Nobody sees the tears.

I see the look on Zabel's face. Annoyed. Like he couldn't open a tough jar of peanut butter.

And then there is pain. I talk, spill everything I've ever known or will know about the stone. I'm not sure how long it takes. I talk until I stop, and then Zabel asks another question and I talk again. It becomes a kind of confession, but Zabel becomes impatient whenever I get too personal. He cares not one tiny shit about my tortured soul. Just the facts, man.

And I'm weeping. Telling it all over again. It has been so long, so many years. To talk to somebody and have them talk back. But he's finished before I am. I want to tell him so much more, so much I've seen over the years and centuries. Zabel's indifference is like a punch in the face.

Where is Roderick the astrologer buried?

I tell him. Why not? I'd tell him anything. Just please keep talking to me.

The Vysehrad. Prague's other castle.

FORTY-FOUR

"Where's he going?" Allen asked.

"I sent him away," Zabel said. "It was almost as difficult as summoning him in the first place."

"Did you find out? What did he say?"

"The Vysehrad," Zabel said. "That's where Roderick is buried. There's a cemetery there. I imagine that's where he is."

"What's the Vysehrad?" Allen asked.

"South," Amy said. "It's a fort."

"Tell us the rest," Allen said. "What else did he say?"

"Come with me." Zabel headed for the hatch in the roof.

Allen hesitated. "Where are you going?"

"This is important," Zabel said. "Hurry." He disappeared down the hatch.

"Come on," Amy said.

They followed Zabel down the spiral stairs and then down to the first floor. Zabel glanced over his shoulder to make sure they were still following. He led them through a cramped kitchen. Another door. More stairs. Down.

In the basement. Allen glanced around. A cupboard. A chair. Shelves with bottles and jars of who-knew-what. A small table with a dirty tablecloth. It was a small room, dimly lit. "What are we doing here?"

"Please," Zabel said. "Stand over by that wall." He pointed to the only wall bare of shelves or other furnishings.

Amy and Allen stood against the wall.

"Hold out your hands," Zabel said.

Amy and Allen looked at each other.

An impatient sigh from Zabel. "Come on, come on."

Amy and Allen each held out their right hand. Zabel placed a smooth chunk of quartz into each upturned palm, muttered a smattering of unintelligible words.

Allen felt himself go rock-solid stiff.

He tried to turn his head, blink his eyes. No go. He was a statue. He couldn't even glance sideways to see if the same thing had happened to Amy, although he assumed it had. He couldn't even feel himself breathing.

"You're both okay," Zabel said. "But I need to keep you on ice while I check this out. It's still hard to believe. The philosopher's stone. But if it is true . . . well, that's the wizard's jackpot, isn't it?"

Allen thought, *Eat shit, cocksucker* as loud as he could on the off chance wizards could read minds.

"I might have more questions for you," Zabel said. "So I'm keeping you until I can confirm or deny this fairy tale. I'll need to go up to my office, gather some things, look up a few spells. Then I suppose I'm off to the cemetery. Now, don't go anywhere, you two."

He went back upstairs.

Allen tried to move any part of his body—finger, toe, tongue, eyebrow. He might as well have been carved from marble. How many minutes slipped by? Thirty? Forty? An hour? It was amazingly difficult to measure the passage of time when one was forced to remain utterly motionless. No windows. No sounds. This could drive him mad in no time flat. He could not stop trying to look at Amy.

Allen heard something, almost like a faint scratching. He would have whipped his head around to look if he hadn't been frozen. The door creaked open. Footfalls came down the steps, a strange clicking. Oh, hell. What was coming for them? Maybe Zabel had decided he didn't need them after all and had come to tie up loose ends.

Allen tried one more time to move any part of his body. Stone still.

The wolf's head came into view. There was still an instinctual moment of fear before relief flooded him. Penny. Thank God. He tried to will the wolf to action. *Come on, knock the quartz out of my hand. You can do it. Come on, figure it out.*

The wolf looked back and forth between Allen and Amy, pacing anxiously. Penny emitted a questioned sound halfway between a whine and a growl, then sat in front of Allen, head cocked.

Get the quartz. Come on. Fetch.

Penny pawed at the air, edged forward, and put her paw on Allen's leg. The wolf snorted. When Allen didn't reply, she got up on her hind legs, put her paws on his chest. Her full enormous wolf weight knocked him back into the wall. His whole body shifted, and the quartz slipped out of his hand, rattled on the stone floor.

Feeling flooded back into Allen's body.

"Oh . . . *shit.*"

Hot needles scorched his knees and the elbow of the arm he'd used to hold up the stone. He collapsed to the floor, moaned, rubbed the circulation back into his elbow. Who knew standing still could be so grueling?

Wolf Penny licked his ear.

"Turn back into a girl before you do that, okay?" Allen moaned again, rolled over and looked up at the wolf. "Did he see you come in?"

Penny shook her head.

Allen looked at Amy. She still stared straight ahead at nothing, mouth slightly open, hand outstretched, the chunk of quartz still in the center of her palm. "The rock in her hand," Allen said. "Get rid of it."

Penny bumped the bottom of Amy's hand with her head, and the quartz went flying.

"Motherfucker." Amy fell back against the wall, slid into a sitting position, rubbed her elbow, and stretched out her legs. "I need to start doing yoga or something."

Allen looked at the wolf. "You going to change back?"

Penny shook her head.

"She doesn't have any clothes," Amy said.

"Oh yeah."

Amy stood, stomped her feet trying to get the feeling back. "We've got to get out of here. Maybe we can sneak back up the front stairs without Zabel hearing. Run out the front door."

"No," Allen said. "He still has the Kelley diary."

"So what?"

"I'm not leaving without it."

"When did you get all action hero all of a sudden?"

"There's information in it," Allen said. "We've come too far just to let it go."

"Let's look around." Amy headed for a cupboard against the far wall. "Maybe there's something we can use for a weapon."

She opened the cupboard, her hand going to her mouth to stifle a scream. She jumped back. Penny growled.

Allen's eyes went big and round, his mouth falling open.

"Damn, that light's bright," said one of the severed heads in the cupboard.

Six heads. Three on the top shelf, another three on the bottom.

"It talked," Amy said.

The wolf whined, hid behind Allen's legs.

"What day is it?" asked one of the top-shelf heads, who had a thick black moustache and eyebrows. "Can you take me outside? I haven't seen the sun in so long."

"Stop complaining," said the head next to him. "I've been in here longer than any of you."

"You'll have to excuse us, miss," said a bald, bottom-shelf head. "It gets a little tedious in here. Hard to pass the time."

"We could start the choir again," suggested the moustache head.

"All you know are fucking Journey songs," said baldy.

"Jesus," Allen said. "Close the cupboard."

"No!" all the heads said together.

"Let's just leave," Amy said.

"Wait!" said the freshest-looking head. "I know you, don't I? London, about two weeks ago."

Amy squinted at the head. "Pascal?"

"Yes. I'm sorry, but I've forgotten your name."

"Amy."

Allen said, "You *know* him?"

"He's a Society official," she told him. "What happened to you, Pascal?"

"It's a long story," Pascal said. "You've got to get me out of here."

"Us too," said one of the other heads.

"Shut up," Pascal snapped. "I'm talking to somebody."

"We can't leave yet," Allen told the head. "Zabel has something of ours, and we need to get it back."

"Where's Zabel now?" Pascal asked.

"He said he was going to his office," Amy said. "Maybe he's still there."

"Don't go to his office," Pascal said. "He's got it rigged with subliminal messages. You'll be helpless."

Allen looked at the wolf. "How did you get in here, anyway? The front door?"

Penny shook her head.

"Did you find an open window?"

The wolf nodded.

"Can you get on the roof?"

The wolf nodded.

Allen scratched his chin, thought for a moment. "Okay, people, here's the plan."

Amy raised an eyebrow, the hint of a smile tugging at the corners of her mouth. "You're making plans now?"

"Just huddle up and listen," Allen said. "Amy, I want you on the street. At least one of us needs to get away clean. Head, you're with me. I need inside information. Now pay attention. Here's how it's going to go down."

They eased up the stairs from the basement. When they reached the ground floor, they split up. The wolf padded back to the kitchen to the open window she'd come through in the first place. Amy slipped out the front door, closed it behind her as gently as possible.

"Okay, head, it's just me and you now," Allen whispered. "Where's Zabel's office?"

"Will you stop calling me head? My name's Pascal."

"Why does your voice sound weird?"

"I have a stone in my mouth," Pascal said.

"Why don't you spit it out?"

"Because I'll die," Pascal said. "The office is upstairs."

Allen started up the stairs with the head under his arm. He stopped every few steps to listen. Had Zabel already gone? If so, maybe he'd left the diary behind. Allen could do with a bit of good luck. They reached the second floor. Allen paused again but didn't hear anything.

"Turn right," Pascal whispered. "The office is all the way at the end of the hall."

"You said there was a window that faced the street?"

"Yes, and a small balcony beyond, or maybe it was just a large flowerbox. I didn't get a good look."

"Okay," Allen said. "Come on."

He tiptoed down the hall to the office, pressed his ear against the door but heard nothing. He knelt, looked through the keyhole. He couldn't see much. No movement.

"I don't think he's in there," Allen said.

"Let me have a look," Pascal said.

Allen held the head up to the keyhole.

"I think you're right," Pascal said. "His desk is right across from the door, and I don't see him."

Allen tucked the head back under his arm, tried the doorknob. Unlocked. He pushed it open slowly, stuck his head inside. Nobody there.

The Kelley diary sat in plain sight in the center of the desk.

"Sweet," Allen said. "Let's grab it and get the hell out of here."

"Not so fast," came a voice from behind Allen.

Damn. Allen's heart sank. He turned very slowly. Zabel stood there, an automatic pistol trained on Allen.

"Damn your eyes," Pascal said. "That's my gun."

"I saw no reason to throw it out," Zabel said. "Looks like it came in handy. Pull the trigger on this end, and the bullet comes out the other end, right? Pretty simple."

"You are a giant douche," Pascal said. "Just look at me. This isn't over."

"I think I might take you up on the roof after this, Pascal. See what the crows make of you." Zabel waved the gun at Allen. "Stand back. We're going to have a little talk. For starters, I'd like to know how you got out of the basement."

Allen sighed. "I'm sorry, Pascal."

"Sorry for what?" asked the head.

"This."

Allen tossed the head into the air. It went nearly as high as the ceiling, then arced toward Zabel, who titled his head back to see Pascal's face screaming down at him.

Allen leaped on Zabel, a hand going to his gun wrist. They twisted, went to the ground. The head came down and bounced off Zabel's skull. Zabel winced, let go of the gun.

Allen grabbed it and stood, pointed it at Zabel. "Hold it."

Zabel didn't hold it. He stood slowly, rubbing the top of his head. "That hurt."

"I'll be taking that diary now," Allen said. "Nobody has to get shot here."

"Don't be ridiculous."

Allen lifted the pistol. "You don't think I'll do it?"

Zabel stomped his foot, pretended to jump at Allen. "Boo!"

Allen yelped, thrust the gun at Zabel, and tried to pull the trigger.

But he couldn't.

He looked at the gun, incredulous, pointed it at Zabel again. No matter how hard he tried to pull the trigger, Allen couldn't make his finger obey.

Zabel laughed. "You didn't think it would be that easy, did you? I have protections all over my house to keep people like you from doing me any harm."

"I told you!" Pascal was on the floor, facing a corner. "Damn it, what's happening? Turn me around."

"Lars, come here," called Zabel.

"Oh, shit," said the head.

Allen was still trying to pull the trigger. He couldn't believe it.

"For Christ's sake," Zabel said. "Give me that gun before you hurt yourself. You can't harm me, but you'll shoot your own foot off if you keep—"

The window exploded behind him, the wolf leaping onto the desk amid a glittering rain of glass. Penny wore a torn strip of tablecloth around her eyes to protect herself from the subliminal spells.

Zabel screamed.

Allen, who'd known it was going to happen, screamed anyway.

"I can't see," yelled the head. "What's happening?"

The wolf zeroed in on Zabel, snapping its jaws, growling. Zabel tried to retreat, but Penny's powerful jaws clamped down on his upper arm. He screamed again, hit the wolf on the side of the head with his free hand. "Lars!"

Allen tossed the gun aside, leaped forward, and grabbed the Kelley diary off the desk. As he turned, he bounced off the chest of a gigantic wooden monster. He sat down hard on the floor, then looked up at the thing made of patchwork bits of wood, like some kind of murderous arts and crafts project gone horribly wrong.

The monster reached out.

I'm going to die, Allen thought.

The monster grabbed the wolf by the scruff of the neck, flung it against the far wall. The wolf crashed with a pained yelp, knocked pictures off the wall.

Allen crawled past the golem's legs, the diary tucked under one arm. "Everybody out!"

"How am I supposed to do that?" shouted the head. "I have no legs."

Allen scooped him up by the hair and dashed from the room. He took the stairs three at a time, hit the ground floor hard, and sprinted for the front door. He opened it, ran through, didn't bother closing it behind him. He hit the middle of the street, searching for Amy.

He glanced back at Zabel's second-floor window. Had Penny made it out? The plan had been to scatter after Allen got his hands on the diary, but if Penny needed help then —

Fire exploded from the second-floor window, shook the street, chunks of brick and mortar pelting Allen and the sidewalk and street. Tourists screamed and scattered.

Another blast of fire, and the wolf flew through the window, fell limply, changing in midair, fur melting back to flesh. By the time Penny hit the street she was human again, naked and smoking.

"No!"

Allen rushed to her, knelt, set Pascal's head aside and scooped her into his arms. She was unconscious but alive, hair and eyebrows singed, covered with scrapes and bruises. "It's okay, Penny. I'm here. You're fine. You're okay."

Amy appeared at his shoulder. "Oh, my God."

"I thought you were getting a taxi," Allen said.

"I did." She gestured at the smoking window. "He took off when the world exploded."

The head faced Zabel's house. "Ha. Burn, baby, burn. Take that you son of a—ack!" The head choked, coughed, and spit out the bloodstone.

"Oh sh—" Pascal's eyes rolled up, and he was gone.

Allen cradled Penny to his chest. "She should never have come for us. She should have called for help instead."

"She did," came a voice from behind them.

Allen whipped his head around, saw Father Paul standing there with another big priest.

"We've got a van around the corner," Father Paul said. "Bring her and hurry. In about two minutes this place will be a logjam of police and firemen."

FORTY-FIVE

Ten seconds after Allen left with the priests, a wooden monster emerged from the smoking doorway of Zabel's home. The golem carried Zabel like a hurt child.

Once they cleared the doorway, Zabel coughed and wiped his sweaty, ash-smudged eyes on a sleeve. "Let me down, Lars. I can walk now."

The golem set him on the ground. Zabel leaned over, put his hands on his knees, gulped clean air. He stood straight and looked back at his home, flames in the windows and doorway. In the distance, the sirens grew louder.

So many of his tools and materials, valuable items he'd collected over a lifetime. All up in smoke. Damn them.

He replayed recent events in his mind. It had happened so fast.

The wolf had burst in and attacked him, would have likely savaged him to death if Lars hadn't pulled it off of him. Then Zabel had unleashed his most deadly spell, but the wolf had darted behind his desk, and the sturdy piece of furniture had absorbed the brunt of the firestorm. A second spell had blasted the beast back out the window, but not before half his office had been aflame. The smoke had overwhelmed him. He would surely have suffocated if Lars hadn't carried him out.

He motioned the golem to follow him, and they ducked down an alley. Lars was not exactly inconspicuous, but Zabel had some quality ingredients stashed in his car. He could put together a few spells, form a plan to make them pay.

One thing was for sure. Sooner or later they'd show up at the Vysehrad cemetery.

A particularly large raven perched atop a rusty weathervane across the street from Zabel's burning home. Everything it heard was heard by its master, Jackson Fay. Everything the raven saw, Fay saw. Everything it tasted, Fay tasted. This included a caterpillar and two especially sour black beetles.

Fay didn't enjoy that.

The raven watched as Zabel emerged from the smoking doorway, then led his wooden behemoth down a back alley. He wondered why Zabel had used wood. Maybe that was all that had been handy. Cheap material. Economical.

When Pascal had not returned from Prague, Fay had strongly suspected he would need to pay Zabel a visit. Probably the man knew something of the stone as well. Whatever Zabel knew, Fay would know soon enough.

Fay watched as Zabel instructed the golem to lie down in the back of an older model Mercedes. He threw a blanket over the golem, then climbed into the driver's seat, started the car, and began to drive.

Fay commanded the raven to follow.

Zabel would be a good test of Fay's strength. Zabel was a decent enough wizard, but Fay felt confident he had the edge in talent and experience.

He'd make damn well sure he had the element of surprise.

✻   ✻   ✻

Margaret floated through the gray void. She regretted the spell that had put her in this predicament. Her motivations were good—to warn her fellow Society members they might be in harm's way. Fay was a dangerous rogue.

Only one last task kept her tethered to the real world. She had to find Amy. But really, what did she care anymore? The balance of magic. Evil wizards.

Such worries were for the living.

FORTY-SIX

The walls were mint green and chipped. Fluorescent lights buzzed overhead. A twenty-year-old refrigerator rattled its swan song in the corner. Allen looked at the furniture, the chairs, the table; wooden and plain, scratched. A countertop next to the fridge held what appeared to be the first ever coffeemaker to roll off the assembly line.

Commie surplus. That made him chuckle. He put his head down on the table, tried not to see Penny's limp body, tried not to hear the explosion again, glass and bits of brick raining down.

Father Paul had taken him across town, to the basement of a small Catholic church. The rooms below were surprisingly plain and bureaucratic, like the offices for the Department of Motor Vehicles in his hometown. Bland and depressing.

Allen heard somebody come in the room, and he picked his head up.

"She's doing fine," Father Paul said.

Allen sighed relief, sank in his chair. He was suddenly exhausted.

"She can absorb a lot of abuse in wolf form," said the priest. "You saw Zabel cast the spell?"

Allen shook his head. "Just the aftermath. I told you. I was down on the street."

"I know." Father Paul lit a cigarette. "Just double checking some things. Quite a story."

Allen looked around the room. "What is this place?"

Father Paul blew out a long stream of cigarette smoke before answering. "It was built by a secret order of albino monks."

"What?"

The priest laughed. "I'm just fucking with you. KGB. It was the KGB who built it, back during the iron curtain days. The church was a trap to spy on Catholic dissidents. There was a group of priests back then opposing Soviet rule. Anyway, the bishop arranged for us to use the place for a while."

"Am I under arrest?"

Father Paul shook his head. "We're priests, Allen. Not cops. We can't arrest anyone. I mean, we can *kill* you, but not arrest you. But don't worry, we won't kill you either. We really were trying to rescue you when we busted into the Society safe house."

"That's what Penny said too."

"Do you want some coffee?" asked Father Paul. "I'm going to have some."

"How about a Coke?"

The priest got up and looked in the fridge. "No Coke. Pepsi."

"Okay."

Father Paul poured himself a cup of coffee in a paper cup, brought Allen a can of Pepsi, and sat down again. He puffed the cigarette, waited.

"At first I just wanted to go home," Allen said. "But now . . ." He shrugged. "I'm not sure how to explain it."

"Try."

Allen thought for a moment, then said, "I don't want to go home not knowing how all this turned out."

Father Paul smiled. "We should make a Jesuit out of you."

Allen smiled too. "No, thanks."

"Your other friend. What's up with her?"

"Amy?"

"One of that Society lot," Father Paul said. "She doesn't much care for my type." Father Paul tapped his white collar with his pinkie finger. "You think we can get her to work with us?"

"I couldn't say," Allen admitted. "Do you need her?"

"The Society and the Vatican are on the same page for this one. Nobody wants to see the philosopher's stone fall into the wrong hands. Nobody's exactly sure what the damn thing can do." A pause for a cigarette puff. "You've told me what you read in the Kelley diary, the caverns beneath St. Vitus and the strange machine the astrologer built. Why do you think the vampire wants the stone?"

Allen felt his eye twitch and looked away. He felt uncomfortable discussing Cassandra. "I don't know."

"She never mentioned anything while you were . . . together?"

"No."

Father Paul nodded slowly. "Okay." Puff. "You want to see her?"

Allen's eyes widened. See her? Of course not! And yet . . .

"Penny, I mean," the priest said. "She's up and around now, I think. I know you were worried about her."

Allen sighed and nodded. "Sure."

Father Paul pushed away from the table. "Follow me."

The priests had stashed Amy in a small office. A desk, a chair, a small bathroom. They'd politely given her a bottle of water when she'd asked for a drink. They hadn't treated her like the enemy, but it was clear they meant for her to stay put until they were ready to deal with her.

Where was Allen? Was Penny okay? All she could do was pace the tiny, bland room.

Eventually her bladder forced her into the small bathroom.

She peed, washed her hands at the sink. She lingered, massaging the warm soap into her palms, rubbed the knuckles. She looked at herself and was surprised she didn't appear more haggard. She felt like she could sleep for days. The cracked mirror above the sink fogged over, the room becoming suddenly chill. Her arms and legs breaking out in gooseflesh. Her breath came out as fog too. The bathroom was suddenly freezing.

Writing appeared in the fog on the mirror: *Are you Amy?*

Amy's eyes grew big. *Oh, shit.* She held her breath, not knowing what to do.

More writing: *Hello? Are you there?*

"I'm Amy," she said in a small voice. "I'm here."

The apparition came into focus slowly, right in front of Amy—an old woman with hollow eyes, skin tight across her face, making her look nearly skeletal. Her features were pinched and jagged. "Amy?"

"Who are you?"

"It's me, Amy. Margaret."

Amy gasped. "What happened?"

"What year is it?" the ghost asked. "So long. So many years wandering, looking for you. I got lost in there. You can't imagine what it's like."

"What are you talking about?"

"Never mind. It doesn't matter," Margaret's ghost said. "I've found you. I can rest. Fulfill my purpose and rest at long last."

Amy hugged herself, shivering now. "I d-don't understand."

"The Society is smashed," the ghost told her. "Fay has betrayed us. Beware of him. The Council is broken. He murdered me, Amy. I hung on to warn as many as I could. I have to go now. So long since I've felt the sun on my skin. I must fade now into the gray. It's pulling me. Like some kind of cosmic undertow." She began to fade.

"W-wait," Amy called after her. "What d-do I do now? I don't know what to do."

"I'm going now." The ghost's voice was a faint echo. "It's taking me. Beware of Fay. Beware."

The ghost vanished totally. Amy shivered, waited another few seconds but nothing else happened. She stumbled out of the bathroom and into the warmth, sat at the little desk, blowing on her hands.

She began to cry, not even completely sure who she was crying for.

Father Paul led Allen down a short hall to another door. Finnegan leaned against the wall waiting for them.

"I brought her some clothes," Finnegan said. "She's putting them on now."

Father Paul knocked. "You decent?"

"It's okay," Penny called from within.

They opened the door and entered. Penny wore a pair of blue gym shorts and a tourist T-shirt with the Czech flag on the front. Allen noticed Penny's legs, pale but smooth and well-toned. He noticed things like that now.

Penny bent over, tying a pair of white deck shoes. She stood and grunted.

"Are you okay?" Allen asked.

"My ribs are bruised," she said, "but it could have been a lot worse. I'll make it."

Penny handed a large, red bra back to Finnegan. "I appreciate that you think I can fill this thing, but I think I'll skip it."

The sheepish grin made the big priest look like some humble, friendly farmer. "Sorry, lass. I don't have a lot of experience buying such things."

"I think we're all glad to hear that," Father Paul said.

"You scared the hell out of me," Allen said gently. "Glad you're not dead."

A smile flickered across Penny's face. "Me too."

The door opened and Amy entered with a tall black priest behind her. Amy saw Penny and flashed her a big smile. "You're okay!"

"A few bumps," Penny said. "I've had worse."

"Thanks for bringing her, Father Starkes." Father Paul turned to Amy. "The Society and the Vatican have often been adversaries, young lady. But I think this time we need to work together. Perhaps if I could convince—"

"I'll help you," Amy said.

Father Paul blinked. "At the very least, I thought you'd need to check with your Council."

Amy sighed. "No. I don't need to check with them anymore."

Father Paul rubbed his hands together. "Okay, then. Let's go dig up a dead guy."

FORTY-SEVEN

High atop a rocky cliff, guarding the Vltava, the Vysehrad was much more a fortress than a palace. A zigzagging path climbed the cliff on the river side. A tram let off tourists on the other side. More respectable guidebooks than *The Rogue's Guide* suggested a scenic walking tour that started at the tram stop, passed the highlights of the Vysehrad, including Dvořák's tomb in the cemetery, and then took the zigzag path down the cliff to the river.

Allen, Amy, Penny, and the priests had elected to come up from the other direction; that was why Allen was puffing and wheezing and finally collapsed when they made it to the top. "Why is every place I need to go in this town uphill?"

Finnegan reached down, hooked Allen under one arm, and pulled him to his feet. "You're out of shape, lad."

"It's been a rough couple of days."

"The trams don't run this time of night, and it's likely that side of the Vysehrad will be more closely watched," Father Paul said. "More stealthy to come up this way."

"Unless they hear young Cabbot's heart pounding," Finnegan said.

Allen wondered if he'd go to hell for giving a priest the finger.

Two o'clock in the morning. This is exactly what Allen didn't want, to be skulking around at night with a vampire on the loose. He supposed a trio of battle priests, a werewolf, and a pretend witch might provide some measure of protection, but Allen didn't feel protected. He clutched the crowbar tight. It was part of his grave-robbing gear, but Allen was ready and willing to smash anything in the face that tried to kill him or suck his blood. The others carried a variety of pickaxes and shovels. Allen also wore a backpack loaded with a flashlight and sundry other gear. Most important, he carried the Kelley diary. He refused to let it out of his possession.

"Let's keep it quiet from here on," Father Paul said. "This way to the cemetery. It's behind the Cathedral of St. Paul and Peter."

The winding paths, pleasant and open by day, were poorly lit at night, jagged shadows making the castle grounds seem eerie and dangerous. Penny walked very close to Allen, Amy just as close on the other side. If they hadn't all been holding pickaxes, shovels, and crowbars, Allen's instinct would have been to take each of the girls by the hand. A kindergarten flashback.

"This is starting to seem like a bad idea," Penny whispered.

"*Starting* to seem like a bad idea?" Allen said.

"At least you can turn into a werewolf," Amy said to Penny.

"Lycanthrope," Penny said. "And I haven't seen you tossing around a lot of mighty witch magic. Why didn't you turn Zabel into a rabbit or something?"

"You know that's not how it works," snapped Amy.

Father Paul looked back and shushed them.

The girls lapsed into embarrassed silence.

The path took them to the cathedral. They circled behind it and found an iron gate. Padlocked. Father Starkes clipped it off with a sturdy pair of bolt cutters, and they all filed into the boneyard, Finnegan closing the gate behind them. Ahead of them lay tombs, monuments, mausoleums, with narrow paths in between. Expensive and ornate stonework, crosses, and stars of David.

"Hallowed ground," Father Paul said.

"What's that?" Allen asked.

"The vampire can't come here." Father Paul patted Allen on the shoulder. "That's why she needed a patsy."

"Thanks."

"A lot of dead folk in here," Finnegan said. "This might take a while."

"I think you're right," Father Paul said. "Let's break into two teams. We can cover more ground."

"Split up?" Penny didn't like the idea.

Neither did Allen. "I've seen enough episodes of *Scooby Doo* to know that's a bad idea."

"Father Starkes will go with you and Penny," Father Paul told Allen. "Amy will come with me and Finnegan. Don't worry. We're trained for this. But we can't take all night. We have to divide up and find Roderick's tomb."

They split up, each team going a different direction. They raked monuments with flashlights, glimpsing names, trying to hurry. An hour later, Allen's team ran back into Father Paul's.

"This is getting us nowhere," Allen said. "There's got to be a way to narrow the search."

Father Paul nodded. "I think you're right. Finnegan, break out the laptop. I want an uplink."

The big Irish priest slung off the backpack, pulled out a thin laptop computer, and booted it up. He set the computer on top of a tomb, the screen's glow eerie in the cemetery. "We'll have the satellite in a few seconds. Okay. Got it."

"Let me try," Allen said.

"Give it to him, Finnegan," Father Paul said.

Allen's fingers flew across the keyboard, cross-referencing

historical databases, Google, Wikipedia. He blinked at the computer screen, read the information again to be sure. "Oh . . . shit."

Father Paul read the screen over Allen's shoulder. "What is it?"

"The cemetery was founded in 1869," Allen said. "Two hundred and sixty plus years after Roderick died. There's no way he could be buried here."

"But the ghost said the Vysehrad cemetery," Penny insisted. "Zabel was clear about it."

Allen shook his head. "No. He said the Vysehrad—the castle. Remember? Zabel just assumed the cemetery."

"We can't search the whole castle, all the grounds," Finnegan said. "It would take hours and hours."

"More like days." Father Paul sighed, shook a fresh cigarette from his pack.

"Wait," Allen said. "Just nobody panic, okay? It's just another research project, right?"

The priests looked at one another. Father Paul said, "What do you have in mind?"

"Let's think it through. Hallowed ground, remember? If it were anywhere else in the Vysehrad, Cassandra could fetch it herself."

Father Paul nodded. "Good point."

"Right." Allen's hands went back to the keyboard. "So we concentrate on the cathedral and the cemetery."

The priests and the girls watched Allen go at it, calling up databases, following links to other links, web pages to dead ends, backing up, starting again. He became one with the machine, a virtual explorer in an endless world of bits and bytes and information.

I am the Matrix. That made him chuckle.

"What is it?" Penny asked.

"Nothing."

He arrived at the home page for a European architectural society, which took him to something about the castles of Europe. *Click*. The castles and palaces of Prague. *Click*. The Vysehrad. *Click*.

"This is all in Czech," Allen said.

"Hold on, lad." Finnegan took over the computer, his thick fingers entering information with surprising alacrity. "I've downloaded a translation program from the Vatican mainframe. It works fast. There you go."

"Thanks." Allen took over the computer again.

His eyes took in the words almost by osmosis. Vysehrad constructed in the tenth century. Stonework. Bulwarks. Battlements. Masons.

Freemasons.

Allen cleared his throat. "Listen to this. A Mason hall was constructed to house all the stoneworkers during the construction of the Vysehrad. The hall stood until 1701, when it was gutted by a fire and the stone blocks were looted for other construction projects. But the stone foundation was reused later, when the cathedral was built around 1869."

"What do Freemasons have to do with it?" Father Starkes asked.

"You've been neglecting your history lessons, Starkes." Father Paul looked at Amy. "Our lady friend can tell you."

Amy nodded slowly. "The Society hasn't been part of the Freemasons in hundreds of years. But way the hell back then . . . yeah."

"Edward Kelley had some sort of association with the Society," Allen said. "I'm not exactly sure. There was no time to read the journal completely. Some sort of alliance, I think."

Father Paul dropped the cigarette, mashed it out with his shoe. "Finnegan, get on the laptop and send the bishop an email. He can read it when he wakes up in the morning. Tell him we apologize, but we're going to have to bust into one of his cathedrals."

FORTY-EIGHT

Zabel watched them from the V of two trees about fifty yards away. The glow of the computer screen lit the small group. What were they doing? Obviously, finding Roderick's grave hadn't been so easy. Zabel had perhaps been strangely lucky. Better to let the priests and the college kids do the hard work, then Zabel could move in afterward and take the stone.

Six of them against one of him. He was regretting leaving Lars in the car. This might get tricky. Best to watch and wait for the right opportunity.

They were moving now.

He watched as the priests and the kids clustered around the door to the cathedral. Were they going in? The big priest approached the front door with a crowbar. A loud crack and the rattle of a falling chain. They were *breaking* in!

A large raven landed on a tree branch near Zabel. It flapped wings, squawked.

Shut up, you stupid bird.

He turned his attention back to the cathedral. They were going inside, but they left the tall black guy out front. A lookout. This gave Zabel an idea. He reached into his bag of tricks, took out a jar of goo, rubbed some on the palm of his hands. He bent down, grabbed a handful of loose dirt in each hand, and spread the dirt in a circular motion while chanting arcane words.

A mist seeped out of the ground around him, swirled around his feet. A thick fog. It began to spread.

The raven squawked again, and Zabel frowned at it. Many considered the raven to be a bad omen. A good thing Zabel wasn't superstitious.

"Find the light, Finnegan," Father Paul said.

"Right."

The Irish priest went fumbling into the dark, and sixty seconds later the lights, small electric bulbs made to resemble candlelight; came on. Charming. Every historical inch of Prague had been done over for the tourists.

Not nearly as grand and impressive as St. Vitus Cathedral, the Cathedral of St. Paul and Peter was nonetheless large and ornate, with rows of pews, hanging chandeliers, an altar with much gold, and other shiny stuff.

"Spread out," Father Paul told everyone.

Allen asked, "What are we looking for?"

"Let's hope we know it when we see it."

Allen strolled the aisle between a row of pews and a stone wall, glancing at the floor and ceiling. A narrow wooden door led to a small anteroom. Another door beyond that, stairs leading down. He descended into a small basement, where he had to feel along the wall for an old push-button light switch, which brought a naked high-watt bulb blazing to life overhead. Barrels and crates. Storage.

Think. Don't just wander around aimlessly. Who were these people?

Masons. Stoneworkers.

Allen got on his hands and knees and ran his hands over the

smooth, wide stones, trying get a fingernail in the crack where the stones met. Allen new nothing of stonework, but this seemed to be solid stuff. He frowned at his dirty hands. The floor was covered in thick dust. Nobody had been down here in a good long time.

He continued to crawl along, knees scraping a trail in the dust. He crawled between barrels and crates, smearing dust on his sweaty face. Back and legs aching, he gave up at last. He stood, looked back at the dust trail. He looked down at his clothes. *What a mess.*

Allen stood there with his hands on his hips. *Think, moron.* But his mind went blank. He simply gazed at the floor, the mental equivalent of a test pattern droning in his head.

He noticed something.

The trail his knees had left in the dust was interrupted by a clean line that ran across it. No dust at all. He bent down for a closer look. A perfectly straight line. No dust. Right down the center of the line was another crack where two of the big floor stones met. Was it his imagination, or was this crack very slightly wider than the others?

He put his face right down next to the crack and held his breath. A slight waft of cool air touched his cheek. That's what kept the dust from gathering along the crack. He crawled again, followed the crack. It went under a crate.

Allen stood, put a shoulder against the wooden crate and pushed. It didn't budge at first, so Allen got lower, gained leverage, pushed again. It edged out of the way. Allen heaved again, his face going red, until he'd moved the crate completely off the crack.

He slumped against the wall, sucked air for a few seconds before bending over to examine the stone beneath the crate.

Something was carved into the far end of the stone, almost up against the wall. It was about as big around as a drink coaster and worn almost smooth. Allen shifted around so he wouldn't block the light. He examined it again.

The Freemason symbol with the pentagram in the middle. Exactly like Amy's tattoo.

He jammed his crowbar into the crack, tried to pry up the stone. It barely budged. He grunted, his face almost going purple this time. No. He backed off. He would rupture himself.

He ran back upstairs. He spotted the big Irish priest, Finnegan, searching the altar with Penny. "Where is everyone?"

"Searching," Finnegan said. "You find something?"

"Maybe," Allen said. "But I need some muscle."

They followed him down to the basement. He showed them the Freemason symbol, explaining how he'd discovered it.

"Okay, lad, get on the other side," Finnegan said. "Put your weight into that pry bar when I give the word."

"Right." Allen jammed the crowbar into the crack, and stood ready.

Finnegan positioned his crowbar on the other side. "Now."

They both grunted, sweat breaking out on their foreheads. Penny stood back.

The stone block was thicker than Allen had guessed, but they finally lifted it high enough to shove it aside, stone grinding on stone, a whoosh of air sending puffs of dust between their legs.

They slid the stone aside, revealing a three-foot hole down into deep darkness and a narrow set of stairs that could accommodate one person at a time. Finnegan shone the flashlight down but couldn't see much.

Allen got on his belly, shoved his own flashlight into the opening. "A chamber. And a tunnel, I think." He put his foot on the top step. "Let's go."

"Hold on," Finnegan said. "Best we fetch the others first. It wouldn't be polite to go off and get killed, letting the others wonder what happened."

Allen felt something tug at him, some force urging him down the stairs and into the tunnel, but he resisted. "Okay."

While Finnegan was gone, the compulsion to go ahead, not

to wait for the others, nearly overwhelmed him. Part of him recognized this as Cassandra's doing. He had to face it. There was still some intermittent hold on him, something that only kicked in at certain key moments. It was Cassandra's will that he go down those steps. *Don't wait.* He had a mission to complete for her, and every second he delayed increased his discomfort, a deep sense of uneasiness at a task uncompleted.

"Are you okay?" Penny touched his arm with soft, cool fingers.

Allen closed his eyes tight, opened them again, and looked at her. He realized he was standing rigidly, with a white-knuckle grip on the crowbar. He took a deep breath and let it out. "I'm a little nervous is all."

Penny smiled crookedly. "Vampires and philosopher's stones? I can't imagine why anyone would be nervous."

Finnegan returned with Amy and Father Paul. They all leaned over, gazed down into the dark black hole.

Father Paul said, "Okay. Everyone wait here. I'll have a look."

"No way," Allen said. "I found it. I'm going too."

"If he's going, I'm going," Penny said.

"If she's going, I'm going," Amy said.

Father Paul grimaced. "Fine. Don't touch anything. Be careful."

Amy smirked. "Did you really just say to be careful?"

Father Paul ignored her, flipped on his flashlight, and descended the stairs. "Let's go."

The stairs delved deeper than expected, heading straight down at first before turning into a tight curve and spiraling. Allen noticed that the passage had been carved from raw stone. It grew colder as they went.

The stairs terminated in a round, twenty-by-twenty-foot chamber, the walls carved smooth. Their flashlight beams played over the walls before coming to rest on the circular door in front of them, carved pillars on either side. A larger version of the

Freemason symbol with the pentagram in the middle had been carved neatly and deeply into the center of the door.

A foot below the symbol was a phrase in another language.

"It looks familiar," Allen said. "Not Czech."

"It's Latin," Father Paul said. " *'Here dwell our dead, for nowhere else can they find rest.'*"

"I think it's a Mortality Motel," Amy said. "Sort of a slang term the Society uses for these burial places."

Father Paul shot her a questioning glance.

"I've heard talk about them," Amy explained. "Often a Society member would get branded a heretic, all that witchcraft, you know. They couldn't be buried in regular church cemeteries."

"There's an iron lever here." Finnegan gestured to the left of the door.

Father Paul said, "Pull it."

Finnegan grabbed the lever and pulled with both hands. It made a rusty, scraping noise as he pulled it down. There was the distant, muffled sound of grinding machinery, and the circular door rolled aside. There was a *whoosh*, and all of their ears popped, a gust of stale air escaping from the door crack.

"It's been sealed a long time," Amy said.

Penny stepped closer to Allen. "I'd rather it stayed sealed."

They entered, all of them clustered together. Father Paul stepped on a stone, which shifted. More muffled sounds echoed throughout the cavern.

"Uh-oh."

Allen said, " 'Uh-oh'? What do you mean, 'uh-oh'?"

On high shelves lining both sides of the hall, tiny flames sprang to life. The group flinched at the sudden pops of flame.

"What is it?" There was a bit of panic in Penny's voice.

"It's okay," Father Paul said. "I think I just hit the light switch."

Amy said, "Oil lamps. A spark spell to light them. Very simple to set up a remote-control trigger."

Penny raised an eyebrow. "You know, I've yet to see you do one bit of magic."

Amy gave her the middle finger.

The flickering lamps provided ample light, and they took a good look at the long hall. A vaulted ceiling arched twenty feet over their heads. The hall was fifty feet wide and twice again as long. Unadorned tombs cut from plain stone lined the walls. Clay urns sat on low pillars throughout the chamber. A dozen empty suits of armor stood along each wall, holding up swords in eternal salute, lamplight playing across dull metal breastplates.

Finnegan lifted the nearest urn carefully from its pillar, removed the lid, and peeked inside. "Looks like it's full of dust."

"Ashes, I would imagine," Father Paul said. "I think you have somebody's remains there."

"Bloody hell." Finnegan promptly returned the urn to its pillar.

"There." Allen pointed to the large tomb all the way at the other end of the hall. Some instinct drew him on.

They followed Allen to the tomb. Again it was plain, except for a single word carved into the center of the lid: *Roderick.* Allen felt his heart beat faster.

Finnegan stepped forward. "One more time, lad."

They jammed their crowbars into the slight crack of the tomb's lid. The great slab of stone was unbelievably heavy. Allen felt the muscles strain along his arms and back. The Irishman's face turned the color of a ripe tomato. Once the lid started moving, it went fast, tumbling over the other side, crashing to the stone floor with a racket to wake the dead.

No, I hope not, Allen thought. *Let's not wake the dead.*

They crowded around the open tomb.

Within lay the mortal remains of Roderick, astrologer at the court of Rudolph II. Bones. The remnants of a dark robe. Roderick laughed at them with hollow skull eyes. In his thin, skeletal hands, he clutched a lead box the size of carry-on luggage. The heavy box had crushed his chest, nestled in his rib cage like it was a bird's nest.

"Well," Father Paul said in a voice barely above a whisper. "There it is."

They all stood frozen a moment, the weight of history demanding a little respect.

"Let's get the show on the road then." Finnegan reached for the box.

"No!" Allen had not meant to shout. The idea of somebody else taking the stone suddenly panicked him. "I've come a long way for this. Let me."

Finnegan looked to Father Paul, who nodded.

Allen reached inside and grabbed the box by the handle on either end. Heavy. He tried to lift it. *Really* fucking heavy.

Finnegan said, "Lad, maybe I should—"

"No, no," Allen said. "I got it."

With a final heave, Allen was barely able to lift it out. Roderick's skeletal fingers slid from the box. The skull's mouth opened.

And screamed.

The shriek was painful. They clapped their hands over their ears—all except Allen, who refused to let go of the box. The scream seemed as much in his mind as in his ears. After an eternal five seconds, the scream stopped.

And something else moved.

The suits of armor along the walls began to take lumbering steps toward them, their swords lifted high.

"Oh, shit," Penny said.

Finnegan and Father Paul drew pistols. "I think Roderick sounded the burglar alarm."

The suits of armor creaked and clanked, seemed to be working out the kinks, moving faster to cut off the group's escape route back to the surface.

"Run!" shouted Father Paul.

Allen was already moving, Amy and Penny right behind him. He heard the pistol shots at his back, the metallic *tunk*s of slugs piercing armor. He didn't look back. He had the stone. He would take it to his mistress.

Allen and the girls made it past the ghost knights right before they closed the circle. He hit the stairs and went up, grunting as he carried the box, sweat oozing from every pore. Gunshots echoed behind him.

He kept going. Up and up.

Father Paul watched Allen and the girls make it past the knights, but the suits of armor closed in, cutting him off. He and Finnegan had been surrounded.

They fired until their magazines clicked empty, the shots punching useless holes in the armor plating.

"No good, Boss," Finnegan said. "Got any magic wands?"

Father Paul grabbed an urn off a nearby pillar, launched it at the nearest knight with a two-handed throw. It struck the helmet, exploded in a cloud of ash, the helmet clattering away, shards of clay flying. The knight dropped its sword, began to twirl in a lost circle without its head to guide it.

Finnegan dove for the sword, grabbed it, popped to his feet and swung the blade, lopped off the metal arm of a knight that had been coming up behind Father Paul, who knelt and scooped up another sword.

They parried clumsy blows from the ghost knights. The clattering suits of armor were slow and awkward, but sheer numbers threatened to swamp the priests.

"Cut your way to the door," Father Paul shouted over the clanging weapons.

They hacked at limbs, sent helmets flying.

They were almost to the door when a knight thrust a long blade into Finnegan's chest. The big Irishman yelled, kicked away the empty suit of armor, pulled the sword out of himself, and let it fall to the floor. Blood gushed. He stumbled after Father Paul through the door to the other side. He collapsed, rolled onto his back.

"Oh, no." Father Paul knelt next to Finnegan.

"The door." Blood gurgled from Finnegan's mouth.

Ghost knights still lumbered after them.

Father Paul grabbed the lever, shoved it back into place. The door began to roll shut just as one of the ghost knights attempted to step through. The heavy stone door tried to close, jammed the suit of armor, slowly crushing it like an old car at a junkyard. It stayed jammed like that, a few of the ghost knight's gauntleted fingers still twitching, helmet crushed flat.

Father Paul returned to Finnegan. "We'll get you to a doctor. Hang on."

Finnegan laughed, his teeth stained red. "Don't kid me, okay? Get out of here."

"Shut up, you stupid Irish lump. Just stay still. I'll find a phone, and then we'll call in some help. It won't take too long to—"

Father Paul realized he wasn't talking to anyone anymore. Finnegan's eyes stared at nothing, lifeless and empty.

It had been a long time since Father Paul had performed last rites; he stumbled though them half blind, tears blurring his vision.

FORTY-NINE

Allen's shoulders and forearms burned with effort. The metal handles of the lead box dug harshly into his fingers, ground against the bones.

The girls were screeching something high-pitched and panicked behind him. He tuned it out. He had to deliver the stone or die trying. The compulsion throbbing within him was almost painful now.

Panting, he made it to the top of the stairs. He staggered through the cathedral to the front door, pausing only once to breathe deeply and lean against a pew.

"Wait!" Penny called after him. "We have to go back for Father Paul."

Allen didn't wait; he jogged to the front door and kicked it open.

And froze in his tracks.

A thick fog had rolled in, gray and damp. It completely shrouded the cathedral. Allen couldn't see three feet in front of him. Amy and Penny halted behind Allen, gaping at the fog.

"Where did this come from?" Penny asked.

Amy shook her head. "I don't think it's natural."

"I have to go." Allen began to walk into the fog.

Penny and Amy both grabbed him.

"What?" He shrugged them off. "Let me go."

"What's wrong with you?" Amy tightened her grip on Allen.

A steady gust of wind, nearly arctic, blew their hair back from their faces. They shrunk from it, startled.

The fog began to swirl. It split apart, a passage through the gray opening up before them. A tunnel in the mist.

There she stood at the end, an eerie blue glow around her.

"Cassandra," breathed Allen. He stumbled toward her.

Penny grabbed for him but missed. "What are you doing, idiot?"

"We've got to help him," Amy said. "She's controlling him."

Amy ran toward Allen, but Cassandra moved like a blur, was in front of the girl in a split second, catching her across the jaw with a sharp backhand. Amy yelped and crumpled to the ground.

Allen fell at Cassandra's feet, pushed the box toward her, panting, almost unconscious from the exertion. "I b-brought it. Please. Just like you asked."

Cassandra reached down, brushed her fingers against Allen's check. Her touch felt like ice. "My wonderful brave boy."

"Hands off, bitch." Penny stood twenty feet away. She kicked off her deck shoes. "He's mine."

Cassandra's slow smile didn't touch her eyes. "Go away, little girl. Before you get hurt."

"It's go time." Penny flexed her hands. Her face twitched. The transformation was abrupt and shocking, fur sprouting and spreading, mouth deforming, long savage teeth growing. Arms and shoulders stretching the fabric of the T-shirt but not ripping it. Razor claws at the ends of her long fingers.

Allen looked up from his place at the vampire's feet, eyes wide. He'd seen the wolf, but he hadn't seen her like this. She'd changed into some stage between human and wolf. It was still

Penny's face, but vicious, snarling, covered in fur. Penny preferred the term *lycanthrope*, but there was no doubt in Allen's mind.

This was a werewolf.

Cassandra's smile showed genuine amusement this time. "One of the old lupine clan. I'd heard there were still some of your kind about. This might prove sporting after all."

Cassandra darted at Penny with lightning speed, hands outstretched, but the werewolf ducked under her reach raked claws across the vampire's belly. Cassandra hissed pain, retaliated with a swift backhand, a glancing blow to Penny's head. She growled, backed away. They squared off, circling around each other.

Penny leaped, claws out. Cassandra put a foot against her chest and fell back, kicked, used Penny's own weight to send her sailing into the fog. Cassandra stood, fists up. Everything went dead quiet. A sad little part of Allen's brain told him to get the hell up and run, but he only lay there. Watching and waiting.

Penny flew snarling out of the fog, striking at Cassandra's face, three long rents in the flesh of the vampire's cheek. No blood. Allen watched in amazement as the wounds closed over, the skin smooth once more.

The werewolf attacked again.

Cassandra stepped forward, caught Penny in midleap, held her by the throat, lifted her off the ground. The werewolf snarled and kicked. Cassandra balled up her fist and punched Penny with alarming might square in the forehead. Penny made the sound of a wounded animal, head flopped, dazed. Cassandra lifted the werewolf with both hands, hurled her flailing into the fog.

Allen heard her land with a crunch and a yelp.

The silence stretched. Penny didn't return.

Cassandra smiled down at Allen. "That little distraction has been taken care of. Come. Bring the stone."

Allen tried to lift the box. He had nothing left and collapsed to the ground. "I can't."

"Never mind, my darling." Cassandra lifted the box like it was a basket of laundry, tucked it under one arm. With her other hand she lifted Allen to his feet. "Let us be going."

Allen hesitated. "You have the stone. Can't I stay? I . . . I'm so tired."

Her eyes caught his. "Allen."

The bite mark on his inner thigh flared hot. Desire for her radiated from it, soaked into every part of his body.

"Come along, Allen."

A dreamy grin split Allen's face. "Yes, of course. I obey, mistress."

She took him by the hand, and they disappeared into the fog.

Amy felt a throbbing in her head, dirt and grit on her face. How long had she been lying there on the ground? Only a few minutes maybe. She started to push herself up, felt hands lifting her. She turned, fist ready to strike.

"It's just me," Father Paul said. "Easy does it."

He helped her up. She immediately looked around, peering into the fog. "Oh, God. Where are they?"

"I just got here," the priest said.

She told him about Cassandra. "I don't know what happened after that."

"The vampire took him," came a voice from the fog.

Penny limped through the mist. She looked pale, hair matted. She held her side. "I landed kind of far away."

Father Paul rushed to her side, helped hold her up. "What happened?"

"She has Allen. And the philosopher's stone."

"Damn."

Another figure emerged from the fog, startling them. It was Father Starkes.

"Where have you been?" Father Paul didn't try to hide his irritation. "I told you to guard the door."

"Sorry," Starkes said. "I thought I heard something out there and went to take a look."

Father Paul rubbed his eyes. "Forget it." He looked up. "The fog is clearing."

"Where's Finnegan?" Amy asked.

"He didn't make it."

Amy gasped. Penny hung her head.

"We need to regroup," Father Paul said. "And then we get Allen back. And the stone too."

They limped away, bruised but determined.

None of them saw the watchful raven following them.

FIFTY

Allen awoke in a cavern lit by torches. There was a water-wheel, and a contraption with lenses hanging over a raised dais. A memory triggered something he'd read in the Kelley diary.

This was it. The machine for the philosopher's stone.

The trip from the Vysehrad to the woods behind Prague Castle had been a blur. He only knew he had to follow Cassandra; his whole purpose in life was to serve her. He didn't know what she wanted with the stone. It didn't matter. Whatever it was, Allen would do his best to make it happen, to earn her love, her kisses, her touch.

They'd entered the caverns beneath the castle through a hidden entrance in the woods. Cassandra told him it had taken her about five years to find it, but that had been a century ago. She couldn't use the entrance beneath St. Vitus any more than she could enter the Cathedral of St. Paul and Peter. Hallowed ground.

His stomach rumbled. How long since he'd eaten?

Allen had fallen asleep poring over Kelley's diary, had tried to make sure he knew how to operate the machine, the proper order to pull the levers that positioned the lenses. He was pretty sure he'd installed the lead box properly. He'd barely overcome a perverse desire to open the box and look at the stone.

What would this do to his beloved Cassandra? He couldn't guess, but he was determined to do it right and please her. They needed only to wait for daylight in the aboveground world. The power of the stone in conjunction with sunlight—that was the trick according to the diary. Allen didn't need to understand. He just had to make sure he followed directions.

His stomach growled again. He couldn't remember ever being this hungry.

A little brown spider scurried between his shoes. He snatched it up, shoved it in his mouth, chewed, swallowed.

Wait. That's not right.

Allen strongly suspected he needed to be rescued.

It was just after dawn, and they'd barely had any rest—just a quick meal and cups of coffee. They were back in the KGB basement of the small Catholic church. Nuns had come in to wrap Penny's bruised ribs and bandage a deep scratch on her forehead.

They stood around a conference table filled with automatic weapons and various explosive devices.

"Soon they'll be able to use the machine," Father Paul said, checking the magazine on a .45 Colt. "God knows what will happen. Father Starkes and I have to go. It's our job. I won't think less of you two if you decide to sit this one out."

Amy and Penny exchanged glances.

"No offense, Father," Amy said, "but fuck you."

Penny's tone was somewhat more respectful. "Father Paul, I have to tell you, I've invested quite a lot of time into Allen. I'd hate to see him killed now. I think I'd better come along."

A wan smile unfolded across Father Paul's face. "Okay then. Let's gear up." He gestured at the arsenal spread across the table. "I don't know if we'll be up against animated suits of armor again. Frankly, I have no clue what we're in for. But Father Starkes and I are going to carry twelve-gauge shotguns. Maybe that can knock apart some armor plating. Select what you want."

Amy put her hand on an enormous pistol, lifted it. Heavy.

"That's a .50-caliber Desert Eagle," Father Paul said. "Might be a little too much gun for you."

Amy frowned. "Why?"

"The kick will knock you back into the last century." Father Paul handed her a small .32 revolver. "Maybe this."

She took the revolver but kept casting longing glances at the Desert Eagle.

In a quiet moment, Amy found herself standing shoulder to shoulder with Penny, going over the equipment, while Father Paul and Starkes were off doing something else. Amy cleared her throat and said, "I think I need to apologize to you. I think it's my fault about Allen."

Penny shot her a sideways glance. "What are you talking about?"

"Remember the morning in the art museum? God, that seems, like, a hundred years ago." Amy told Penny about Allen and Cassandra. "I suspected Allen might not be in full control of himself. I should have said something."

Penny lapsed into sickly silence.

"I'm sorry," Amy said.

"It's okay," Penny said. "I'm glad you told me."

They went about their business in silence. Starkes and Father Paul thumbed double-aught shells into their pump-action twelve-gauges. They hung bandoliers of additional shells over their shoulders. Shoulder holsters with .45 automatics. The priests pried open a crate, revealing a stash of hand grenades. They passed the grenades around, along with extra ammunition. Kevlar vests. Utility belts with flashlights and miniature, compact tools. Combat boots. Black fatigues with the Vatican Battle Jesuit patch on the sleeves.

"This stuff is weighing me down." Penny stripped off the Kevlar, kicked off the combat boots. "And I have to be able to transform quickly." She put the deck shoes back on, picked out a small black T-shirt with the Battle Jesuit crest over the pocket.

"I like the boots and the pants and the belt, but I want a T-shirt too," Amy said. "That stuff you wear is too hot."

"Fine," Father Paul said. "I'm not sure Kevlar is likely to stop what we might encounter anyway."

He grabbed a pair of pickaxes, handed one to Starkes. "Let's roll."

The morning sun was well into the sky when the four black-clad strangers armed with pistols and shotguns walked through the courtyards of Prague Castle toward St. Vitus Cathedral. Tourists scattered before them.

"We seem to be causing a scene," Penny said.

Father Paul didn't break stride. "No time to be subtle."

Two security guards in blue shirts with silver badges stopped in front of them, holding up their hands and yelling at them in Czech.

Father Paul flashed his Jesuit ID. "Vatican business, gentlemen. Stand aside."

The guards looked at each other. They stood aside.

"You can do that?" Penny asked.

"Apparently."

They entered the cathedral, more tourists scurrying out of their way. They headed for the entrance to the burial vault. A tour group stood aside to let them around the velvet rope and down the stairs to the chambers beneath St. Vitus.

"Allen told me it was all the way at the end," Father Paul said. "At least that's what he read in the diary."

They marched past the tombs, and the chamber ended in a black wall of whitewashed brick. Father Paul lifted a pickax. "Man, I hope this is the right place."

He swung the pickax and it bit deeply into brick and mortar. Starkes took his place next to him. They destroyed the wall in three minutes flat, opening a passage to the tunnel beyond, tall and wide enough for two people to pass through.

And that's when the zombies spilled out.

FIFTY-ONE

"I think it's time."

Allen looked up from the Kelley diary, beaming his adoration at Cassandra. "Yes?"

"Yes."

The vampire climbed the steps of the dais, unfastened her dress, and let it fall. She stood naked, smooth and white, the power of her sexuality radiating, seeming to fill the cavern. The bite mark on Allen's thigh flared again. His longing for her made him ache.

Cassandra lay on the table, folded her hands over her breasts. "Begin."

"Yes, mistress."

Allen rushed up the steps of the dais, the Kelley diary in his hands. He began to pull levers, always double-checking the diary as he went. The cavern echoed with the sound of reluctant machinery forced to move after being dormant for hundreds of years. The sound of rushing water filled their ears. At first the waterwheel didn't budge, but finally it groaned and creaked as it began to turn, slowly at first, but then more rapidly.

More levers. Allen's heart pounded so hard that it threatened to leap from his chest. The gizmo above the dais lowered, the lenses spinning into place to the racket of machinery and rushing water. Allen pushed another lever to activate the sunlight shafts and reflectors. The sunlight hit the lenses.

Then the sunlight hit Cassandra.

She screamed, writhing, on the table. Thin tendrils of smoke rose from her body.

Vampire + sunlight = bad idea.

"The stone!" she screamed. "Activate the stone."

Allen flew down the dais steps, stumbled and went down. He picked himself up, ran behind the protective lead wall, and pulled the final lever.

The cavern exploded with light. The sound of a thousand howling souls assaulted Allen's brain. He dove to the floor, eyes shut tight, hands over his ears. The floor shook, the cavern rumbled.

It felt like the end of the world.

He forced himself to stand. It had been long enough. He pushed the lever back into place, and the white light dimmed. He ran back to the dais, shut off the waterwheel. He pushed more levers, the lenses lifting back out of the way.

He backed down the steps, watched the woman on the table, his mouth hanging open, eyes wide. He waited.

At last, she sat up, swung her legs around slowly to stand on the floor. She looked at her own hand. It shook. She blinked away tears in her eyes. "Alive. Oh, my God. After a thousand years, walking the earth as undead." She laughed and cried at the same time.

"Allen, I'm alive again."

"They're dead!" Father Paul yelled.

He pumped a shell into the chamber and blasted a load of buckshot into the zombies that crowded the room. They kept coming, dozens of them, crawling over one another to reach the priests and the girls.

The zombies were half skeletal, leather chunks of flesh dropping off as they attacked. Mouths half full of yellow-brown teeth chewing at nothing.

Starkes and Father Paul kept pumping buckshot into the crowd, limbs and bits of flesh and teeth flying. Undead corpses piled up at their feet. A half dozen zombies surged past the priests to attack the girls.

Penny screamed.

A skeletal hand grabbed Amy by the shoulder. She gasped and jumped back. The zombie's arm came loose, hanging from her shoulder, where it still held on.

"I think the warranty has expired on these things." Amy pried the fingers from her shoulder. She used the zombie arm as a club, swung hard, knocking its undead head across the room. It bounced off a tomb, rolled around on the floor.

Penny kicked the leg of the zombie closest to her. The leg snapped and the zombie fell into a pile of bones and dried flesh. "She's right. These things are . . . well, kind of pathetic."

Amy reached into a zombie's mouth, pried out a tooth. "Souvenir."

Father Paul stopped firing the shotgun. The zombies crowded around him, pawed feebly at his chest. "Okay, this is just silly. These things have been decaying for centuries. They might as well be made out of tissue paper. Push them out of the way and let's get going."

They shoved the zombies aside, pushing them into piles of bones, kicking legs out from under them. They entered the hole Father Paul and Starkes had knocked into the wall, trudged through the dark passage beyond until they heard the sound of rushing water ahead.

Cassandra descended the dais steps to stand in front of Allen. She was as beautiful as ever, but there was something different about her too. A flush of pink in her cheeks. She touched Allen's face with warm fingers.

She was alive. She was a woman.

"You can't know what it was like, Allen." Her smile was warm, genuine. "Walking around, half cold to life, only half feeling everything that was happening to me." She ran both her hands over Allen's chest. "I can feel you. I mean really feel you, one human being to another." A pained expression struck her face. She looked away. "All the things I've done. A vampire can't feel remorse, Allen. God, I've done such terrible things. But I'm going to live now. It'll be different. Never again will I—"

A line of warm, red blood trickled from her left nostril. She wiped it away, surprised. "It must be some side effect. But look. It's warm. My blood is warm and human. Allen, this is the best thing that's ever—"

Another trickle of blood from the other nostril. Cassandra wiped it away, smearing red across her lips.

"Are you okay?" Allen asked.

"I don't know." She blinked, and blood ran from the corners of her eyes. She wiped it away, looked at the blood on her hands. "Something's wrong."

Do you remember when I used the machine to bring the emperor's cousin back to life? I suppose now is a good time to show you everything that happened.

Pay attention.

1601

Kelley looked at the cousin's smooth face again. Had he deserved to die so young? Was he a good person? Kelley had never met him in life. Maybe God had selected him for death. Perhaps he was wicked and cruel, and it was a kindness to the world to be rid of him. Who was Kelley to decide his life or death? Kelley tried to convince himself he wasn't deciding anything. Roderick had built the machine. Rudolph had given the orders.

Kelley was simply pulling the levers.

"What's happening over there?" Rudolph called from behind the wall.

Kelley frowned, ignoring the emperor.

The alchemist circled to the other side of the dais, where a row of twenty levers connected to gears and pulleys and flywheels. He pulled the first lever, and the sound of rushing water filled the cavern. The waterwheel turned, slowly at first, then more rapidly. The other levers determined the order of the lenses, the flow of light, lowering the whole apparatus. It all had to be done in the exact order. Kelley had been over the scribbled instructions in his journal a thousand times. He knew the procedure by heart.

"Do you hear me?" shouted the emperor. "What's happening?"

Shut up, you lunatic. I'm working.

Kelley began to pull levers. The lenses lowered, surrounded the table. Overhead, gears meshed. Powered by the waterwheel, they began to spin. The big lens in the middle lowered until it was directly over the emperor's cousin, three feet from his chest. Portals opened overhead. Sunlight from above, reflected and reflected through lenses and mirrors, poured through the shafts, struck the lenses brilliantly white.

Kelley had expected it, but he flinched anyway.

Rudolph stuck his head around the corner and squinted into the light. "Damn you, alchemist. Don't you hear me talking to you?"

"If you want to live, Highness, get back behind the protective barrier."

Rudolph frowned but ducked back behind the lead wall.

Arrogant fool. Hatred and resentment swelled within Kelley. Who was this insane ruler to defy the will of God, to squander the resources of an empire for his mad schemes? How many had died and suffered for Rudolph's vanity? Kelley's need to defy the emperor compelled him at that moment like no other force on earth, his need to rebel palpable.

Kelley glanced back over his shoulder. Rudolph and his men could not see him, would not witness what he was about to do. Roderick's words floated through Kelley's mind. *Everything must be exact. Perfect. The smallest thing can ruin it all, prevent the light beams from flowing properly.*

Kelley put his hand down the back of his pants and stuck his thumb up his own ass. He wiggled it around where it was moist and warm. He brought his hand out again, then stuck his thumb in the dead center of the lens hanging over the emperor's cousin. Kelley's every thought was bent on hatred for Rudolph. Kelley mashed his thumb hard against the glass, leaving a big, greasy thumbprint.

Fuck your immortality.

Not my most mature moment. But effective.

It seems the sweat and fecal matter had hardened over the years, the thumbprint crystallizing on the surface of the lens. Such a small thing, the tiniest imperfection. But it caused the beam to be off, kept the lens from doing its job exactly right. Roderick would have been able to explain the physics, would have been able to talk of particles and waves. I only know what happened in the simplest terms.

I fucked things up.

FIFTY-TWO

"**A**llen, help me!"

Cassandra clung to him, panic in her eyes. Blood spilled from her ears, left bright red trails down her white skin. An eyeball popped and oozed.

Allen backed away, shaking his head, eyes wide and horrified. "I don't know. I don't know what to do."

"What went wrong? I can't believe this." Bitterness laced Cassandra's voice. "All the time and effort. So many plans." The skin under her eyes came loose, began to slide down her face. "Damn it. This is bulls—"

Her bottom jaw fell off, landed with a wet splat on the cavern floor. Teeth knocked loose rattled on the stone. The rest of the skin melted off her body, revealing organs and bone, a beating heart.

Allen screamed. He took a dozen steps backward but was unable to avert his eyes. He was transfixed by the woman coming apart in front of him.

Cassandra cried a final, strangled scream before collapsing into a pile of steaming meat.

There was no psychotherapy on earth that would ever erase

that image from Allen's mind, but he felt something unclench in his chest, a veil lift from his eyes. He was free.

Cassandra was gone, and Allen was in possession of his own soul once again.

Father Paul led them over the dam, down the narrow stairs to the stream below, kept walking until the waterwheel came into view. He saw flickering torchlight. Someone was definitely down here. He kept his shotgun ready, motioned for the others behind him to stay alert.

He spotted Allen sitting on the bottom step of a raised dais, strange gizmos hanging over him, big glass discs. This must have been the machine he'd described before.

Father Paul jogged toward Allen. "Are you okay? We came as fast as we—what the hell is *THAT*?" He backed away from the still-melting heap of flesh and bone.

The others arrived and saw it too. Penny groaned. Amy turned away, made a gagging sound but managed to refrain from vomiting.

"That's Cassandra," Allen told them. "Or what's left of her. She'd wanted to use the machine on herself all along. I guess she was tired of being a vampire, wanted to be human again. I can't believe I'm going to say this, but I felt sorry for her. I saw the whole thing. She came apart right before my eyes. It was awful, the worst thing I've ever seen."

Father Paul looked at the machine, then back at the melted pile of Cassandra. "What went wrong?"

Allen shrugged. "No clue. Maybe the thing never worked at all." He hung his head, rubbed his eyes with his palms.

"It's all over now," Father Paul said. "I'll take the stone back to the Vatican, hide it in the secret room where we keep the Ark of the Covenant."

Allen looked up at the priest. "What?"

Father Paul laughed. "Just fucking with you. But we'll put it in a safe place."

The sound of a shotgun shell being pumped into a chamber forced all eyes to Father Starkes.

"Change of plan." Starkes leveled the shotgun at Father Paul. "The stone comes with me. Drop the weapons, and I won't splatter you with buckshot."

Father Paul said, "I have to say, Starkes, this comes as a bit of a surprise."

"You want a surprise?" Starkes smirked. "Check this out." He held the shotgun on Father Paul one-handed while he pulled a thin vial of red liquid from his pants pocket with the other. He thumbed out the cork, drank the liquid in one rapid motion.

Starkes's face began to twitch, the skin going rubbery. It stretched and distorted, then re-formed itself into the leering likeness of Abraham Zabel.

"It's that asshole," Amy said.

"I'm the asshole? You little fuckers burn down my whole house, and *I'm* the asshole?"

"You paralyzed us in your basement," Amy shot back.

"Oh, yeah," Zabel said. "Well, tough shit."

Penny took a step back, kicked off her deck shoes.

Zabel frowned. "What the hell is she doing?"

"This." Penny grunted, fur spreading across her body as she transformed into the half-wolf.

She sprang at Zabel, claws extended.

Zabel flung his hand up, barked a command word. Lightning sprang from his fingertips, caught Penny in midair. Her body convulsed with the electrical impact. She fell, hit the stone floor hard, and lay still.

Allen leaped to his feet. "Penny!"

Father Paul already had the .45 out of his shoulder holster. He ran for cover while squeezing the trigger, four quick blasts shaking the cavern.

Zabel blasted with the shotgun. Buckshot ricocheted off stone. He pumped in another shell, blasted again. Penny dove for cover one way, Allen another. Zabel and Father Paul exchanged fire. The priest scurried behind the protective lead wall, and Zabel followed him with the shotgun, pumping, blasting, and pumping in another shell.

"Stupid goddamn priest," Zabel shouted. "All I wanted was the stone. Now it's got to be hard. You want it hard? You got it."

Zabel scooped three gray pebbles from his pocket, blew on them, and tossed them to the floor of the cavern. They grew into armored spiders the size of beagles. They scurried behind the lead wall to attack Father Paul.

Father Paul's .45 thundered behind the wall. He ran out, the last spider pursuing him. It jumped at him, and Father Paul squeezed the trigger twice. The spider crumbled in midair, fell and rolled over on its back, legs curling up.

But Father Paul had broken cover. Zabel leveled the shotgun and squeezed the trigger. It bucked in his hands, buckshot scorching Father Paul's chest and belly. The priest spun and fell to the ground, hand going to his guts, blood oozing between his fingers.

"No!" Allen shouted. How had it come to this?

"Okay then," Zabel said. "Anyone else want to get dead? I didn't think so. Now, I'm taking that stone, and I'm going to walk straight out of—"

The shotgun suddenly glowed fiery orange in his hands. "Shit!" He dropped the shotgun, blew on his scorched palms. "What the hell?"

"Sorry for the dramatic entrance." Jackson Fay stood by the waterwheel, hands on hips, a manic gleam in his eye. "Hope I'm not interrupting anything."

FIFTY-THREE

"I realize I'm a little late to the party," Fay said. "And what I'm about to say isn't very original, but I'm afraid the philosopher's stone is coming with me. I'd say something too about standing aside or getting hurt, but the fact is, I have absolutely no problem hurting every single person here."

Zabel said, "I don't know who you are, dickhead, but you just bit off a mouthful of trouble."

"But I know who *you* are, Mr. Zabel," Fay said. "You are a sad, second-rate magician with delusions of grandeur. What do you think you would possibly do with the stone? You'd only hurt yourself. You make a good living as a hired spell-peddler. Stick with what you know."

Allen watched, held his breath.

"Okay, you know who I am," Zabel said. "Now tell me your name. I want to be able to tell everyone who I killed."

"My name is Jackson Fay."

"Uh . . ." Zabel slowly turned pale. "Yes. I've heard of you."

"Nothing unflattering, I hope."

"It doesn't matter," Zabel said. "I'll pit my skills against yours any day. Still, maybe we can talk this out, eh?" He wiped the sweat off his forehead with his fingertips. "So tell me. What do you think of *this*?"

He flicked his fingers at Fay, the sweat droplets flying through the air. Harsh syllables spilled from Zabel's mouth, and the droplets elongated and hardened, became flashing silver blades, slicing through the air toward Fay's face.

Fay spat words in return, blew a puff of air when the blades were six inches from his face. The blades jerked to a halt, transformed into silver butterflies, which flapped harmlessly away.

Fay laughed. "Not even close."

But Zabel was already running toward one of the torches on the wall. He tossed a pinch of dust into the torch flame, followed by elaborate, arcane hand gestures. The flame shot up into an arc and poured itself onto the floor between himself and Fay. The fire formed itself into a flaming bull.

Allen belly-crawled to Father Paul, put two fingers on his throat. A weak pulse. He glanced up, saw Amy trying to get to Penny. Maybe they could all sneak out of here while the wizards dueled.

The flame bull snorted, charged Fay.

Fay cast a spell at the stream that ran to the waterwheel. A giant hand emerged from the stream on a long column of water, reared up like a snake. The palm was ten feet wide. Fay made a swatting gesture, and the hand came down hard and flat on the flame bull.

The water hand exploded on contact, obliterating the bull in a hiss of steam. A ton of warm water surged across the cavern floor, knocked into Allen and Father Paul.

The priest opened his eyes, coughed. "Allen."

"It's me. Hold on. We'll figure out something."

Father Paul's chest rose and fell with a wheeze. "Everything's all wrecked inside me. I'm not going anywhere."

Allen couldn't think of anything comforting to say.

"Take this. Maybe it'll come in handy." The priest slipped

something cold and heavy into Allen's hand. "You'll only have a few . . . a few seconds . . ." His eyes rolled up.

And Father Paul was no more.

"Thank you, Mr. Zabel," Fay said. "You've been amusing. I liked the bull. I'd have formed it into a minotaur. That would have added a little flare, don't you think?"

"Fuck you."

Fay frowned. "Time to end it."

Fay gestured with both hands at the waterwheel, spoke the words. The waterwheel shook, broke loose from its base, and lifted into the air. It started to spin, faster and faster, then flew straight at Zabel.

Zabel threw up his hands, screamed the words to the counter-spell. The waterwheel halted a foot from his face. He pushed back, sent the waterwheel flying at Fay.

"No, you don't!" Fay grunted as he willed the waterwheel back toward Zabel.

Allen watched the two wizards struggle, the waterwheel hovering a dozen feet in the air between them. Now was the time.

He dashed toward Amy and Penny, his footfalls splashing water. He was relieved to find Penny still breathing.

"She's unconscious," Amy said. "Can you lift her?"

Allen lifted her, put her over his shoulder. "Let's get the hell out of here."

"What about the stone?" Amy asked.

"Forget it. I don't want to be under that waterwheel when it comes down."

They ran back toward the dam. Two seconds later a cata-clysmic crash echoed though the cave, wood splintering, stone crumbling.

"Keep going," Allen shouted.

They climbed the stairs up the side of the dam. When they reached the top, they paused to look back.

"Oh, hell," Allen said.

Jackson Fay hovered ten feet in the air, green light glowing around him. He flew toward them, arms outstretched, a maniacal expression twisting his face.

"We've got to hurry."

"No," Amy said. "He'll come after us. He'll follow us and kill us. We've got to end this now."

Fay floated closer.

Allen said, "Unless you've got a Sherman tank in your pocket, I suggest we haul ass out of here *right now.*"

Amy leaned in close, whispered in his ear, "You know how you don't think I have any magical powers?"

Allen nodded.

Amy grinned. "Well, you're right."

She jogged out toward the dam.

"What? Come back! You'll get killed."

Amy picked her way along the top of the dam until she stood in the very center. She faced Fay and waited. He floated to within twenty feet of her, then stopped and hovered there.

"You defeated Zabel," Amy said.

"Yes," Fay said. "I must admit he was somewhat more formidable than I had anticipated. Good thing I disposed of him. He might have actually been able to do something with the stone if he'd obtained it."

"I talked to Margaret," Amy told him. "You're a traitorous bastard."

"Margaret?" Genuine surprise in his voice. "Well, the old bat had one last trick up her sleeve. Interesting."

"You got past Zabel," Amy said. "But you won't get past me."

"I'm sorry, but are you high or something?"

"I've been studying my craft. I'm more powerful than you think. Much more powerful than Zabel."

Fay held his belly and laughed hard. He wiped a tear from his eye. "Oh, yeah. You're one mighty sorceress. Just like your friend Clover. You should have seen the surprised look on her face when I killed her."

Amy went red, fury boiling within her.

"Tell you what," Fay said. "I'll just float here. You go first. Seriously. You cast your mightiest spell." He laughed again. "I mean it. Let's see what you got."

"Okay." Amy raised her hands, formed an arcane gesture. "You asked for it."

"Let's go," Fay urged. "Cast away."

"Right." She reached behind her under her shirt and came out with the .50-caliber Desert Eagle. "Suck on this, mother-fucker."

She squeezed the trigger, and the pistol bucked and thundered. Blood and flesh erupted from Fay's shoulder. He spun in midair, screamed.

Fay tried to right himself, twirling slowly in midair like some lazy weather vane. He reached out with one hand and flayed Amy with a weak blast of blue lightning.

Amy contorted, spasms of shock spreading to every inch of her body. She threw her head back, eyes shut tight. The electricity dissipated, and Amy went to her knees with a splash, barely catching herself before falling back into the pool of icy water.

Fay had stabilized, floated toward Amy with both hands outstretched, hellfire in his eyes. "Bitch! That's cheating."

Amy lifted the heavy pistol, closed one eye, sighted along the barrel.

She fired twice more, flame flashing from the gun. The slugs smacked into Fay's side, exploded out his back. His mouth fell open in a noiseless gasp; eyes wide with disbelief. He crumbled and plummeted, trailing blood in the air. He landed with a splash and a crunch.

Amy turned and ran from the dam to join Allen on the narrow path that led back up to St. Vitus Cathedral. She stumbled, fell forward.

Allen barely caught her. "Are you okay?"

She nodded, panting. "Just a little woozy. Let's get out of here."

"One more thing," Allen said. "Can you take her? Are you strong enough?"

Amy grabbed Penny under each armpit, dragged her up the path. "Hurry."

Allen went to the edge of the dam, peered over. Fay lay at the bottom, still moving. The wizard looked up and saw Allen. "You . . . little shits. I'm going to h-heal. Going to heal up and then I'll d-drink wine out of your f-fucking skulls." He coughed, flecks of blood covering his bottom lip.

"I don't think so," Allen said.

He pulled the grenade Father Paul had given him from his pocket, jammed it into a niche between two stones. He pulled the pin and ran.

He just made it to the passage back to the daylight when he heard the explosion behind him.

FIFTY-FOUR

When the grenade went off, I saw the whole thing. A pretty good show.

The small explosion only damaged the dam a little at first, rocks and dust flying. But Allen had put the grenade in just the right spot. Never underestimate dumb luck. Geysers spouted from the dam, opening fissures. Jackson Fay had a front-row seat when the dam finally broke, tons and tons of water and rock tumbling down on him.

The water swept through the caverns, wrecking Roderick's machine, smashing lenses, washing away bodies.

The rush of water was so powerful that it even sent the lead box with the philosopher's stone rolling and tumbling along deep underground caverns, through a shaft that emptied itself into the Vlatva. The box sank into the mud at the bottom of the river.

What happened to it after that, I can't say. I've come to the end of my part in the story.

I didn't know that at first, but I know it now. I can feel it. I'm going someplace. Events have come to fruition, and I've been released. I know now that I've waited centuries to finish this, to witness, to tell you about it. I don't know what happens next.

I see the big, deep gray loom before me, and I'm afraid. I don't want to go. For hundreds of years I've prayed for release, but now I don't want to go.

I can help you.

Who is this?

You know who this is.

You're me, aren't you?

I'm you an hour from now. You know how funny time works here.

What are you doing here?

It was difficult, so I've come back to help you.

How can you help?

You need to start thinking. You need to face up to some things. It'll go quicker if you start now. I resisted, and it took longer. It was . . . uncomfortable.

What do you mean?

Think about what you're doing here. Why are you a ghost? What happened?

Nothing happened. I don't know what you're talking about.

Yes, you do.

Go away. I don't need your help.

Remember Roderick. Remember how he died, the agony. From exposing himself to the stone.

Is it because of the emperor's cousin? Am I being punished for that? He died just like the vampire. Because I smudged the lens. Is that it? It was worth it. Rudolph sealed up the caverns after that. He didn't think the machine worked. It was a good thing. I'm sorry about the emperor's cousin, but it was good he thought the machine a failure.

You know that's not what I'm talking about.

I don't want to speak to you anymore.

Remember Roderick's agony. How he withered away. You were exposed to the stone too.

Shut up.

You didn't want to die like that, did you? So much pain.

Shut up!

So what did you do?

I didn't do anything. Go away.

WHAT DID YOU DO?

I t-took a rope. A noose. I put it around my neck. Oh, God.

It's okay.

Oh, God. I remember. Oh, my God.

Let it out.

I wept. I don't know how long. It's hard to tell when you're dis-embodied, when you can't feel warm tears roll down your cheek. I wept and wept.

There. Feel better?

I don't know. I feel tired.

I'm going on ahead. I'll see you there soon. You'll make it okay now.

Okay.

And I feel myself being pulled along. Not like when Zabel summoned me to his rooftop. More like floating along with a gentle current. I'm floating into the gray. There's no tunnel of light. No choir of angels. Just the long gray. And I'm going there.

Toward an ending. And a beginning.

Into all things.

FIFTY-FIVE

After fleeing St. Vitus Cathedral and Prague Castle, they returned to Penny's apartment, where Allen and Amy laid Penny on her bed. She woke several hours later, pleasantly surprised to be in her own room. Allen and Amy filled her in on what she'd missed.

Penny cried for Father Paul.

They all slept, aches and bruises and fatigue forcing them into the deepest slumber of their lives.

The next day, Allen and Penny walked Amy to the nearest tram stop. Amy wore a pink T-shirt, white shorts, and sandals, her toenails painted the same pink as the T-shirt. She wore a small backpack over one shoulder. She looked like she was on her way to a sorority beach party.

"I knew I never had any powers," Amy said wistfully. "But to be a member of the Society, to have a place. I'm not very independent, I guess. I needed to belong."

"What are you going to do now?" Allen asked.

She shrugged. "Maybe in the fall I'll go back to school. Finish my dissertation in astrophysics."

Astrophysics?

"Until then I suppose I'll bum around," Amy said. "I'll take the tram to the train station. Catch the express to Vienna. It'll be nice to be an ordinary tourist."

Penny offered her hand, and they shook. "I know we didn't hit it off at first, but I hope we see you again."

Amy smiled. "I'd like that."

The tram pulled up to the stop, and Amy climbed aboard.

She suddenly jumped off, grabbed Allen's face, and planted a hard kiss right on his lips. Allen stood speechless.

Amy flashed a devilish grin at Penny. "I know he's all yours. But he sure is cute, isn't he?"

She hopped back aboard the tram as it pulled out, and they watched Amy wave from the back window. The tram rounded a corner and trundled out of sight.

Penny and Allen strolled the sidewalk.

"It just occurred to me," Allen said. "I don't have to research a chapter on Kafka for Professor Evergreen anymore. Looks like I have a whole summer and nothing to do."

Penny's hand found his, and their fingers laced. "Well, I just don't know what you're going to do. I hear Prague's kind of a dull town."

Allen's face grew somber. "I think there's something I need to tell you, Penny. Something about me and Cassandra."

"Never mind," she said. "Amy told me all about it."

"You don't care?"

"I can't say I'm *thrilled*," she admitted, "but it wasn't your fault." She stopped him, stood in front of him, head tilted up. "Besides, you're mine. I *earned* you. So try to be worth it, okay?"

"Looks like I know what I'm doing this summer."

He kissed her long and hard.

It was good.

Much better than a Brontë novel.

A NOTE FOR HISTORIANS

Much of this novel was inspired by actual events. Holy Roman Emperor Rudolph II really did keep alchemists prisoner in Prague Castle to work on the secret of the philosopher's stone. Edward Kelley and John Dee were real people. Read up on this stuff. It's interesting.

But please be aware that the author has recklessly deviated from actual history for his own purposes. Liberties were taken. Dates screwed with. Serious historians should avail themselves of a grain of salt.

ACKNOWLEDGMENTS

Thanks to all the folks at Team Touchstone, most notably Zach Schisgal, Shawna Lietzke, and Jessica Roth. Much gratitude to David Hale Smith (and Shauyi!) for V8 agenting with hybrid efficiency. As always, thanks to Sean Doolittle and Anthony Neil Smith for support, advice, very bad (but fun) golf outings, and smacks upside the head when needed. A special special special special thanks to all those readers who "get it." Much obliged to my son, Emery, for all the "Jedi Training," (i.e. whacking each other in the backyard with the lightsabers Santa brought us for Christmas.) And best for last, thanks to my wife, Jackie, who spent a month with me in Prague and put up with my "writer bullshit."

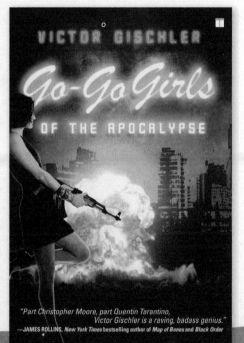